NIGHTINGALE STREET

LETA NASTA

PublishAmerica
Baltimore

First printing

ISBN: 1-60703-285-6
PUBLISHED BY PUBLISHAMERICA, LLLP
www.publishamerica.com
Baltimore

Printed in the United States of America

I dedicate this novel to my parents—they made me what I am and I got here because of their hard work.

I would like to thank Michael, my editor, who believed in this novel, Catrinel Serghie and Paul Aalders who offered me good advice, and of course my daughter who did the research for finding the best publishing house.

Motto: Should we fear dark? What about the daylight? Is life only insecurity and hell? Could we dream of heaven or at least of a piece of it?

Prologue

The last glimpse of light vanished. He checked the road behind him, and stopped his car on the side of the road, in a small parking lot, turning off the noisy engine, which had kept stealing his thoughts by then. Nevertheless, with all the silence around, he couldn't grab the slightest shred of thought.

Tired, extremely tired, as if he hadn't slept for days, and he actually hadn't, he put his head on his crossed hands, sighing deeply, as he could find no way out of the wry situation.

He feared the day to come. Fear was like a hairy spider crawling over its body along his spine, crawling, making him feel shivers of deep despair.

He had already chosen the only reasonable thing to do and, even though he had some afterthoughts, he couldn't clearly seize or understand them. It was like a glimpse of what he was supposed to be and wasn't. Somewhere, deep inside, he knew that his plan did not feel right, but, as he had always been told, a man had to do what a man had to do. Sure, it sounded such a cliché but he felt the words were true.

Chapter One

The sharp scream burst out in the night, filling the air with fear. She woke up scared, shivering and panting, as if she had just had a nightmare. Nevertheless, the nightmare hadn't even started yet.

Turning the light on, she discovered John, her lazy and chubby John, lying next to her, clinging to the blanket covering his chest covered with curly, white hair. His eyes were wide open. There was pure and mere horror on his face.

None of them could say or do anything. The screamed paralysed their minds and bodies. They were watching each other—big eyes and pale faces. They couldn't imagine—actually, they did not want to try their imagination, and sort things out, to understand what that horrible scream, having spoiled their night, could have meant.

After a few more moments of painful silence, John said in a low voice—not to awake any possible ghost, lying in the dark:

"What the hell was that, Doris? Did you hear?"

"Of course, I heard, you stupid!" she burst out. "Why do you think I'm staring to the walls in the middle of the night? You must go out and see what's going on", she said with some rush in her voice, her determination screeching in the man's ears.

He looked at her completely puzzled. He couldn't even believe his ears. Her words stirred a torrent of anger in his mind and everything was piling/building up somewhere in his chest.

"You have thought a lot, haven't you?" he replied bitterly. "Do you think I've got the guts to go out in the night after that?"

For one single moment, she said nothing but her eyes said everything he would have wanted to know. It was nothing new there. He knew her feelings for a long time. There were years since she had looked at him differently, with warmth and delight.

"Oh, God, you're so pathetic! You're a real pussy!" she exclaimed ironically, knowing that the simple uttering of such a word might make him move.

She knew what moves to make and what words to say. Over time, she had learnt to use everything in her favour and to gain every move she'd make.

"This time, you can say whatever you want, my dear... This time, it won't work", John replied with some resignation.

There was also laziness in his words, as if he had no care in the world.

"Please, believe me! I don't care at all for the moment. I won't go out only to make you happy. It sounded as if it had come out directly from hell, you know it, and, besides, hell and I have nothing in common, you know", he reminded her of his favourite reply.

"I know, I know, don't remind me!" she said reluctantly and a bit annoyed. She would know his replies by heart. They had been living together for too long to be anything new left to be said.

"But maybe someone needs some help and we just stay here wasting time and speaking nonsense."

"If you are so brave, you should go there", said he, stressing the words. "But, you must know, I don't advise you to do it. You're crazy, I have to tell you".

"I don't think so", she replied, grumpily. One could sense small victory in her voice. She seemed to have sharpened her ears to catch the slightest move.

"I hear fast steps outside. I think our neighbour, Mr Thompson, has woken up too... I think there are also others. What are you saying now?" she tried to challenge him.

She could imagine he wouldn't feel too good if he didn't go out now. Men were like that. You could have dared them without the slightest trouble. They would always try to show they were better and stronger and braver than any other man in the bucket.

"All right, back off!" he snapped feeling a bit petty. "If he is there, I'll go too. Now, shut up, back off and let me get dressed", replied the man, angrily, cornered by his nagging wife.

He got up and went to the bathroom to take his bathrobe. His gestures were abrupt, crying his anger out loud.

Then, he went downstairs growling some nasty remarks about his nosey wife, who was still in bed, waiting for news from him. Of course, she didn't have enough courage to get up and go to look through the window, at least, as she would always do, he thought ironically.

Opening the front door, he saw light at all the windows in the little street and felt like having paced into an unreal world. Not even at Christmas did their street show so much light. Then, he saw three men heading to his yard, speaking one to the other, and when he saw what they were looking at, his blood ran cold.

On his lawn, a body was lying in the light of the moon that had just got out of the clouds. In an instant, he could see the blonde hair and the white dress, completely torn out and stained with blood and the green of the grass. The body's right hand laid in full sight, with the fingers curved, as if they had been trying to catch something in the air, but there was no drop of life in them to end their movement.

Then, the smell hit him: a little sweet and sour the same time. It was that type of smell one couldn't forget too easily or too soon. He could bet his last quid in the bank that the scent would last there for days or maybe more.

He suddenly felt dizzy, and for a moment, he had the strange feeling that his body had lost substance. Then, nausea hit him, like a fist in his belly, pumping the air out, leaving his lungs longing for the comfort of a good breath. He could have used it.

Suddenly, he bent in a weird position. He reminded at a perfect angle of ninety degrees. He couldn't find a way to breathe even if he'd made serious efforts and he felt his head was spinning making him lose focus.

Now he could see everything only like through a dense fog: Mr Thompson was there and he had just bent over the body on the lawn. He was saying something, waving his hand to Mr Reid, the one who was living in the third house across the road, that Mr Reid with his weird wife.

Mr Reid answered something back, and Mr Dobbs found it quite strange that he couldn't catch any of his words. He couldn't understand them: they made no sense to him.

Then he caught a glimpse of a shadow in the dark, in the corner of the house. He felt it like an imperious threat, although he was aware that it was effectively foolish because nothing could have happened to him, there, where he was staying.

However, he was far from a young lad with no knowledge about life. He felt sweat running down under the collar of his wardrobe. Fear caught his heart in a strong fist and shivers were running along his spine. A drop of sweat tickled his spine along its way downwards.

He had no logical explanation but couldn't control the tremble of his fingers. They got a life of their own.

Lack of air and fear, bare fear, were too much for him to hold together. He was not very brave on his best days, but now he was old and he did not have the advantage of youth's stupidity and ignorance that had kept him on the line in his fresh years.

He lost his posture completely at once, falling on the veranda like a log, in his fall making a loud noise that turned all heads towards him.

Now, everything went black and completely silent around him and only a terrible pain seized his chest on the left side for a few moments. Then it was something like long wished peace. He welcomed it as if it were an awkward friend liberating him of fear and the unknown. It was a secure way out although he had never thought of feeling like that when the day would come for him.

From upstairs, in her bed, Doris had sharpened her ears to catch the slightest sound, and she could hear Mr Reid saying loudly:

"Oh, I think Mr Dobbs has fainted. We should call his wife too, not only the police. Maybe a doctor or something, I think".

Mrs Dobbs started trembling overwhelmed by black thoughts. She felt her heart crumbling and she tried to get out of her bed but her legs were shaking and were of not much help for her.

She couldn't find her slippers. She couldn't pull herself together sensing that something very bad had happened.

She knew John quite well after so many years. He was a little lazy and sometimes too stubborn for his own sake, but she knew well he wasn't a coward or a pussycat, as she'd called him just before he went out. She also knew that he had never fainted before, however bad the situation would have been.

However she would put it, he used to be quite a fellow. He'd never given in and she could rely on him in bad weather. He used to be her realm for years no matter what had come and, actually, there were times when things had not been too good.

Now, if he had fainted, she realised things looked pretty bad. She felt something, like a huge burden, touching her heart. It was guilt, strap bare guilt. If it hadn't been for her, her husband wouldn't have gone outside at all and he would have kept lying next to her, in their old bed.

Her husband wasn't a curious person, and no one could care less of what was going on in the street or in his neighbours' houses. He was the type of person that would have believed in each one's right of privacy and he'd never approved with spying on people next door.

She went downstairs, trying to keep her balance, leaning against the walls. She was all in a tremble now, and she couldn't control herself at all, no matter how hard she tried. She felt beside her wit for good. Something cold had overwhelmed her mind and soul. No thoughts could overcome her bleak premonition. The worst thing had just happened.

She managed to control her wild panic for one tiny moment and, suddenly, she had the strange feeling that things wouldn't ever be the same for her from that very moment on.

She could have told that something irreparable had happened: she could have bet on it. With that, she could have won the big pot, she was sure.

She knew her life was going to change for good in a few seconds. She couldn't put her finger on for sure, but the feeling and the pain were terribly strong.

This thought made her get downstairs as fast as her shaking legs allowed her. When she got into the hall, she saw the front door opening and, only for one moment, she felt airless watching the slow movement of the door. It was only then that she heard the steps. She saw two men—she didn't recognise them at first sight, getting inside with her John in their arms. This one seemed lifeless and she knew that something very bad had happened to him, too, not only to the person having screamed earlier.

She finally recognized her next door neighbours, Mr Thompson and Mr Reid.

She stared at them motionless and then, after a long while, as she felt, Mr Thompson said:

"Don't be afraid, Mrs Dobbs. I think Mr Dobbs has only fainted, that's all. I only hope he doesn't have a weak heart. What he saw there is not for a person with a weak heart. Where should we put him? The doctor is on his way. He'll be here in a minute. Mrs Dobbs?"

He kept talking and talking but no word was filtered by her mind. She realised she was watching him speaking, his lips moving on, but, actually, she hadn't heard a word of what he was saying.

She shook her head, as if she had wanted to get rid of the dizziness in her head and to seize the sense of the words flowing around.

Mr Thompson, noticing her puzzlement, repeated slowly, uttering each word:

"Mrs Dobbs, are you feeling well? Where should we put poor Mr Dobbs?"

She finally managed to pull herself together and said:

"On the sofa, I think. Yes, on the sofa", she repeated louder, trying to recover and be quite her old self again. "I think that this is the best place for him now. Thank you, Mr Thompson. Have you said the doctor was coming?"

"Yes, Mrs Dobbs, right now. I've asked Mr Brown to call him here. We've called the police too. They're on their way."

"What happened, Mr Thompson?" asked she, somehow reluctantly, as if she hadn't wanted to know anything.

And that was strange for Mrs Dobbs. She was always the first that found out what was going on around. She was the first to know if any neighbour had a row with his wife or with another neighbour or when the Porters' little

Patsy eloped with that good-looking young man, or when the Davidsons were going to divorce.

"You'd better not know, Mrs Dobbs. It is too awful, I think. Here's the doctor. I know the sound of his car. I'll go to bring him inside".

She sat down on an armchair near the sofa and watched her husband. The colour of his face was weird and his lips had no colour at all. His left arm was grabbing his bathrobe and seemed stuck there. His right hand was lying on one side of the sofa completely lifeless. She couldn't hear him breathing at all and that made her feel uncomfortable.

And, then, she knew. The doctor needn't come. Her husband didn't need the doctor. He was gone.

She couldn't move at all. She was staring at him and only one thought was coming up from the darkness of her mind: "He's dead, certainly. Oh, God, he's dead!" The thought kept coming up like a mantra; she couldn't stop hearing it louder and louder in her head. Then, she fell like a puppet with the strings suddenly cut. Now, she finally had peace. Nothing could bother her anymore. There was only dark, and pain had hidden somewhere inside. There was no pain at all. It had gone away. She had got rid of any feeling.

***

All the people in the street gathered in front of the Dobbs' house as always people sense death and despair and they cannot help to be part of that. They saw the known doctor coming and getting into the house and, here and there, a rumour could be heard. People were whispering. Words spread out.

They were saying that poor Mr Dobbs had had a heart attack and that, probably, he had already been dead before the nice doctor could come.

Nevertheless, they couldn't imagine why his wife hadn't come out and why they hadn't heard a thing of her. That was quite strange of her.

They knew very well she was a too nosey woman to stay inside when something like that was going on in the street, and moreover, in her own yard. It was even unthinkable.

Then, they heard the sirens of the police cars approaching the lane. They immediately shut up and watched the cars driving up Nightingale Street.

They left more space between them and the Dobbs' yard, as if they wanted to take distance and show that they were not involved in the mess on their lawn. It was their lawn and their mess.

The cars stopped in front the Dobbs' house and some people came out of the cars and headed to the lawn. Some were in police uniform but others weren't.

People watched curiously at those carrying some big black cases in their hands. All of them seem preoccupied and they swept the public with a quick look.

All of them seemed to start talking almost the same time. One of the policemen seemed to notice the crowd in the street for the first time and shouted to another:

"James, ask them for their names and addresses and send them home. We'll talk to them later. Now I want more space here and no on-lookers in front of the house. There've been too many by here already, and, probably, they've spoilt the evidence".

"Yes, sir", said the young man and headed to the people in the street taking a little black book out of his pocket. He seemed confident in his ability of having the job done and the rough voice of his superior didn't seem to bother him at all.

He went to each of them, and asked their names and addresses, and if they had seen anything before the murder happened. However, no one saw anything. They had heard only that inhuman scream and woken up. Then, they had gone out and seen that person lying on the lawn exactly in the same position. They couldn't see the face of the body because Mr Thompson had told them that they shouldn't move the body until the police came.

They also told James about poor Mr Dobbs, who had fainted in front of the house and then they left, somehow reluctantly, and went to their homes.

James came back to the other policemen and told everything to his boss, the very man who'd sent him to ask questions to the people.

His boss listened to him and then replied:

"Ok, James. Good job! Now go and see what's with that Mr Dobbs. I think I've just seen two men getting into his house. I want to talk to him and to them, too".

James nodded and went to the Dobbs' front door. He went inside without knocking on the door because the door was already open. He heard some people whispering somewhere on the right and headed there, following their voices.

When he got into the room, he saw the doctor checking the pulse of a woman.

This one wasn't young but she wasn't too old either. She was somewhere between forty or fifty. Nevertheless, he knew he could be wrong about her age. The woman had no colour in her cheeks and seemed completely run down.

He couldn't figure out anything from how she was looking. She seemed completely lifeless. He knocked on the door and said:

"Good evening. I'm sorry for disturbing you. I'm sergeant detective James and I've been sent here to see Mr Dobbs".

That very moment, as if that was the signal she really needed, the woman burst into tears. The other two men remained shocked for one moment, and then, one of them, apparently the doctor, said watching her:

"Finally, she cries. It is better for her. She should have done it sooner or later", he also commented, and then turned to the sergeant and said: "I'm sorry, sergeant, but Mr Dobbs died a few moments earlier. He had a massive heart attack and I couldn't do anything for him. I think the shock was more than he could have bore".

"I see", nodded James, actually wondering why the shock was so devastating, and then continued: "All right, then. I leave you now, but sir, when you have finished here, we must talk to you. And to you", he said to Mr Thompson turning to him. "Who are you, sir?"

"I'm Thompson. I'm Daniel Thompson".

"Oh, I see. You're the one who told the others not to touch the body. They told me so".

"In deed,sir! I've been in the Navy for some while before and I know something about such things. I'll come at once. I must only finish talking to good Mr Connolly. Is that all right?"

"No rush, sir, because we still have some things to solve outside now", said James stressing the words and then left the room.

He went outside and saw his boss, Inspector-Chief McNamara, talking with one of the forensics. He headed to him, waited for him to finish and then said:

"I'm sorry, sir, but Mr Dobbs died. He has just had a heart attack. His wife is quite shocked now and I don't think we could talk to her. However, Mr Thompson will come out at once with the doctor, sir".

"Oh, damn it! What a bad luck! I think he saw something if he died so suddenly. We'll see", said he in a low voice, "we'll see".

Thoughtfully, he turned to the older man next to him:

"So, doctor, what do you say?"

"Not very much now, but I can say she had her throat cut and she was stabbed a few times before. She didn't die easily. I cannot be sure now, but she died within a period between an hour and only a few minutes, maybe a quarter of an hour, something like that. Before having her throat cut, she was beaten up badly, for a few days. You see, the bruises on her body have different age. Their colour doesn't seem the same. Her face is beyond any recognition, I'm afraid. You have to identify her differently. I'll tell you more later. I have to perform her autopsy first".

"All right, David", replied the man understandingly. "However, if we consider the phone call we got, people heard that terrible scream they told us about only fifteen minutes before, so we may presume that she died then", said Inspector-Chief McNamara. "James, go and see if she has any ID in her purse. I think I saw her purse on the ground there".

James took the purse from the ground and looked inside. He found the ID and said:

"It's Patsy Porter, sir. She was quite young, I'm afraid. She was only sixteen and she was living right on this street, sir", continued he, with some amazement in his voice.

"Good, James. We should go and see her family this morning and tell them about the sad news. We'll talk to them later. However, they must come and identify the body at the morgue tomorrow during the day".

McNamara made a sign to the two men waiting near a stretcher with a plastic bag in their hand.

"You may take her now".

Then, the body was taken from the lawn and carried to the ambulance in the black plastic bag. The forensics started searching the place and gathered what little evidence they could find in the area. They couldn't find the weapon used to kill her, but they didn't hope to find it, either. It would have been too nice to be true. Afterwards they left.

***

Peace descended in the little street again, but, this time, silence wasn't a comfort and people didn't feel safe anymore. They'd known such things kept happening in other places, but they had nothing similar so close to their house. Suddenly, their peace seemed to have been broken and they couldn't bring it back anymore, no matter what they'd have done. It seemed even hopeless to think about it now. Therefore, they started thinking about their own lives and tried to send the story they had witnessed a few moments earlier somewhere deep in their mind.

Only Mrs Dobbs kept watching out through the window in the night, trying to see what could have made her husband die.

She'd asked to be left alone, saying she'd be all right and she'd manage. She didn't feel any curiosity towards what was going on in the street, but she couldn't stop thinking that she had to find the thing that killed her husband. At the same time, she felt so lonely that she couldn't bear it. She felt emptied and deserted completely.

She hadn't been in love with her husband anymore; that was true. Too much time had passed, and their life had been too dull for the two of them. However, she'd cared of him and she kept caring of him, even if he wasn't there anymore.

She couldn't stop thinking that they were meant to be together, in a way, and they'd had a good life together, even though a sort of boredom could be felt after twenty years of marriage.

She knew he was at the morgue now and she couldn't stop shivering thinking of the cold table he was lying on. The loss was deep and her insecurity made it deeper.

Then, there was also guilt. She was the one having sent him to see what was going on in the street. Moreover, she hadn't even known that his heart was weak. She was so selfish that she hadn't paid attention to any of his complaints about his health, and now it was too late to do anything about that or to remember what he used to say.

She kept looking into the night outside and, in a certain moment, she had the feeling she saw someone crossing the lawn. The person had a flashlight in his hand. He seemed to look for something fallen on the ground. She didn't know who the person was and she didn't even think that she could be in danger because the light in the room was projecting her image in the dark. She presumed that police were looking for evidence on the ground. Nothing more.

Nevertheless, the person in the shadow saw her looking into the yard and knew very well her way of being and her gossiping. She wasn't a person to keep her mouth shut.

In a single moment, the shadow made a decision and, therefore, made a detour and went to the back door. He tried to open it slowly, without any noise. He wasn't heard. It was done.

Chapter Two

It was almost ten o'clock in the morning when McNamara, together with James, came back in Nightingale Street to ask questions about the murder.

First, they went directly to the Porters, and knocked on their door. Waiting—waiting seemed to be so much part of their life that they didn't even bother to think of it anymore—they heard some hurried steps on the stairs and then, the voice of a woman yelling:

"One moment, please. I'll come at once!"

After very little time, the door opened before them. The woman in the door, looking at them inquiringly, was short and a little plump. Her face wore signs of acute tiredness and seemed so strangely old that they could presume that her age was between forty and sixty.

"Yes. Who are you, please?" she asked, quite amazed to see some unknown people at her door in the morning. They didn't seem to be salesmen or those marketing people—the ones making those seemingly pointless studies. She felt a bit awkward because she opened the door only because she expected to see her friend, Mrs Brown.

"We're with the police, ma'am. Here are our badges", said the tall one showing her his badge. "I'm Inspector Chief McNamara and this is Sergeant Detective James. May we come in and talk with you, please?"

She let them inside, bending her head, but said nothing. She only stepped aside, her heart crunching with a bad feeling.

She had tried hard to chase away the words she'd heard the night before about a girl lying dead in the Dobbs' yard but they kept haunting her over and over.

The previous night, she had not gone out because she felt too lonely and she had been quite afraid, despite having seen her neighbours out when she found the courage to look out of the window.

Moreover, she couldn't stand such a show. She never could. Even when she saw an accident on the road, she used to turn her head. Nausea would have hit her and kept being present for the entire day otherwise.

She led them into a living room that seemed to have had better days. She said nothing at all, and, with a trembling hand, she showed them the sofa to sit down.

The policemen sat down and McNamara tried to find a way to tell her that, probably, her daughter was at the morgue.

Experience had taught him that there was no perfect way to tell such a truth and hurt less. Therefore, he tried to delay the dreadful moment asking her some routine questions:

"Where's Mr Porter, please?"

He imagined it would have been easier for her if she had someone on her side to comfort her after their leaving. He knew that, generally, people would bear such things easier when they were together, regardless what their mutual feelings had been.

Hardly had he asked the question, than he noticed with horror that tears filled her eyes. For a few moments he thought she would burst into tears but then she said slowly and a little ashamed, as if she had had some painful and shameful sin:

"He left, you know. A week after Patsy, my daughter had left, he left too. He was so angry with Patsy and me. Oh, dear! He said I was to blame for the girl's leaving with that boy".

"What boy, ma'am? Do you know his name?" McNamara asked hoping he found a lead. So far, he had not found out anything about any possible connections to his victim.

"Oh, yes! He was a good-looking boy with some too smooth talk but he was good. He used to work for Mr Brown's pub at the other end of the street. He left the same time with Patsy's leaving home, I can say. I don't know where they're now".

"Do you know his name?" McNamara asked her again.

"I think, Peter. I'm not sure. I didn't ask Patsy because I didn't know she was going out with him until she'd left the note and went away, but that was written on the note.

That she was leaving with Peter from the pub on the corner, and then, I was too ashamed to go to the Browns and ask them. However, what's the matter? Has something happened to my husband or Patsy?"

Her voice was almost bagging for a negative answer although she could read everything in McNamara's eyes. His eyes were dark as well as his face. She could see that he had something bad to tell her, and her heart crouched to appease the news she was going to be broken to.

McNamara, cursing himself for not having sent Jo to deal with Mrs Porter, tried to find suitable words to tell her in a soft voice that, apparently, her daughter had been found dead in the Dobbs' yard or they were thinking that, at least, but he couldn't utter any word, even though he'd done such a thing before and not only one time.

The woman seemed so fragile that he couldn't tell her the truth bluntly in the way he'd have done before in other circumstances. He was afraid she'd have fallen into pieces in front of him and he did not feel like gathering the pieces afterwards. He was not quite the type of man to do it. Damn it! He even didn't know how to do it.

Looking her straight in her eyes, he was trying hard to decide what to do. The silence was so acute that all of them could feel it scratching their skin and deafening their ears. Finally, when she felt she couldn't bear the silence anymore, Mrs Porter whispered with the last drop of courage of someone on the edge of the abyss:

"It is bad, isn't it? Which one of them, please? I hope it isn't Patsy!"

She looked up in McNamara's eyes to guess the answer and then she knew. His eyes were telling everything she wanted to know. It was Patsy. Another painful thought penetrated the fog of her mind: she was the one in the Dobbs' yard last night.

For one moment, she had the strange feeling that her heart stopped beating but she was wrong. Her heart kept beating but her mind didn't work anymore. That is why she could not notice the beating. For one moment, only one moment, she didn't react at all. She remained stoned with her hands joined in her lap and with a grimace in the corner of her mouth.

McNamara saw recognition in her eyes and on her face. He stood up to put his hand on her shoulder comfortingly but surprising this thought he almost started inside. He'd never had such inclinations. He always tried to remain cold and detached from anything. Only finding answers and convicting killers counted.

Then, something broke inside the woman. First, she groaned and then, she burst into tears. Somewhere in her mind, she has a vision of her plans for Patsy, for the day she'd have come back home but that day would never come anymore and the vanity of her plans kicked her in her stomach leaving behind only pain, sharp and devastating pain.

McNamara watched James hoping for help from his side but then he dropped the idea. He tried to say in a voice sounding as if he were apologizing.

"I'm sorry, Mrs Porter, but I must ask you to come down to the morgue and identify the body just to be sure".

A glimpse of hope nested in her soul but died almost instantly. She knew it was useless to think that police had been wrong. She'd already felt it in her soul: her Patsy was gone and left behind only the amazement for such a short life.

She had been feeling some acute loss during the last two weeks, as if the time had stopped and nothing new would have ever come again. She hadn't believed in such things before. She'd called them crap. But now she was thinking that such presentments really existed.

Then, she managed to utter a few words with difficulty:

"When do you want me to come?"

"When you feel able to, but sooner the better... Do you want me to send you a car to take you this afternoon?" McNamara offered to help her.

"No, thank you, but I'll come by myself. Maybe I'll ask my friend, Mary, you know, Mary Brown, to fetch me. I don't think she'd get upset".

She realised she was talking twaddle and she gave up.

"All right, Mrs Porter, then we'll see you there at noon. Now, I think we'd better leave you alone", said McNamara, standing up from the sofa again.

He felt a huge rush to go because he didn't know what he could do for her and he knew quite well that he wasn't the comforting type of person. He felt sorry again because he hadn't sent another one instead of him to give her the bad news.

Mrs Porter nodded, but said nothing. She stood up with difficulty and led the two policemen to the door. She opened the door and, after their leaving, she closed the door easily to make no noise.

She leaned against the wall for a few seconds and then she slid down. She remained like that for a while and then she burst badly into tears.

***

"Come on, James. Let's call on Mrs Dobbs to see how she is. She might have something to tell us now and she might want to see someone", McNamara said.

"Yes, sir, I think this is a good idea", James said going with him down the street.

They headed to Mrs Dobbs's house. When they got to the door, they knocked, but no answer came from inside. They watched each other questioningly and then they knocked again. James stepped back a little and watched the first floor.

"Sir, I think something's odd. It's ten o'clock and there's still light on the first floor".

"Who knows why? However, we should go at the back too. She might be there. It's clear she's at home if there is light. Stay here and keep knocking, maybe she hears you.

I'm going to see at the back of the house", McNamara said. "I call you if there's something".

He went with big steps to the back of the house watching thoughtfully the lit window James had noticed. Maybe the woman fell asleep, who knows? She might not have woken up yet. Perhaps, she was exhausted after the previous night. He knew he shouldn't think of the worst things. It wasn't good to anticipate such things. One could be wrong too easily.

He got to the back of the house and wanted to knock on the door when he noticed the door wasn't closed but a little open. He pushed it more open and called:

"Mrs Dobbs, are you at home? We're with the police".

No answer came from inside. He heard only his own voice. Then he went to a side of the house and shouted:

"James, come here. Something's wrong".

James left the front door and went to the back of the house. When he got to the back door, he found McNamara waiting for him. McNamara made him a sign and both entered the house slowly, ready to fight back if a possible attack had occurred.

They looked inside the first room and saw there was the kitchen. It was clean with no sign of recent use. They kept heading onto the corridor and making extremely little noise. They opened the door on the left and saw the pantry. They reached the entrance hall. Another small corridor was lying before them and, on the left, they could see the stairs. Near the stairs, there was a door and on the right another.

James checked the room on the left, but could see only an empty small but cosy drawing room. McNamara opened the door on the right of the stairs but saw only the dining room and no one inside.

They started to go on the corridor to a small room on the left. It was the living room and behind the door, there was a trace of blood. However, before anything else, the smell hit them strongly. They knew it very well. They felt it too much before to be wrong now.

McNamara watched behind the door and with no word made a sign to James to watch too. When he watched, James felt a slight nausea in his throat. It would always happen the same thing. He resigned with the thought he wouldn't ever get used to it.

Mrs Dobbs was lying on her belly and there was a splash of blood almost completely coagulated under her. Around, there was a small table knocked down and a broken vase with flowers. The water wetted the floor parquet and the flowers were a little aside.

"She seems to have heard something and come to the door. She tried to defend herself when she was caught, I think, but she had no chance" McNamara said. "Probably, because the person was stronger... And of course there was the surprise, too".

"I call to the headquarters, boss, to send the coroner and the forensics",

"All right, James. Till they come, let's wait in the front hall. I don't think you want to stay here too much. Neither do I".

***

Mrs Thompson saw the cars crowding in front the Dobbs' house. After the night before, she was more than curious, so, she went outside with a determination she did not usually feel and headed to Sergeant James who was speaking to a man dressed in a brown jacket. She'd already seen James a night before when he had spoken to them.

"Do you mind, sir? What's happened now?"

"You'd better go inside, ma'am. We'll come to you later and explain you everything".

Alice Thompson didn't want to leave, but she couldn't find an excuse or something smart to say. When such a thing happened, she behaved obediently and she didn't know how to refuse an order, even though James made it sound like a mere request. Slightly thoughtful, she headed to her house when she heard someone calling her name:

"Alice, what's going on?" asked her a lady in a light outfit, although it was quite cool. The summer was on the verge of end. Autumn was already felt in the air and in the colour of leaves.

It was Mary Reid, her neighbour. She also heard the police cars, and, after the night before, obviously she was thinking of worse. However, she wasn't far from truth.

Mary was a woman about thirty, a little plump, swarthy-faced and green-eyed. She'd got married one or two years before, Alice didn't know very well because they'd moved in the area only half a year before, after having bought the house from Mr MacDonald's grandsons. Poor Mr MacDonald died one year before.

Alice and Mary made friends a little but only because they used to stay at home in the morning, while their husbands went to town for work. However, they weren't very close, even though the difference in age wasn't big between them. The truth was that both of them had completely different interests.

They weren't fit to be friends. Alice was the typical and obedient housewife that would take care only of her house and husband, while Mary was nothing of this kind. She was an independent woman. Obviously, Mary didn't seem to need her husband's opinions. She even used to do always what she wanted regardless what the poor guy would have said. The quarrels heard from their house were a clear proof sustaining that.

"I don't know, Mary", answered Alice. "I'm afraid, something bad happened at the Dobbs'. I think something happened to Mrs Dobbs. That young policeman over there didn't want to tell me anything... He sent me away quite fast... He said they were going to talk to us later", Alice replied.

She headed to her house, failing the chance to see the grin on Mary's face, but suddenly she turned back and said:

“What do you think, Mary, would you come to drink some tea, oh, sorry, I’d better invite you to a coffee. I know you don’t like tea, although I don’t understand why”.

“I don’t know, Alice”, Mary said without noticing the other one’s reproach. She seemed to think a little. “All right, I’ll come. I can’t work now anyway. I’ll think only of what happened there. I’d make a lot of speculations. All right, I’ll come. Thus, I’ll relax a little and then, I’ll be able to work more and even better”, said Mary following Alice.

Hearing about her work, Mrs Thompson turned up her nose, but Mary didn’t see her. She had learnt how to avoid Alice’s disapproval. Alice didn’t like to hear of Mary’s work. She didn’t think it was a dignified occupation for a married woman. She was pretty sure that Mary should have taken more care of her household, and she shouldn’t have wasted her time with absurd things.

Alice opened the door and invited her in the house. They went into the kitchen, and Mary sat down at the kitchen table while Alice started making coffee for Mary and tea for herself. She seemed willing to say something but she was shrinking from saying it.

Mary was watching her face amused. She knew Alice wanted to say something, probably a small wife-to-wife reproach, but she didn’t seem to have the courage to start. She was bored but decided to push her a little. However, she didn’t pay attention to what Alice would say. She never paid attention to her but now and then she liked to play around.

"Say it, Alice. If you have something to say, say it. You shouldn't shrink from do it. I couldn't get mad with you", Mary said, adding in her mind: "You're far too stupid and have no spine, so I couldn't get upset on you".

Alice tried to find the most appropriate words, and then, she started hesitating:

"You, know Mary, I've heard your husband yelling at you yesterday afternoon. You know, I don't want to advise you how to run your marriage, far from me that. I think everyone should do whatever they want", she said, thinking exactly the opposite. "But", she continued, as if she had no two-faced thought, "maybe if you took more care of him and if you did more household jobs... I mean, a wife should always put her husband first and only then the other things that could interest only her".

"I know you think like this, Alice. But I don't" replied Mary decisively, enjoying herself. She liked throwing Alice's opinions back into her face. "A husband may be here today. Tomorrow he might be with another woman, and, believe me my dear, nothing could stop it, if it's meant to be. If it's to happen, it happens. You cannot stop it even if you cook perfectly and your house is spotless. But, you see, if Michael leaves, even if tomorrow, I won't have to ask him money to live and I won't have to expect for alimony each month, being afraid that he might want to punish me a little or might not care a bit of me to send me the money on time. I'll go on with my work. I'll have that whatever the circumstances. However, I couldn't stay all day in the kitchen, cooking his favourite dishes. I'd die with boredom. He knows it, and he also knows he isn't everything in my life. He's not sure on me now, and he might think twice before leaving me. Nevertheless, if he does so, and I don't think it is impossible, I won't be a deserted woman, left with nothing".

"I don't believe what you say", said Alice. "A husband always appreciates when his wife makes small things for him. He appreciates her if she's there for him. If he knows he is the first and the most important thing in her life, then he appreciates and loves his wife more and he won't desert her. I saw it to Mr Thompson. I know what I say".

"You know nothing, damn it!" said Mary to herself. She knew better what the "wonderful" Mr Thompson could do, but she couldn't say it to her friend. However, she was sure Alice wouldn't have believed a word, and would have accused her of being envious. Instead, she said:

"Maybe, Alice. Maybe you're right", she repeated even though she didn't think that. "I saw my mother, you must know. She was exactly like you: the typical housewife. She didn't think of anything else but her husband and his pleasures all the time. Then, she was left alone with three children to bring up and no money in her pockets, and even with no friend. Friends were his, not hers. She had to start all over again... If you think about it, she had no training. It was very difficult for her; I can say it to you. The only thing she could do was to clean people's houses. That was everything she could do. She didn't know anything else. Therefore, Alice, I'm sorry, but I prefer being exactly in the way I am. If Michael leaves one day, and he might do it, who knows, I won't be left having no job, money or friends. And, by the way, I prefer having my own friends, if you understand me, not his".

Alice couldn't say anything for the moment, but she couldn't stop herself thinking that Mary was wrong. Who knows? Maybe her mother wasn't good enough. If you stop thinking, usually daughters behave exactly like their mothers, and considering the way Mary was behaving...

She knew that if you were doing your best and as well as you could, it was impossible to be deserted. Her husband wouldn't do that, unlike Mary's, who would do it. She was sure of that.

Mary was too lazy and did nothing for him. She didn't cook and bought everything already cooked from the grocer's. She didn't take care of his clothes too much and she didn't think at least that he could be too tired when he got back from work. She used to ask him to mow the lawn and do various things in the house. She even heard her telling him to clean the house and dust if he wanted to have a neat house and iron his clothes if he wanted ironed clothes. It was inadmissible. A wife shouldn't do that. She knew she wouldn't.

Mary, on the other hand, thought Alice was a simpleton, even if she was the one older with some years. Mary knew, as everyone in the street did, that Mr Thompson was seeing Ann, the young typist living in the same street.

That's why he was so tired when he came home. And, maybe, who knows, there might have been others, too.

Alice didn't use to ask him to do anything in the house and he was like a king in his own castle. He had Alice for cleaning and cooking and taking care of his clothes, and he also had Ann for his soul and for fun.

However, she couldn't tell that to Alice. It would have been too cruel. The little wife satisfied with her marriage and her husband! However, who knows, maybe, Alice wasn't as satisfied as she pretended. God knew!

Alice drank her tea keeping silent, but she couldn't stop herself from feeling some bitterness thinking that Daniel wasn't as loving as he used to be before, at the beginning, the first months. However, she couldn't deal with his passion, so, maybe, who knows, it was better like that. Nevertheless, she'd have liked to have something else. She felt that something was missing from her life but she couldn't say what. She didn't want to think of that, so she turned her eyes to Mary and asked her:

"What are you writing these days?"

Actually, she wasn't interested in what Mary was writing at all. She didn't read anything else but some magazines and sometimes the newspapers Daniel brought at home in the evening.

"A little story with ghosts", Mary cheered up. She liked talking about her work because she felt on a safe territory. "The ghost of a man falls in love with a living woman and pursues her everywhere. It is something romantic and comic the same time. All sorts of funny things happen".

"I wouldn't like to read it!" Mrs Thompson exclaimed, horrified of such an idea, because she was a too pragmatic woman, in her way, of course, to taste such things.

"Don't worry!" answered Mary back harshly. "There are a lot of people that like to read such things. My editor told me that I could earn a lot of money with it and this is important, don't you think? I want to visit Egypt one day and, who knows, maybe this little story might help me see my dream come true", said Mary winking, gesture she knew Alice didn't like at all. She saw her grinning a few times.

"However, I hope you manage", Alice grumbled. "Do you want some more coffee, Mary?" she asked, being suddenly bored with Mary and hoping this one would leave.

'No, thank you" replied Mary, inferring what the other woman was feeling. "I think I must go. I have enough to write, so I'd better leave you now. See you soon. Maybe we'll see each other later".

After Mary left, Alice washed the cups and put them back in the closet. She started thinking of Mary's weird marriage with Michael Reid and their terrible fights. She could hear them even though she was living two houses away. Actually, she knew the entire street could hear them. They'd become quite famous. They were a reason for fun in the little street where usually nothing happened. Well, at least so far.

However, she was sure their marriage wouldn't last. Mary was too selfish to keep it. She didn't make the smallest effort for that.

Michael would get bored with her some day, and leave her with her stupid stories. She'd wanted to see what Mary would say then. Certainly, she'd lose some of her self-confidence. It couldn't be otherwise. She'd have lost some of her identity. A husband could offer you that, Alice thought, and felt a sort of fondness thinking of poor Daniel, who would come tired to death in the evening, working so hard to offer her a better life than she'd had before meeting him.

Chapter Three

While she was thinking of Mary and her husband, although she was completely absorbed by her thoughts and had remained still in front of the sink where she'd washed the cups, she heard a knock on the door. She went and opened the door. James, the policeman she talked to earlier, and another man were in front of the door and greeted her asking her some time to speak with her. She invited them inside politely, as she'd been taught, and led them to the living room. She showed them to sit down and then sat before them.

"Mrs Thompson", started the older man, "I'm Inspector-Chief McNamara and you already know Sergeant-Detective James. I'm sorry to tell you so directly, but Mrs Dobbs was killed last night".

"Oh, God! I knew that was something wrong when I saw the police. In addition, she didn't come out at all this morning. She would come out in the yard early in the morning. Well, I thought she might not have felt well after everything happened last night", said Alice, stopping herself when she realised she was talking nonsense. She pulled herself together and asked: “What happened? Who killed her?”

“We don’t know now, but we’ll find out, that’s sure”, replied McNamara a little annoyed because everyone was expecting miracles from them, and everyone wanted police had some answers on spot. They were supposed to tide things up at once and usually, unfortunately, things were quite far from that. It was necessary some work, even a lot of work. He went on: “I’d like to know if you or maybe your husband heard something last night. You live practically across and maybe who knows...”

“Oh, I don’t know if he heard or saw anything, but I didn’t hear a thing. You know, after I heard about that girl on the Dobbs’ lawn, I took a sleeping pill, because I knew I’d been thinking too much of that and wouldn’t have slept at all. Usually, I don’t do that. I mean, taking pills, but now I had to. I fell asleep in ten minutes, I think. I had just woken up since a quarter of an hour when you came. I’m sorry, but I can’t really tell you anything. After you left last night, I don’t know what happened”.

“When is your husband going to come back at home today, ma’am?” asked McNamara. “We’d like to talk to him too. Maybe he knows something, he saw something...”

“I’m not very sure. He might come at six; he should come at the hour, normally, but sometimes he has unsolved problems and must stay at work till later, even quite often lately. He happened to come at home only at ten or later. Sometimes I don’t even see him in the evening.

He says it's meaningless I wait for him. He doesn't want me to get too tired".

"All right, ma'am", said McNamara, who already saw how the things were. "Where does he work? Maybe we'll call him and ask him a few questions on the phone and finish with this discussion".

"Well, he is an accountant", said Alice proudly. "He works for Expert Audit Co. It is in town, you know. He has to travel every day. We've moved here because we prefer the peace and quietness of suburbs. It is different from the town, isn't it?"

"Hmm", grumbled McNamara, sick of hearing her holding forth with no use. "Well, ma'am. Can you tell us a few things about Patsy Porter? You must know her as she was leaving next door."

"Well, I can tell you what I know, but unfortunately, I don't know much. She is not that kind of girl to whom I pay too much attention", she said plainly, to have her opinions about the girl clearly understood. "I think she's sixteen or something like that. I know I heard she left school. It was a serious scandal at her house that day. They shouted one to the other for hours. Poor Mrs Porter was very upset then. Patsy is a very beautiful girl for her age, well, if you like dyed hair and very long and thin legs, as she has. She's not very smart and she's even shallow, if you know what I mean. I've heard she left the house with a young man working for Mr Brown's pub. I, myself, don't know him very well. I think I've seen him only once or twice when he led her at home, if he was. That's it. However, when I saw them, I didn't think they were so close. She didn't seem too fond of him. I don't know where she is now and I think my husband doesn't either. He wasn't too interested in what was going on at the neighbours'. I've told you he is quite tired when he comes back home and I can't bore him with such things".

"I see, ma'am", said McNamara, already tired to hear her so decisive and bitter opinions. "However, if you remember anything, you can call us. Here's my card," he said taking a card out of his coat pocket.

"Of course, sir", said Alice taking the business card. "By the way, sir, has anything happened to Patsy?" she asked curiously, although she'd have wanted to hide her curiousness.

"We don't know yet", lied McNamara. "For the time being we only presume things, ma'am. Thank you a lot. We're leaving now, but if you remember anything, please contact us", he said pointing to the card in her hand.

"Of course, sir", Alice said putting the card in the pocket of the apron. "But I don't think I know anything else", she said seeing them off.

After the door closed behind them and they reached the street, James looked at McNamara and said:

"Sir, don't you think that Mr Thompson plays on two fronts?"

"Yes, I do. I might be wrong and he might have something to do at the office. Who knows? What's interesting is the fact that the woman hasn't thought at least a second that Patsy could be the girl found on the lawn. I don't think she's very smart or if she is, then she's very absent-minded or completely disinterested in the entire situation, and I don't buy it. She couldn't hide curiousness in her voice".

James accepted, nodding.

"However, let's go and see the woman we saw visiting Mrs Thompson this morning and after we talk to her, we go and see the people next door. I think it's about Mrs Reid", presumed McNamara, looking on a page in his little black book.

They went and rang at the Reids' door. After a while, Mary Reid came and opened the door smiling when she saw the two men.

"I've been waiting for you", she explained them her smile, when she saw their look. "I was sure you'd ask questions to everyone in the street. I know this is the procedure. I also read thrillers now and then. Please, get into", she said showing them into the house.

They got inside and followed their hostess in a room that seemed to be her study.

"I'm sorry I've brought you here", apologised Mary with no conviction, "but this is the most comfortable room in the whole house, at least for me. I don't like to stay in the living room, I feel it's of no use when I don't have guests, and I don't have a drawing room. This one should have been the drawing room. I turned it into a study for me. It looks good, doesn't it?"

McNamara, almost exasperated because of so many useless explanations looked around and, noticing the computer on the desk, asked their talkative hostess:

"What do you work, ma'am?"

"Ah, I write stories", she said blushing. "I'm not a famous writer or something like that, and I won't become, I'm sure", she said quickly not to leave them the impression that she was dreaming to become more than she was. "I make some money, that's all. Of course, I can't say I don't like what I do. It's interesting to make your imagination work instead of being an accountant or something like that," she continued making grimaces as if someone had put a lemon before her. "You must understand me, I'm sure. Your work also involves imagination, I think. You have to think of various scenarios and find solutions all the time, don't you?"

McNamara smiled to the woman. In deed, he liked her, in a way, even though she was wasting his time with useless discussions. He always thought that you must know the people you were dealing with during an investigation, and the woman revealed herself quite fast.

She was like an open book, completely different from Mrs Thompson. Her nature was like fresh air after they had just talked to Alice Thompson, who was rather a stiff woman and didn't have an agile mind like the woman before them that moment. Alice Thompson was too full of her role of a wife to be truly sincere.

"In deed, ma'am", he approved her presumption concerning their work. "I'd like to know if you heard or saw anything last night after we'd left here".

"To tell you, sincerely, I couldn't hear anything even if I wanted... You know, I had a monstrous scandal with my husband last night" she admitted with some hesitation, blushing slightly, although she wanted to seem nonchalant. Despite her blush, she seemed quite used to that, though. "You know" she continued "he was really upset with me because I'd gone out in the street with my gown... Nevertheless, I must admit that my gown is quite short and thin. Actually, it doesn't hide too much, maybe almost nothing. The matter is I put on the first thing I saw when I heard that scream and went out. Imagine how furious he got when he saw me! I was quite happy he was concerned with what happened to that girl and then to Mr Dobbs in the street. I wouldn't have liked to have a row with him before the others in the street—these people talk too much and about us, they talk most of the time. This is, actually, their main concern. I know they listen to our quarrels with interest because they don't have too much fun over here. Moreover, I know my husband well, even very well. He couldn't have stopped himself from yelling at me if he saw me dressed like that before getting inside. However, that's it. He saw me in the end, you know, when we got inside, and I had to listen to all his accusations. Of course, I also told him what I thought of his behaviour. He was right in a way, I don't say no" she tried to seem reasonable, "but he should have thought I hadn't done it on purpose. I didn't have enough time to choose the right gown to go out in such circumstances. Would you have thought what to wear if you had heard such a scream? It was horrible!" she explained, and the mimic of her face was telling everything.

"No, in deed" answer McNamara without stopping a smile hearing her explanations.

He could also see that she had a great body, even if she was a little plump. He was sure that if he had been her husband, he'd have done the same thing as Mr Reid. He'd been horrified. He wouldn't have liked that anyone else could see that body, but him.

"So, I'm sorry, but I couldn't hear a thing" Mary continued peacefully. "We yelled for at least two hours, if not more. It wasn't a great night," she grinned. "We didn't even talk to each other this morning. He prepared breakfast for himself and left at work with no word," she said without seeming upset at all that things were so bad between her and her husband.

James, completely amazed couldn't refrain from asking her:

"And don't you mind, ma'am, at all?"

"What should I mind? That he doesn't speak to me? No, I'm used to that. He does that every two days. It is not a real problem", she sent the hypothesis away with a gesture. “He always does so. He finds something to make a scandal: my dress or tights, I’ve forgotten to prepare dinner or I haven’t ironed his shirts... However, I don’t do that and he should’ve known it already. I know I warned him at the beginning. I told him I’m not the household type and he shouldn’t expect such things”.

The two men were very astonished now. They’d never seen such a wife or one to admit so openly such things.

“However, how can you bear?” asked James again, although he was actually thinking of her poor husband who should bear her laziness.

James thought that, if he were in his place, he wouldn’t have lived with her for at least a day. He wouldn’t have accepted that his wife dressed in the way she did or didn’t do anything in the house.

“But it’s really interesting, you know?” she told them smiling widely. “If we got along just fine, with no quarrels and scandals, I’d die of boredom! I’m sure I’d die!” she insisted. “Quarrels bring something fresh in our lives, in my opinion, and thus we won’t get bored one with the other too soon. Today I’ll play my usual role of upset and hurt woman and tomorrow he’ll try his best to make me happy. Isn’t he nice?” she said smiling sweetly, maybe too sweetly.

James was completely knocked down. McNamara couldn’t bear anymore. He wanted to go out and laugh as much as he could. Therefore, even though he hadn’t had a chance to ask her about Patsy, he thought it was time to do it later. He stood up and said:

"Then we leave, ma'am, and keep in touch. We surely have more questions for you and also for your husband".

Mary saw them off and came back to her work, thinking that, actually, they hadn't asked her any pertinent question and that seemed really strange. Soon, she stopped thinking of them and returned to her love story. It was more interesting and, moreover, she had a delivery deadline and she didn't want to miss the chance to gain the big sweepstakes.

Once out of the house, McNamara burst into laughter. James watched him completely amazed.

"Why are you laughing, sir? I don't think it's funny. These two are a little crazy, don't you think so?"

"Oh, no, James, not really... Each of us has their own weirdness... I know these two seem completely mad. However, I think that their life is really interesting, in deed. I'm sure they don't get bored, as Mrs Reid used to say. How could they? However, James, think: we already have two interesting families. On one side, the Thompsons, with Alice, the caring little wife, and Daniel the womaniser, I can bet, and on the other, we have the Reids, with Mary, the little gambler, figuratively speaking, and Michael, jealous and possessive. They are very interesting, aren't they? It's strange that they're so two different families and they have certain relations, though. Who would've believed that Mary had something to talk with Alice and vice versa? They are like oil and water, James".

"Oh, no, sir, I think they're merely crazy, each one in their way, and that's why they get along. I'm from the country, sir, and I don't taste such things", said the policeman coming from a little country village where he hadn't ever had a chance to see things like that.

"Don't bother, James", McNamara said smiling. "Let's see the other people in the street. I can't believe they're more interesting than that. I think we must talk to the Randalls now. They live exactly between the Thompsons and the Reids".

They went to the Randalls' house and rang at the door. They insisted but, in the end, no answer came from inside. After having expected a little, Alice Thompson, having watched them all this time, came out in the door of her house and told them:

"They're not at home now. They have the grocer's shop in the corner and they're there now. Their children are at school, probably, and don't come back until three. I never hear them earlier and you must know they're very noisy usually".

"Thank you, ma'am, then we go to the grocer's and talk to them," said McNamara. "See you soon!"

"Have you seen, James, I think she was watching us from behind the curtains" McNamara said. "What do you think?"

"I have no opinion anymore, sir. With these people I really don't have an opinion", James replied, seeming a little out of balance. They didn't usually run into normal people during their investigations, but he could understand those, in a way or another. They were mostly criminals, but not these.

McNamara and James advanced to the other end of the street. After a few steps, they stopped for a moment in front of a small house on the left, with the windows and door painted in blue and white walls. There was a small garden in front of it with multicoloured flowers, standing proudly under the pale sun.

McNamara watched avidly the little house and flowers. He was sure that at sunset it was a real relish to stay on the house veranda smelling the heavy smell of flowers in the night.

"It's a restful house, don't you think, James?" McNamara asked, pointing with his head to the house with blue transoms, feeling a bit wry for having noticed that.

"I think so, sir. The truth is that almost all little houses from suburbs have a special charm, as far as I could see. But you must know that at home, at my parents, it's more pleasant. The green is greener and there are more birds...", spoke out nostalgia in his heart.

"I see your point, James", said McNamara with a smile in his voice. He found it was funny how such little sentimental notches could lie where you expected less. "In the country, there's a lot of peace ad serenity... You know, I'm curious to see the owner of this house. However, we'll meet this one soon. He must be on the list Mike drew up. And you must know that the contrast with the house next door is welcome".

"Yes, it's a very good combination of white and yellow, sir", James agreed, watching the house next door.

After a few moments, they went away, without realising for a moment that someone was watching them behind the yellow curtain of the house on their right side.

They headed to the grocer's and, on their way they savoured the peace of the little street, whose children were still at school. The street was small, but clean and restful.

The grocer's wasn't too big, but seemed to have enough merchandises if you could believe the advertisements on the outside wall.

The policemen got into and saw a man with a white apron tied on his waist arranging some oranges on the counter. There was a smell of spice in the air and it pinched their noses but it wasn't unpleasant at all.

The grocer looked up and saw the two newly entered, but he didn't have a chance to say anything because one of them said first:

"Good day, Mr Randall, I presume", McNamara said.

"Yes, sir. And you are...?"

"I'm Inspector Chief McNamara, and this is sergeant detective James. We're here to talk to you about the girl found in the Dobbs' yard last night and about Mrs Dobbs".

"Has anything happened to Mrs Dobbs?" Mr Randall asked with a little dreadful fear in his voice. He had heard about poor Mr Dobbs but to think that also something happened to Mrs Dobbs it was really upsetting.

"I'm afraid, so, sir. She was also killed last night".

"Oh, God! Alison, come here, dear!" Mr Randall shouted.

"What happened?" asked a woman getting into the shop from the back.

She was a tall and skinny woman with severe air. She had a lot of wrinkles and her eyes were sharp with no trace of humour in them. She seemed not to have ever smiled in her life.

"Listen, Mrs Dobbs was killed last night!" her husband told her.

"Oh, dear, poor Mrs Dobbs! She was a very nosey woman, I know, and she upset us all the time with her intruding nature, as otherwise all our neighbours, but I couldn't have ever imagined that such a think could happen to her... However, you know, the cat died because it was too curious", she said reproachfully even though she had just heard the woman had died. "How did she die?"

"I think she was stabbed about four times, ma'am. It wasn't too pleasant to see" Mr McNamara said wanting to turn back the reproach he felt in Mrs Randall's voice.

About dead people, only good things, he'd been taught. And here it wasn't about someone having made a lot of wrongdoings, but only about an old, curious and intruding woman, that shouldn't have deserved such a fate, in his opinion, no matter what. He resented Mrs Randall affirmation and he though that she was clearly a woman with a narrow mind.

"Oh, poor thing! How could we help, sir?" asked Mrs Randall, even though without much concern, but feeling hurt for having been so severely admonished.

"Did you hear or see anything last night? Especially after the police had left..."

"I must tell you we saw only the end, when the police came. We woke up with some difficulty because we had a hard day yesterday. We heard that scream like in the dream and, initially, I didn't even want to wake up. My husband woke up with even more difficulty", she said watching her husband reproachfully, but this one kept saying nothing. "And I haven't heard anything from the Dobbs, so far, even if they live next to us. We went to bed as soon as you'd left and I fell asleep at once. I'm afraid we cannot help you too much", Mrs Randall said and her husband, nodding, showed he agreed with her words.

"Well, then. What do you know about Patsy Porter?" McNamara asked, while James kept writing in his little book.

"She's a very stubborn girl and she's even badly brought up, I can say", Mrs Randall began, peevishly, leaving clearly the impression that in their family she was the one talking and making decisions. "She made a lot of problems to her poor mother when she was here, but she didn't know to control her either" she said severely. "Poor Mrs Porter still hurts because her daughter left. She seems to have left one day, a few months, I think. Everyone says she left with that young man who used to work in Mr Brown's pub. He was a hard working boy but the girl stole his minds. He couldn't see anything else before his eyes. I'm sure he was convinced sun was rising up when she turned up".

"Did she love him too?" Mr McNamara asked her.

"I'm sure she didn't", Mrs Randall said quickly wickedly. "She was playing with him, that's all, and therefore I was very amazed hearing they left together. Something wasn't all right. I'm sure about it. It wasn't all right at all".

Seeing the confusion on McNamara's face she explained:

"I couldn't imagine she'd leave with him. And, I'm sure", she said making a large gesture that should've include the entire street, "everyone here was thinking the same. Had she been to leave with a man, then she'd have left with an older one, even a very older one. I remember she was making eyes to all the men in the street that are over thirty. It was really strange her leaving with such a young boy, you should know. But, however, both of them disappeared the same day and I heard they left a note to her mother and she was writing that she was leaving with Peter, so that's it".

"So, you'd never imagined they'd eloped together", wanted McNamara to make sure he understood.

"Not at all", she said decisively. "She wasn't for that boy. She was aiming at something more, you must know. She used to say she didn't go out with children and only an older man could satisfy her taste. And I wasn't the only one hearing her. Many others did. She used to make eyes to my husband too", she said accusatively, and glanced severely to her husband as if he'd been involved in something very bad.

Mr Randall blushed slightly and tried to deny but his wife's eyes didn't leave any place to move and, reluctantly, he admitted she was right although, inside, he was boiling with rage.

"Yes, this is true! She was trying to make eyes to each of us. Mr Reid didn't notice her, you know, but usually he doesn't notice anything else but his wife. I'm afraid he doesn't trust her too much and he's quite jealous, in my opinion. They quarrel all day long, the two of them. You hear them yelling one to the other from far".

"In deed", his wife approved. "One day he'll kill her, I'm sure. I say they should split up, it would be better for both of them. The two of them are not meant to live together. They'd be better with someone else".

"Don't be dolt", Mr Randall contradict her condescendingly. "They only quarrel, that's all. He doesn't beat her or anything. She's a little different from what a wife should be, that's why everything happens. She doesn't seem to care of his needs too much and she doesn't cook or iron. She dressed in the way she likes and she doesn't consider his wishes about that. But she also works and seems to have a certain financial independence. Therefore, she doesn't pay much attention to what he wants. That's all" he replied, making his wife to spring up as if something bit her on her back.

"That's not all", Mrs Randall said meanly. "The man is upset because she dresses so that all men could see her legs up to the top and she doesn't cover at least her breasts too much. All men look at her and they have why, and her husband, of course, doesn't like it. I think it's normal. Don't tell me you'd like me show my legs and breasts to the entire street?" she asked turning warlike to her husband.

This one watched her a little shocked, but as the other two could realise, he wasn't shocked a lot because of the presumption to see her in short skirts or very bare-shouldered, although this could seem really weird to him too. No, he wasn't shocked because of her idea of arousing his jealousy in any way. He'd stopped being jealous on her for a long time, even almost as soon as they'd got married. He couldn't find anything in her to attract him. He couldn't see anything else but her tough eyes and her tight mouth, as well as her moralizing nature. And he couldn't even think that someone else could see something different in her, at least. And that was a pity because thus he might've taken her out of his head and he could've got rid of her.

McNamara and James realised what he was thinking and tried to watch otherwise not to let Mrs Randall understand it too, seeing her husband's thoughts reflected so well in their eyes.

"Did anyone seem interested in Patsy in a special manner?" asked McNamara trying to chase away any of Mrs Randall's thoughts.

"Mr Graham seemed to like her", said Mrs Randall, slightly evasively. "But however", she chased away any idea that could bloom from here, "he wouldn't have done any gesture in her direction, I could swear. You shouldn't think of that".

"Why not" asked James curios to find out why she was so confident in her opinion.

"He's a teacher, you know?" Mr Randall said. "He's a guy that seems serious and I don't think he'd try to seduce a minor. He doesn't look like having such inclination or at least the courage", he said having the satisfaction of seeing his wife narrowing her eyes because he spoke before her and didn't leave her the chance to tell her opinion first.

"I see", said James. "Who else was also interested in her or paid her some attention?"

"Mr Thompson", said Mr Randall fast. "I've the impression he liked her quite a lot. Patsy had the same coloration as his wife, but she was younger than Mrs Thompson and, obviously, much merrier. Mrs Thompson doesn't smile too much and seems interested only in keeping her house clean and her husband well dressed. She doesn't know what a dance means and doesn't go out too much. I've seen them going to a restaurant only once so far, when they were invited to a wedding".

'Don't speak about her like that", his wife interrupted him upset. "Alice is a very good woman, and you rarely can find such a woman these days. She knows taking care of her house and husband. He should be enormously grateful for having such a wife! Not everyone has this luck!" Mrs Randall burst out vehemently. "Think of Mr Reid!"

Randall abandoned the subject. However, James and McNamara had already understood what was about and could imagine why Mr Thompson was paying attention to Patsy. A man sometimes prefers a woman to talk with and have fun with, not only one that keeps the house in good conditions. There are maids for such a thing, if you thought.

"So", interrupted McNamara the silence, "have you seen Patsy or maybe, have you seen Peter lately?"

"Oh, no", Alison answered. "None of them has come back or written or anything else... They left for good, I think", she said with a hardly hidden reproach for Patsy. "Ungrateful child, I've always said. Poor her mother struggled with her alone because her father rarely came home. You know, he's a salesman. And even then he wasn't too interested in what was going on in the house. He was good of no help. Maybe if he was more interested, the girl wouldn't have ended up like that: a mere skirt", she said with total scorn for the girl.

"Very well, Mrs Randall, I thank you. Here's my card and call me if you remember anything, even if you consider it's not very important", McNamara said offering her his card and shortening thus the discussion that had got boring, following the same lines.

After getting outside where no one could hear them, McNamara turned to James and said:

"I think Mr Thompson really liked Patsy. He certainly could see something of his wife in Patsy, but this one should've been less boring and a bit more amusing than his correct and so hardworking wife. He might've made eyes to the girl, in deed, what do you think, James?"

"Yes, sir, it might've been like that. But, you know, I think that the teacher also could be considered a suspect in this concern, as well as Mr Randall. You saw he blushed when his wife mentioned Patsy's habit of encouraging older men, associating him in this game too. Maybe, Mr Reid could be taken out of the list, though, what do you say? He's too possessive and jealous with his wife to have cared of the kid, what do you think?"

"I don't know that yet, James. I first must see and talk to him and only then, I'll make an opinion of him. Maybe he also plays some games with his wife and he might also be sick of so many quarrels in the house, don't you think? No one could enjoy a continuous scandal".

"Maybe, it's so, sir, but don't you think that Mary Reid would've seen something if her husband liked Patsy? She doesn't seem a dolt woman, but her mind is quite sharp, even if she's in the way she is".

"Maybe she is, who knows? And Randall blushed because of fear of his wife, too, I tell you, not only because he'd like the girl, although I also think he'd like her. With such an old crone at home, it would've been impossible to be different. The man doesn't have too much joy in his life with that woman as a wife. Now, let's go and see the Browns too. They are at the pub, or at least they should".

They crossed the street and got into the pub. It was a small pub, specific to suburbs, but it was cosy and the people inside seemed to have a great time.

At the counter, there was a massive man with big hands and red face. He was around forty and had a special allure because of the red curly hair that seemed not to have been combed that day. Actually, his hair always seemed the same. It had its own life. Hadn't been his age and height, he could've been considered a naughty boy, because of his eyes and hair. He had a merry air, and his clients seemed to like him a lot. Anyone could see that the people in the pub felt there like at home, comfortably, and McNamara could imagine that they, probably, came there every day, as generally happens in the pub in a neighbourhood, suburbs or small villages where people know each other and where the pub is the meeting place for most of people, especially men.

People were talking and laughing. Although there were few women inside, in McNamara's opinion, there was a lot of noise, though, and people seemed to talk the same time.

McNamara and James went to the counter and sat on the high chairs in front of it.

Mr Brown, the publican, came to them and said:

"Good day, to both of you! What should it be?"

"Coffee, please, for both of us", ordered McNamara, putting some money on the counter to pay for the drinks and only afterwards he showed his badge. "We're with the police, sir, and we've some questions for you and your wife".

"I see", said Mr Brown leaving the impression that he was trying to figure out what was about. Perhaps it was about what happened a night before. "I can answer your questions, no problem, but my wife has just left. She went to Mrs Porter, at the other end of the street and she said she might have to stay for a while. Mrs Porter seems to have a problem, something. She didn't say what exactly on the phone, but it seemed serious. My Mary said she was crying".

"Well, then, we'll ask you. Do you know to whom Patsy Porter used to make eyes? We've heard that she encouraged more men in the street".

"In deed, it's true. She made eyes almost to everyone in this street and some of men answered back too. Now here's a girl that really brings trouble, if you want to know my opinion. It's that kind of girl that prefers older people, and, between you and me, you know that men usually answer to such things if they're of a certain age. They feel a little flattered and even proud to make an eel to pay them attention, especially if they had the impression their days of seducers had gone".

"Were you also among the men she tried to charm, sir, and that answered to her encouragements?", James asked.

"Oh, no!", said the man smiling openly the same time. "I might've been flattered for a while, you know", he winked to them roguishly. "I'm forty-four already and I think I liked that such a young girl paid me attention. Who wouldn't? She's quite pretty, you know. But, on one hand, how could I put it, I have a happy marriage and I don't say it only to say it. My wife looks great, although she's twenty years older than Patsy, but, otherwise, she's a very merry woman and she satisfies me entirely, if you know what I mean", he said winking to them. "On the other hand, Patsy was doing that with all the men in the street, and, honestly, I don't like this kind of girl... I think a girl should be merry and have a little fun, but shouldn't be only a cheap flirt. If she'd really liked someone in a special way, I'd have understood her, but she hadn't. It wasn't like that. Everything was like a sport to her. She wanted to have an older lover, that's all. You know...nothing serious. She probably thought she'd have more distinction if she'd go out with an older man, possibly with a certain material situation".

"We've heard she left with Peter, the boy who worked for you before", said James.

"I heard that too, but it's too odd, you should know. I think so. That boy wasn't for her. He was too young, only twenty. He used to follow her everywhere, and he looked like a puppy, you know. When I saw them, I told him the girl was mocking of him, but I don't think he could understand such a thing—he was too caught. Therefore, when I heard they'd left together—you know, my wife is a good friend of Mrs Porter and she told her about—I couldn't be more astonished. I wouldn't have thought it was possible. But maybe, I was wrong, who knows?", he continued, seeming very mistrustful, though. One could clearly see that was stuck in his first opinion.

"Wouldn't it have been possible she only said she was leaving with Peter, but actually she'd left with another man?"

"I don't know, to be honest. It could have. But I know he also left the same day she did. He took his weekly check and said he was going to work in town because there he'd be paid better and had friends there".

"After he left, didn't you hear anything of him?" McNamara asked him.

"No, nothing. He didn't come by here or called. I don't know anything of him now. He was a good lad, you should know, very hardworking. And he never left his work unfinished, not even after falling in for Patsy. I really regret him. I hired one afterwards, but I had to fire him because he did nothing right. He was interested only in having a big pay check. He didn't work at all. Many times I had to do his job too, and you see, it didn't work for me at all", he said frowning for the first time.

"But about Patsy, have you heard anything ever since?", McNamara came back to the subject he was interested in.

"No, sir! My wife told me Patsy hadn't even bothered to call her mother and tell her where she was or what she was doing", he said, and they could feel reproach in his voice. "Poor woman is anxious with worries", he said, and the two policemen realised he didn't agree at all with what Patsy was doing.

"Have you heard that Mrs Dobbs was also killed last night?" McNamara asked him watching his face attentively to see if he was trying to hold anything back.

"Oh, no, was she?" Mr Brown exclaimed and he seemed surprised in deed. "I've heard a young girl was killed in the Dobbs' yard, that's all. How was she killed? Mrs Dobbs, I mean?" he asked curiously, without trying even to hide that.

"Well, she was stabbed in her drawing room", McNamara answered to him. "She might've noticed something that could be related to the girl found earlier in the yard and I think the killer saw her too".

"I know we haven't had such a thing around before", Mr Brown said, "but wasn't a burglary?", he tried to express his opinion as if it was more meaningful if she'd been killed due to a burglary than otherwise.

"No, sir", James answered, "nothing was stolen from the house, in our opinion, and in the room there are only signs of a short fight, that's all".

"I see", he murmured. "Poor, Mrs Dobbs! She was an intruding and curious woman, I know, but otherwise she was really good and large hearted", he said. "She shouldn't have died like that", Mr Brown continued, shaking his head as if he still couldn't believe, and McNamara could see that the man was really sad because of the news.

That moment, a man around thirty or forty, came to the counter:

"I'd like a beer, Mr Brown, please".

"Of course, Mr Graham", he said professionally with a smile on his face, although a few seconds before his face was sad because of Mrs Dobbs' death. "As usual, isn't it?"

"Yes, please", said the young man absently, turning around and watching in the room to see someone he knew with whom he could sit down and talk.

Mr Brown turned and took a bottle from the shelf behind him and then put the bottle of beer before the man.

McNamara, hearing the name the publican uttered, already turned to the man and watched him a few moments and then, taking off his badge, he said:

"We're with the police, sir. May we accompany you at a table there and ask you a few questions?"

Mr Graham seemed a little confused that moment, even alarmed, as McNamara thought, but accepted the invitation reluctantly. He couldn't do otherwise. He showed them to a small table in the corner and invited them to sit down on the bench in front of him.

"What's about, sir?" he asked curiously drinking a little from his bottle first, as if to make courage to start the discussion.

"Haven't you heard anything about the girl killed in the Dobbs' yard last night?", asked James shocked, not knowing what kind of game the man was playing. He'd have thought the people would've imagined the police would ask questions about the killed young girl, because that was the usual procedure and even though they hadn't ever had anything to do directly with such an investigation, at least from movies they could've found out how such things were dealt with.

"I've heard nothing", Mr Graham answered a little shocked about the news. "I wasn't at home last night, you should know. I stayed with a girl friend in town and I've come back now. I've just come back. What girl is about? Do we know her?" he asked with a little fear felt in his voice.

"If you weren't at home, then that's understandable", James said without showing him he felt his fear in the voice. "Well, last night a young girl was killed in the Dobbs' yard, and Mr Dobbs died immediately after he had seen her or maybe because he'd seen something else. During this night, after everyone left, inclusively the police, Mrs Dobbs was also killed in the own living room".

McNamara was watching Mr Graham's face attentively and could see he was more than astonished of what he heard. News came fast, a piece after the other, and no piece was too cheering. The man seemed to have known nothing of all of those and was really shocked.

"To fill in the official report, sir", he asked him "could you tell us the name of the person with whom you were last night? I'm sorry, but we must write it down. We must find out what everyone living nearby did last night".

"Of course, no problem", said Graham a little reassured now. "It's about a friend in town. Actually, she also teaches in the same school where I do. Her name's Laura Bradshaw and we've been going out together for a while. We were to some friends last night because they celebrated their first year of marriage and then we went to her house because it was too late and stayed there till this morning when we went together to school. If you want to talk to her, this is her address and phone number", he said, taking a little black book out of his pocket. He tore a sheet of paper and wrote the address and phone number on it and handed it in to McNamara.

"What could you tell us about Patsy Porter, sir?" McNamara asked him.

"Patsy Porter? Is she the girl found in the Dobbs's yard?" in Graham's voice they could feel amazement and also a little grieve for the young girl if not more. Maybe he liked her too, as the others.

"We don't know for sure yet, but she might be Patsy, because she matches the description. However, could you tell us anything about her?" McNamara repeated.

"Well, Patsy was my student for three years and then she left school. She was a really beautiful girl, and she knew it, even very well, and the boys in the school were all crazy about her. However, she didn't use to go out with boys of her age. I saw more men waiting for her in front of the school, of course not all of them at once", a trace of smile could be felt in his voice. "She seemed to prefer men of a certain age, at least with fifteen years older than she. You realise I couldn't know who were the men waiting for her. Edinburgh isn't a small village you know it. You cannot know everyone".

"We've heard she made eyes to all the men in this street, inclusively you, didn't she?" McNamara asked.

Mr Graham blushed a little hearing him and, then, he said a little reluctantly.

"Yes, she did, in deed. Some of the men didn't care of her games, you know, and I didn't either, even if the girl was very attractive. Ok, I liked the girl, a little", he admitted. "Who wouldn't? However, you must realise I couldn't think of her this way because she was my student, and, moreover, she was also minor. I couldn't stop thinking of her age, even after she left school and I wasn't her teacher anymore. I don't want having problems with the law. I can't afford it in my situation. As a teacher, I have a reputation to keep, I hope you understand it", he insisted.

"So you didn't encourage her at all, sir?" James asked him curiously.

"Of course, not!" Mr Graham exclaimed, showing that he considered James' presumption completely outrageous. "She'd always try to draw my attention, of course, as if she did with everyone, but I managed not to let myself caught. Once she wrote me a letter, I remember, and another time, she asked me if I wanted to go with her to a dance in town, to a disco. But I didn't accept it at all. I don't do such things or at least not with kids of her age. I didn't encourage her at all".

"If she hadn't been your student, would you have accepted her invitation?", McNamara asked him thinking that the man seemed quite weak to have accepted.

"No, I've already told you!", Mr Graham burst out already very irritated, unable to keep a low volume to his voice anymore. "She was minor, damn it, and I don't need such problems. I'm a teacher, for God's sake, and I must show some decency and morality! I like the job I'm doing, even if I'm badly paid for it. I can't afford being fired only for having liked a nice face. And she's only that—a nice face. She didn't have anything to offer or at least not to me!".

"I see", McNamara replied, although with some restraint in his voice. "Do you know anything about the men in the street having accepted to go out with her in the end?"

"I cannot be sure, but I think Mr Thompson accepted", he said, thinking that giving that out didn't really matter. In the end they'd have heard of Thompson's adventure with Patsy because he knew other people had seen them together. "I saw them in town once when I was with my girl-friend in a restaurant... Patsy and Mr Thompson passed by the restaurant where we two were dining. I could notice they were having a very serious discussion, and he seemed a little upset, I think".

"When did that happen?" asked James suddenly very interested thinking they finally caught a line of investigation.

"Two weeks ago or maybe two weeks and a half... I was quite surprised, because Mrs Dobbs, you know Mrs Dobbs used to gossip a lot, told me that Patsy had left with a young man who was working in Mr Brown's pub and she wasn't ever wrong when she told something. I even thought then that her infallible nose made a mistake that time".

"Knowing that Patsy preferred older men weren't you surprised that she eloped with a kid of only twenty?" asked McNamara, letting the other one see clearly he didn't believe too much of what he was saying.

"I was a little surprised", he admitted, "but then I thought the girl might've changed her ideas. Peter was five years older than she, though, and he wasn't a student, you know. I thought she'd find something interesting in him and came back to normal, I mean, to be like the other girls of her age. Things like that still happen", he said, trying to convince them he was right.

"I see", McNamara said, although he didn't understand a thing. He couldn't see the logic in what he was saying, because he knew very well that people rarely change and when they do it, the change is only at the surface. Life taught him things like that and he counted more on his experience than in the chit-chat of the man before him.

"And teenagers do such thing all the time", explained the man. "Today they love someone, and next day another one. At fifteen, sixteen they're not at the age when they have steady relations", Mr Graham added with the voice he used in class usually, trying to seem sure of what he was saying even though he wasn't too convinced the two men would buy it.

McNamara studied the face of the man for a few moments and realised that, actually, he wasn't too sure of what he was saying. Now he was convinced Mr Graham was trying to express groundless opinions and that made him wondering if he was as sincere as he tried to seem.

The policeman didn't like Edward Graham's small and dark eyes, either, because he could read in them badly hidden cunning, and he didn't like his mouth, whose line betrayed wickedness. He didn't seem to be a person with a strong nature, and he doubted Graham would've resisted to a young girl like Patsy. He was sure he wouldn't have turned his back to the girl if she'd made him eyes. He'd have found a way to be with her. People always found a way to fulfil their wishes and they always think they are smarter than the people around and, consequently, they would not be caught.

The three men drank each a bit of their drinks and then McNamara thought he'd have to ask him something else when, suddenly, his mobile phone rang.

"McNamara", he said, and then listened frowning.

It was the coroner who had some very interesting news for him, but the problem was the news changed absolutely everything. Nothing he knew made sense anymore. If anything had made so far, he told himself bitterly.

"We have to leave now, James. Thank you, Mr Graham, for everything you've told us. Here's my card. If you remember anything, but anything, please call me at the office or on the mobile phone", he said offering his card to Mr Graham. "We have to leave now, James", he told his subordinate standing up from his chair the same time.

James stood up too. Both waved to Mr Brown and left the pub then.

"What's happened, sir?" asked James, while they were heading to the car they'd parked at the end of the street, not far from the bar, near the square near the little street.

"Apparently, the girl found in the Dobbs' yard is not Patsy Porter. The coroner says her hair wasn't light brown, as we've thought, even though the girl used to dye her hair. Patsy probably dyed her hair too, but she couldn't have it otherwise than light brown, and the girl we found has dark brown hair at origin. Moreover, the height doesn't match Patsy's. This one is taller than she is. Oh, yes, and apparently, Patsy didn't have appendicitis, and this one does. Moreover, she wasn't beaten to death and then had her throat cut off, as we'd initially thought, but the knife did the entire job. Yes, she was beaten first and repeatedly and wildly raped and after more days, she was stabbed with a sharp knife—the kind of knife used for hunting. It's about the same knife used to kill Mrs Dobbs. Ah, and something else very interesting: the girl was pregnant in four months. Moreover, she'd been also tied up for three or four days if not more".

"Oh, God!" James said. "So, we've done nothing else but losing our time this morning, sir. We've asked questions about a girl who's not involved and where we shouldn't, probably, should we?"

"Maybe not, James... It must've been someone that knows various things about this street and the empty house next to the Dobbs', because a stranger couldn't have known such a thing. The house's been empty for five months since the owner died of cancer. I'm very afraid that our killer wanted to kill her there, with no witnesses around, but he couldn't. Maybe the girl escaped from his hands and she had to die in the Dobbs' yard. Certainly, the killer must've known that Mrs Dobbs goes to sleep at nine and therefore he imagined the way was free because otherwise I don't think he'd have risked it. Everyone knew that Mrs Dobbs was a gossiper. And also it's sure that he knew that Mr Thompson usually comes late at home and Mrs Thompson doesn't have the habit to survey her neighbours' houses and the Reids have something else in their mind than watching what's going on in the street. It must've been someone with tight relations with the street, I bet on that", McNamara said decisively. "And however, don't forget we found Patsy's ID in the victim's purse, and this is quite strange. Why was it there and where's the victim's ID" it's quite weird, don't you think? However, at least we've found out something about Patsy and her neighbours and I think this is important, is this? At least we know with whom we're talking".

Thoughtful, the two men watched each other. Then McNamara said:

"Come on, let's go back to office. Let's check the past of each person in this street and we may come back later to question the others. First we must find out who's the dead girl".

Chapter Four

In the police office, there were five men and two women working busily. Two of the men were talking on the phone and the other people were checking some papers. One of the two women was writing something on the computer.

McNamara got into the office with an alert step, with James behind, and asked:

"What's new, boys and girls?"

"Nothing, sir, I must tell you", answered one of them with regret in his voice. "We've found nothing to clear this case up".

"Not really nothing", replied cheerfully a woman with a pony tale that had just got a message on the computer.

"Got something new, Jo?" McNamara asked the young women, the same time putting his coat on the peg near the door. He was sick of wearing the coat.

"In deed, sir! I've managed to find out who the victim is, sir. I've tried to see if her prints are recorded in our database and, hear here, they are. I've just got the answer. The girl was arrested a few weeks ago for shoplifting. She wasn't sent to prison being only at the second arrest, but she had to pay a penal fine and has record now, so her prints are in our database".

"Ok, who was she?" McNamara cut off her talking impatiently.

"Her name was McWilliams, Diane McWilliams, and she was a student until a few months ago when she left school and home the same time. She left school the same time with Patsy Porter, as a teacher I've talked to on the phone told me. But there's something more interesting, sir".

"What the hell could be more interesting? Joan, you're awful! Why can't you give me the information in a certain order and why should you make all sorts of comments besides what's important?" McNamara asked exasperatedly.

"Sorry, sir, I don't know. That's me, I think", Jo smiled defensively. "I must add a little colour or it's got no charm".

However, both she and McNamara knew that he couldn't get angry with her. The policeman even smiled. He couldn't get upset because he knew she was a very smart girl and always she'd come with something more, something the others couldn't find. She had her own special flair. No one could equal her when it came to take something out if that thing was hidden in God knows what corner. She was tenacious and never quitted.

"Ok, girl, take it easy and tell me all the facts, and if possible, only the facts", he underlined, reminding her about her habit of pigmenting everything with personal opinions and all sorts of divagations that not always were of use, a lot of times turning out to be only a waste of time.

"Well, then, I'll try to be brief and stick with the subject", she began. "Diane learnt in the same school with Patsy Porter and, moreover, the girls were classmates. I had also a short conversation five minutes ago with the policeman that arrested Diane last time and he told me that when Diane stole those things in the shop she wasn't alone but together with Patsy. Patsy had to make a statement, too, you know how these things work... Apparently the girls were very good friends and Diane defended Patsy saying she hadn't known a thing about the stolen things or about her intentions to steal. She said it was only her ideas and she didn't bother to inform her friend about what she was going to do before getting into the shop. She assumed the entire guilt so Patsy got loose".

"Well, anything else?" McNamara asked a bit anxious, seeing that Jo couldn't refrain herself from making collateral comments.

"Well, that's it, sir. I haven't had too much time, you know", said Jo explanatorily. "The doctor told us that the victim couldn't be Patsy Porter only one hour ago or even less. So I haven't had enough time to find more so far, but you know very well I'll do", she said convincingly.

"I'm sure you do", McNamara replied, noticing at once that the men in the office were grinning hearing his praises for the policewoman.

“What’s the problem, Mike? What don’t you like?” he started hauling Mike over the cools. As a rule, he was as good as Jo. “When you come with so much information as Jo did and in such a short time, I’ll praise you too, don’t worry. You know I favour no one and never. By then...And now, because you want to put yourself into spot, try to find out everything you can about this girl from her teachers, but don’t tell them she’s dead. Find something! Did you tell it to that teacher, Jo?”, he turned to the young woman watching her questioningly.

“I’m not a beginner, sir. I know when to keep my mouth shut. I presumed you’d like to inform her parents first and then the rest of the world”.

“Exactly! Good job, Jo!”

He was about to get out of the common office and get into his, when he reminds something. He turned back and said with a menacing voice:

“And, by the way, please, take care and don’t let press smell a thing about this business. Only if I hear a single word about the real identity of the victim, I’ll eat you up. I’m going to make some phone calls and then I’m going to Diane’s parents with James. Jo, find me her address, please!”

“I already have it here, sir”, Jo said, waving a piece of paper before his eyes.

McNamara took the paper from her hand, and then, making a sign to James to follow him, he wanted to leave the office, when he reminded of something else:

"Oh, I shouldn't forget. Someone must call Mrs Porter to not come to the morgue anymore. Tell her she's not her daughter. She'd be glad, I'm sure. I only hope she hasn't left already".

"Yes, sir", Jo said, "I'll do it at once", she offered immediately.

After McNamara got out, Jo showed her tongue to Mike who had frowned when McNamara reprimanded him and this one went crazy for good.

"What the hell, do you think you're doing? Do you think you're smarter, or what? All the praises got high in your head and you think you're better?"

"I've always told you, dear", she replied merrily, being in the mood of playing and wanting to make Mike boiling a little. "I'm better than you".

"In your dreams, sweetheart", the young man joined her game guessing with his last traces of reason that she wanted only to make him snap. "If you come with me tonight, I'll show you that I'm the best", he added winking to her roguishly, although he wasn't kidding at all. He even stopped breathing hoping for an affirmative answer. But he should have known better than that.

The woman didn't guess anything and she thought to continue the game.

"Maybe, in your dreams, dear! In your dreams! I'd rather go out with Quinn!" Jo replied, knowing that Mike couldn't stand Quinn, as well as all the others. Actually, Jo didn't like Quinn either. No one liked him because he used to spread all sorts of rumours about others and no one made the illusion he'd be a sincere person, in a way or another. Everyone already knew this one had only one thought: to promote as fast as he could and if he could promote making problems to his colleagues and stepping on bodies, then that's it. He didn't bother absolutely at all. It'd have ruined his sleep such stupid things, he thought. Therefore, he didn't even bother to think of. He knew only that he had to gain no matter the price and that means were never important as long as he could reach his goal. His dear mother had told him so since he was a small child. Only the goal counted in life. What he had to do to reach there, was completely insignificant.

Mike felt hurt because of Jo's words and he turned his back, promising not to pay her attention at all. But, on the other hand, he'd promised that to himself many times before and, as far as he knew, he'd probably do that many times from that moment on. The girl had something that made him forget about the promise and probably that something was related to her freshness and smartness that often troubled him. Mike tried to get rid of the ideas that started turning up in his mind and started to phone people again.

Jo, feeling some remorse for her maliciousness, turned back to her work, a little absent-minded this time. She decided to call Mrs Porter first. Maybe she hadn't left the house yet. And she was lucky.

***

"Let's go to Diane's parents and then to school to see if we find out something else", McNamara said, after he read the coroner's report. "Something must be here. We have the body of one girl and the ID of the other. Something is wrong, I can swear. I'm afraid Patsy is also in trouble. Don't you think, James?"

"Maybe, sir... Or maybe she's involved in her friend's death. It's possible", he said defensively, seeing that his chief was watching him with some doubts.

'Yes, maybe", McNamara accepted, but he wasn't sure of that. "We have only the coroner's report that mentions a thread of hair which doesn't belong to the victim. That's all. Therefore, we have a lot of work to do, to find the killer.

CHAPTER FIVE

McNamara decided to drive himself. James resigned and sat on the left side although he knew his boss was an impulsive driver that wasn't at all decided to respect all the traffic rules. Therefore, James fastened his safety belt with determination, although he feared this one didn't represent a great protection given the manner in which the inspector usually drove, but it was better than nothing.

They drove to another part of Edinburgh, to other suburbs than the ones of the Nightingale Street. There, Diane lived with her parents, or better said, she should've lived if she hadn't been killed.

James was looking out of the window, even though he couldn't manage to see too much. McNamara was driving too fast and used to overcome often because he didn't have enough patience to respect the daily traffic.

After a quarter of an hour and more traffic lights that tried badly his patience, McNamara, finally, arrived in front of Diane's parents and stopped.

Both policemen got off the car under the curious looks of the little dirty boys playing in front of the house whose walls were shrunk and seriously needed new paint and whose windows should've been washed long time before. Watching them, McNamara thought that no one could see anything through them and probably they were kept thus not only because of the laziness but also because it was more practical: no curtains were necessary.

They rang at the door and until someone could come to open, a bigger child, of about ten, with quite shabby clothes and dirty hair as well as dirty hands, came closer to them.

"Mom's not home, you know, she's at the neighbour's", he said showing to the next door.

"But where's your father?" asked McNamara, who'd preferred to break the news to a man, especially after that morning's experience with Mrs Porter.

"He knows where he is", child's answer came. "He left long time ago, as soon as Dennis was born", said the boy raising his shoulders and pointing to a kid about six, who was playing together with other children in the gutter near the sidewalk.

All of them were entirely dirty and they didn't look too neat. McNamara could swear no one had taken care of their faces or clothes for a few days.

"Then, can you go to call your mother, boy?" he asked the child. "Tell her we're from police and have something to talk to her".

The boy stared at him with big eyes and then asked him, as an adult:

"Which one's in trouble this time? Diane or John?"

"You'd better call your mom, kid", James urged him in a kind voice. "We'd better talk to her".

The child nodded and got into the next yard. Although the policemen tried to hear what people were talking there, they heard only an unintelligible murmur. After a few moments, a quite old and slatternly woman turned up from the yard accompanied by the boy they'd just talked with a few moments earlier.

"I'm McWilliams", the woman said in an ineffable and even quarrelsome voice. "What's the matter? Who did what, because they ate me up, these children, I can swear to God!"

"Can we go inside, ma'am?" asked McNamara pointing to the curious children. "Maybe we'd better talk first, with no other ears around".

"Very well, sir, let's get in", the woman opened them the door, although she wasn't very sure if she should let them in. She'd heard enough stories about the police coming and profiting from the lack of attention of the host while planting various incriminating evidence.

However, she said nothing and she was afraid that should've been something more serious than the little pilfering that her son, Richard, usually did, or Diane's usual meetings with the police when she stole from shops because otherwise this kind of cops wouldn't have come. Usually, policemen in uniform came, not detectives.

The policemen followed her in the house and the heavy smell of stuffy food, unwashed clothes and tobacco overwhelmed them. All taken altogether offered a completely unpleasant environment.

The woman showed them in a room that should've been a sort of a drawing room, but the room was full of everything, exactly like an old clothes and lumber shop.

Seeing James's despising look when he noticed the room, the woman said defensively and provoking the same time:

"I know it's not like in your house, but I've only two rooms and enough children to bring up in this house and only with the social help, I can't do too much over here, can I?"

"No one said anything about that, ma'am" McNamara cut her upsurge. "We've come here for something else. We haven't come to criticize your house, you or the way in which you bring up your children, although everything's undesirable, if you want to know my opinion", he said harshly.

Seeing that he annoyed her for good, he tried to calm her down.

"Let's leave all of that aside because we've got more serious things to talk about. I say we all sit down and talk calmly", he said pointing to the dirty sofa that was stained with all sorts of things and on which he was decided not to sit down, though.

James looked there and he decided not to sit down either. He watched the armchair afterwards, but they didn't inspire him any trust, either, and therefore gave up sitting down and decided he'd better stand.

Neither took McNamara a seat, but he went to the window not to seem he dominated the woman with his height. He expected her to sit and then asked her:

"What do you know about your daughter these days ma'am?"

"Honestly, I know nothing", the woman said openly. "She left the house some while ago, I can't say exactly when. I was satisfied I had a mouth less to feed and that's all. It's quite difficult to do it when you don't have with what, I know quite well, no matter what you could think. What she's done now?"

"Don't you know with whom or why she left?" McNamara kept asking her, apparently without noticing she'd asked him something.

"I didn't ask her. She told me she's leaving—that's all. It was enough for me", the woman replied categorically, provoking him with her answer.

"Well, but she's minor", replied James whose scorn for the woman had increased more for the last few minutes, especially because he'd seen she didn't care at all where the girl had gone or what she'd done since she left.

"She'd be, but I have other four children to bring up and I think the girl's at the age to manage by herself. I did so and I didn't manage badly. After all, I've a house at least and I've all my children alive..."

"Not quite", answered McNamara decided not to turn around the subject any more.

If for Mrs Porter he'd felt some compassion and tried to treat her softly, he felt only scorn for the woman before him. He was furious that her negligence and indifference led her elder daughter to death and therefore he considered that he shouldn't show her mercy or any kind of such a consideration.

"What do you mean?", she asked, losing something from her previous defying allure.

"Diane's dead", McNamara answered her, "and you'd better come to the headquarters to make an official recognition. We found out it was she checking the prints in the record".

The woman instantly turned white and tears came into her eyes. Despite her nonchalant voice from before, and of the ideas she emerged so strongly, she actually cared of her children and she'd been quite worried since Diane left home. But she couldn't stop her. The girl hadn't been listening to her for a long while. Neither she nor Richard had.

McNamara was watching her attentively and realised that, actually, despite her misery and indifference, the woman was more than the eye could meet. Despite the tears in her eyes she vainly tried to recover from the brutal strike he'd given her.

“Don’t you really know anything about what she’s done since her leaving?” he asked her, more kindly this time.

“No, I don’t”, she said and suddenly she burst into tears and let go.

The two policemen waited her to calm down, but, after a few minutes, seeing that the situation wasn’t improving at all, McNamara told James:

“Go to the kitchen and bring a glass of water, James, please”.

James got out and went to the kitchen but although he searched attentively, he found no glass. He found only a few cups left on the side of the dirty sink full of dishes. He took a cup and filled it with water and then came back to the room. He gave the cup to the woman who drank the water as if she hadn’t drunk water for days. After a few minutes, she managed to calm down a little and McNamara considered he could continue with his questions.

“Don’t you know anything at all?”

After she kept silent for a while, the woman admitted she knew something. She nodded and started talking:

“Richard, he’s my elder son, you know, told me he met her two weeks ago. He said she looked very good. She was well dressed, even smartly, and she was neat. She told him she was living with a man with money who was taking care of her and maybe he’d marry her. She said she wouldn’t come back in this dump, no matter what she had to do for that. She said she was sick of tasteless and poor food and there's no big deal to work hard and learn when you can have a good life without it.

"Didn't she say who the man was?"

"No, she didn't. However, Richard also told me he saw her one day, less than a week after he talked to her. She was with that guy in front of a shop with expensive clothes. They'd just got out from there. He couldn't talk to them because they took a cab and didn't hear him calling.

"Did he tell you what that man was looking like?"

"He said he was looking good. He was tall and neatly dressed. Unfortunately, my son doesn't have any talent to describe people. He sees nothing else besides clothes".

"When could we talk to him?" McNamara tried to find out.

"I don't know. He comes when he wants. He lives somewhere in town with a friend of his. He left me a phone number to call him if I have something urgent. I have it somewhere in the other room", she said and stood up heavily from the sofa to fetch the phone number.

She went into the other room and the policemen heard the noise of slammed things. After a few minutes, the woman came back and fetched a piece of paper and held the paper out to McNamara because she had realised he was the boss.

"This is his phone number. It's not direct to him", she came back over the words said, "but it's the number of a neighbour. He has no phone where he lives. He told me so".

"Thank you", McNamara said copying the phone number in his little book.

He was about to leave when he turned back to her:

'Didn't Diane have a diary or something like that?"

"Yes", the woman said. "Do you need it? She used to hide it somewhere under the stove. Not because of me she was hiding it because she knew I respected her intimacy. It's about the children. They found it once and laughed at her. She's my only daughter and it's difficult with so many boys around", she said and realised then that she couldn't speak about her in the present and started to cry again.

McNamara tried to talk to her kindly and told her:

"You must come to the morgue, ma'am, and identify her. Ah, and I also want that journal", he added, trying to remind her that she wanted to fetch it to him.

She accepted nodding and went to the kitchen and fetched him a thick notebook full of stains. On the cover there was written the word Journal with calligraphy full of curves.

McNamara took the notebook from her hand and then asked her:

"Do you want us to call you a car, ma'am, to drive you to the morgue?"

"Yes, I think so", she said. "It'd be difficult to me to get there otherwise... May I take my neighbour with me?" she asked entreatingly, wanting desperately to have a support on her side when she was to see her daughter dead.

"Of course, ma'am", McNamara answered to her, knowing that it was better thus, because he knew the girl didn't look good, and it'd have been better that Mrs McWilliams had someone on her side when she was to see her. "Call a car, James", he ordered to the sergeant and then waited him to make the call.

"It comes at once, sir. I also called a policewoman. I think it's better for Mrs McWilliams".

McNamara approved him and then he went outside and called the kid he'd talked to earlier.

"Call your neighbour, kid. Tell her to come urgently to your mother because she needs her now. Come on, go", he urged him seeing that the boy remained watching him.

While the kid was running to the yard next to the house, McNamara came back inside, determined not to let the woman alone until her neighbour had come.

Unfortunately, he couldn't find anything else from her, because the woman wasn't able to say a thing. Stooping, she was only sitting on the dirty sofa and was watching without seeing anything. She didn't even realise that someone was next to her.

She didn't react even when her neighbour came in with the dirty kid behind. McNamara told this one what was about in such a way that the child couldn't hear him. The neighbour shook her had sadly and regretfully and then she went to her friend and held her in her arms. That moment, Mrs McWilliams started crying again, frightening her younger son.

McNamara took the child and led him out of the room in the street. There he told him:

"I think you'd better stay and play a little more with your friends. You also must take care of the younger one", he pointed to the boy's brother. "Your mom must go somewhere, but she'll be back soon, don't worry".

Chapter Six

They stopped in front the school and James seemed really pleased when he got out of the car because this time he'd driven and there'd been no moment when they were in danger, as when McNamara used to drive. James was a more prudent and responsible driver than his boss who drove too fast and unpredictably.

"James, I'm going to talk to the headmaster, and you look for Graham's girl-friend, that Laura Bradshaw he told us about and talk to her", McNamara told him and then split up and headed to the headmaster's office.

He was pretty tired because of the roads and interviews and moreover he had no clear point to start his investigation. Everything was very confused, he thought.

He'd inclined to Thompson, but he couldn't be sure if he was guilty or not, if he had any connection with these, besides the obvious one, because he should've been messed up with Patsy, that was clear.

In the waiting room, at the secretary's desk there was no one so he knocked directly on the door of the headmaster's office and got into when he was answered.

The moment he entered, he found a distinguished and calm woman around forty, who hadn't lost the beauty she was endowed with, yet.

"Yes, sir, what can I do for you?" she asked. "I don't think I know you. Do you have a child in our school?"

"No, ma'am, I'm chief inspector McNamara", he said, and then he showed his ID and badge. "Here's my ID. I came here in relation to an investigation we're carrying on", he added, putting his ID back in his coat pocket.

"I see", she said, although she seemed to have some doubts that she knew what was about. "What can I do for you, sir? I know we don't have extraordinary children in our school—at least most of them, but, unfortunately, this is the fate of the public schools at the border of the cities, nowadays. However, I can't believe that we have here children that could do such things. I refer to things requiring the investigation of a chief inspector", she argued. "Other kind of situations we've had enough, I can't lie, especially shopliftings, breaching the peace, things like that", she added, quite amazed to see a chief inspector coming to investigate in the school.

"It's not about the action of a child in the school", McNamara started, but he didn't have any chance to go on.

The headmaster simply amazed jump off her chair with big eyes and shouted:

"Do you mean that a teacher of the school did something reproachable?"

One could effectively feel panic in her voice. She couldn't imagine that a teacher, who should've been a model for his students, could be involved in something of police's competence.

"No, ma'am! Calm down! I didn't mean that. However, it's about two former students of yours: one was killed and the other is considered missing, for now, while her ID was found next to the body of the former".

The woman stared at him and couldn't believe her ears and for a moment, she couldn't say anything because of the astonishment. She hadn't ever run into such a thing. In deed, they'd had children who stole from shops before. They also had other situations when children fought or got into various bands or started trifling with drugs, doing them or selling them to other colleagues to get the daily dose. However, at least, they'd never had such a thing in school before.

After a few moments of silence, she said:

"I see", although it was obvious, she understood nothing and had reached no conclusion yet, because she couldn't realise what was about. "Who's about, though?" she asked in a voice that tried to be as normal as possible, although one could see that her usual self-confidence had disappeared.

"About the two girls that have abandoned school this year, ma'am", McNamara said.

The headmaster laughed bitterly hearing his words and then said slightly ironically:

"We have more girls who have abandoned school this year, sir. I'm afraid you must be more specific, if possible".

"It's about Diane McWilliams and Patsy Porter, ma'am".

The headmaster tried to remember of the two girls and she managed even at once. The girls had come many times in her office because they would always do something, either minor things, like breaching the internal order rules or more serious things, like stealing.

Diane had also managed to have a record, if she remembered well. And what was more painful for her, it was the fact that both were smart girls that could've learnt well and make themselves a safer future, but they'd chosen other ways to start their lives.

"Which one of them died?" the headmaster asked with her heart crunched of regret for both of them.

"Diane, ma'am", answered McNamara, understanding very well what the woman before him was feeling.

It was a real loss whenever a person lost his life, but when it was about teenagers, the loss was always felt more severely than ever, regardless what kind of people they were.

The headmaster winked a few times to get rid of the tears in her eyes. She had to keep a reputation and she couldn't afford to show her real feelings to anyone when she was in school or in public, anywhere.

"Yes, in deed. A policeman phoned earlier to talk to the girls' teacher. But I didn't imagine... What can I do for you, inspector?" she asked trying not to divagate from the subject, imagining the policeman had enough on his head and that the investigation was pressing him.

"Could you tell me with whom among their colleagues or outside the school they used to hang around here, if you know, obviously?"

"In an ideal world, I should've known all of these", she said with a bitterness she couldn't hide. "But, unfortunately", she continued, "we don't live in an ideal world, inspector. I can tell you for sure that they had no relations with the boys in the school. They didn't have at least a friend among them. They were part of a group of girls who preferred older man, if you know what I mean. I happened, and not only once, to see them leaving with such men. And I must say that, besides two girls that moved out in another side of the country, all the others, and this means a total of about five, abandoned school almost the same time, if I remember well. I asked to have their parents fined, of course, but apparently, they don't know where their girls are or what they do, either. I was told they couldn't control them anymore. Three of them have only a mother, one, this is Diane, had a divorced mother, and Patsy Porter had her father away almost all the time. Although, sincerely, I don't think this is the problem. We have other children in school with only a mother or a father, you must know, and they are quite serious and learn well and try to do something with their lives. I think it's about education, genetic fund", she said on a professorial tone, "but, however, I wouldn't like to annoy you with all my opinions. I think you understand what I mean".

"I do, ma'am", McNamara said, and he really understood because he knew from his own experience what the woman talked about.

He'd been brought up only by his mother. His father had gone away long before his birth, but his mother had tried hard and bothered him a lot to go to school because she considered it was the only way he'd do more than she had. She'd worked for him and she had had the pretension he did his part, to learn. Therefore, he'd tried not to deceive her ever and make himself a better way than hers.

"So there's no one of her friends here to talk to", he drew the conclusion.

"No, unfortunately", the headmaster said. "I can't help you here. They hadn't had relations with the girls over here and I don't think anyone knew whom they met or what they did. They seemed a quite exclusivist group, if you want my opinion".

"Could you give me the names of the other girls' in their group, ma'am?"

"Yes, of course", she said.

She thought a little and searching in a register, she reminded of the names and then she took a piece of paper and wrote down the girls' names and addresses she knew.

"I also can give you the names of the girls having moved out with the address of the schools where they took the transfer, if you want", she added wanting to be as helpful as possible.

"I'd be grateful", McNamara thanked her for her effort.

After having completed all the data, she held out the paper to McNamara who stood up and thanked her for her answers. After shaking the headmaster's hand, he went out, already thinking of the possible lines of investigations opened before him.

He reached the car and because James hadn't come yet, he called to the office.

"Mike", he said, "write down the names I dictate you. Two are in other sides of the country, so, please, get in touch with our colleagues there, and ask them to talk to the girls", he said, and then dictated the girls' names and addresses. "Please have people sent to each of the girls here", he continued, "to talk to their parents, and maybe you ask Jo to check the database to see if anything turns up in relation with them. OK?"

"Yes, sir, I've written everything. I'll give Jo the names of the girls to check them in the database, and I'll call to Bristol and Leeds. As soon as we hear something, we'll call you", Mike said.

"All right, Mike. I leave you now", McNamara said and hung up, watching James who was just coming towards him.

"Well, James, what have you find out?"

"It checked out, sir. Graham was where he said he was. I also talked to the two colleagues that had celebrated one year of marriage and to whom he said he'd been and the statements corroborated so he's all right. He couldn't be on Nightingale Street the same time. Have you found out something, sir?"

"Not very much, but let's hope Mike and Jo will come with details later", McNamara replied.

"It'd be better, sir", said James, watching the watch. "It's almost five thirty. Are we going back to ask questions to the others in the street, sir?"

"Yes, James, I think so. However, we can't do anything else. We have no other starting point".

Chapter Seven

"Hello, dear! Have you just come back from work?" asked Mrs Stevens, who was leaning on the sash, to her much younger neighbour Miss McNeil, who had just parked her car in front of the house.

"Oh, yes, I've really had a busy day. A new book came up and, apparently, I think it'll become a best seller soon. A lot of people came in the shop expressively to buy this book and, believe me, I found it difficult to satisfy all the requests. I can't split in more, unfortunately. However, we've talked enough about me, I don't want to annoy you with that. I know you don't like it. What have you done today? Have you had any pains?"

"A little, dear!" the old woman admitted. "You're very nice to ask me about. What do you think, will you have tea with me or you have other plans in your mind?"

Bryony McNeil seemed to think a little of her neighbour's proposition. The truth was she was awfully tired and she'd have liked to put her legs somewhere up and lain for a while, but she knew that she couldn't, anyway. She still had a lot of work to do with the ledgers to catch up. So she smiled to Mrs Stevens and then nodded, saying:

"Of course, why not? Wouldn't you prefer to come with me for tea? I've just bought some chocolate cakes from the teahouse near my bookshop and I'm sure you'll like them. I'm madly fond of them, really. What do you say?"

"Well, then", accepted the old woman that knew her tastes very well and knew that Bryony wouldn't have brought anything she hadn't liked. "I'll come to you", she said, "let me only take my walking stick".

Mrs Stevens disappeared from the window and after a few minutes, she came out leaning on her walking stick. Her gait was quite difficult and her younger neighbour pitied her from all her heart for the pains the old woman frequently experienced.

The two women got into Miss McNeil's house, the house McNamara admired that morning, painted in white and with blue windows and door, and Bryony showed old Mrs Stevens to her drawing room and helped her sit down on her favourite seat. Then, she went into the kitchen to prepare the tea and put the cakes onto a plate.

While the water for tea was boiling, she prepared some small sandwiches with butter, cucumber and cheese they both liked a lot.

She'd just got into the drawing room and put the tray with the cups, tea and plates onto the table, when she heard the bell at the door.

"Do you expect someone, dear?" Mrs Stevens asked her curiously, because she knew very well that since Bryony quarrelled with Ann Goddard from the end of the street, no one had called on her—it wasn't anyone, maybe Mrs Reid or Brown, but their visits were very rare.

"No, I'm not waiting for anyone. I'm going to see who's at the door and I'll come at once", promised Bryony leaving the room.

She opened the front door and looked at the two men in front of the door, a little shocked, because she hadn't thought a moment to see some strangers. She had imagined it was Mary Reid or maybe Mrs Brown. They called on her now and then to borrow a book or ask her to bring them something from the bookshop.

However, the two men, she'd never seen before. The man on the right was about forty-five, very tall and well-built, dark brown-haired and green-eyed. His allure was a little rough and his face wasn't handsome at all, but however it was something interesting to see. He seemed to have lived many things in his life and know quite plenty of things about the dark side of the world.

The one on the left was very young, by contrast, maybe about twenty-five. He wasn't as tall as his fellow and seemed absolutely different from this one. His hair was very dark, somehow like the Gaelic type, black with bluish reflections and his eyes were blue. This one seemed a freshman in life stuff, in opposition to his friend. His smile was open and warm and reached even to his eyes, while the smile of his fellow seemed rather cold, cynical and distant. Even his eyes were cold with no shadow of smile in them.

Bryony didn't realise she had been watching the two men without saying a thing and she pulled herself together only when she saw the ironic smile flourishing on the older one's lips.

This one had already analyzed the woman in front of him. He'd glanced to her at the beginning, but he'd seen everything he'd wanted to and although he didn't feel like admitting that, he liked what he saw. However, he tried to not let her know it.

That moment, feeling a bit embarrassed, Bryony asked them a little ironically:

"Well, who are you and what do you want? Do you sell anything? However, I'm sorry for you, I don't buy anything, I don't need anything", she said with a big smile and opening her arms.

McNamara didn't appreciate at all her presumption that they were salesmen and showed it at once, frowning at her. A quite deep furrow appeared between his eyebrows and he seemed even tougher than before, if it were possible, or at least she thought so watching him. McNamara wasn't that kind of person caring of people's opinions, but, however, by then no one had mistaken him with a salesman. In addition, he had his share of dislike for salesmen.

"We're from the police, ma'am. We must ask you some questions", he said emphatically and the same time severely, although, generally, he was agreeable when he interviewed people. Usually, his voice was calm and pleasant and thus he made people answer his questions quite easily, a thing to not let go for a policeman.

James seemed a little troubled hearing his boss's voice. He'd never heard him speaking like that when they were questioning people and he tried to smile even sweeter, hoping thus to sweeten a little McNamara's answer and make up for his boss's apparent lack of politeness.

"I see", she said in a cold voice, while coldness reached the light of her eyes too. "What happened?" she asked. "Haven't I paid a fine or has someone reclaimed me?" she continued ironically, thinking that there was no other explanation for their visit.

McNamara seemed to get angrier because of her insolence, but he controlled his temper somehow and replied reproachfully, without trying to hide his irritation.

"We're not in uniform, ma'am, so I don't think you could mistake us for constables. We're investigating two crimes, ma'am, and I've no time to exchange amiable replies with you. So..."

"Two murders!" she jumped and interrupted him, suddenly, in complete shock. "My Lord! I know of no crime! Who died? And when?" asked she not being aware that she asked questions too fast to get an answer to them.

The two men looked her astonished because they didn't think it was possible to live practically next door and not know that two people had been murdered next to your house.

She felt what they were thinking and told them as if she apologized, even though she couldn't imagine why she'd do it:

"I know you might find it a bit strange, but if the two murders you're speaking about took place last night, this morning or during this day, you must know I came at home only at eight thirty last night and saw no one. I worked in the kitchen for a while because I started work during dinner. Then, I didn't want to move out because it seemed quite comfortable. Afterwards, because I had a headache—you know I had a beginning of a migraine and my migraines are awful—and as I couldn't sleep at all, I took a sleeping pill, although I rarely do it. I'm not used to this kind of drug and I slept like a log and I heard nothing all night. Oh, yes, and I met no one this morning when I left for work or in the afternoon in my way home. Mrs Stevens, with whom I'm having tea right now, seemed to want to tell me something, but here you've come and thus I've had no chance to hear a thing. However, if you want to ask me some questions, come in!" she tried to attenuate somehow the harshness and irony shown before, because she felt a little guilty for having shown shallowness when the situation seemed quite serious.

She stepped aside and let them inside, closed the door behind them and showed them to the drawing room, inviting to take a seat on the sofa. Then, she introduced them to Mrs Stevens:

"These two gentlemen are from police, dear. I'm sorry, I don't remember your names", she said a little ironically, turning to them, letting them understand they hadn't introduced themselves accordingly.

McNamara resented her mute reproach and frowned again, although he couldn't explain himself his sudden irritability, but then, realising they hadn't introduced themselves as they were supposed to do it, he said:

"I'm Chief Inspector McNamara and this is sergeant detective James".

James stood up and shook politely Miss McNeil's hand and then Mrs Stevens's but McNamara didn't stand up at all from the sofa, didn't shake their hands or said anything more, keeping his unwonted air he'd shown at the door and, as James thought he knew him quite well, he felt completely awkward.

McNamara didn't like the young woman's behaviour, although he couldn't point out exactly why and he felt a need to be respected more, even if, actually, it was his duty to be polite to the people he was talking to. But, this time, he chased away from his mind all norms inspired during all years he spent in the force.

Bryony McNeil didn't seem to care of his rudeness, and, apologizing for a few moments, she went to the kitchen to fetch cups and plates for the two men.

When she came back, she poured them tea in cups and offered each one a cup of tea.

"Please, take as much sugar as you want and maybe milk. Ah, and please help yourselves to sandwiches and cakes", she said smiling nicely to James, but without smiling to McNamara too, because he'd been driving her crazy since the very moment she opened the door.

James blushed a little. He really liked the young woman and felt flattered to have been offered tea and sandwiches as if they'd been invited to tea, while they actually had come to ask questions. Not everyone was so kind when police was knocking on their door.

McNamara, who was feeling very hungry because he hadn't had a chance to have lunch that day, took two sandwiches and dropped two pieces of sugar in his tea, absently, and then he asked Mrs Stevens, turning to her:

"Have you heard anything about the two murders having taken place in your street, ma'am?"

"Of course, I've heard", this one said with a voice showing clearly that she felt hurt if they considered she wasn't in touch with what was going on in their small community. "I've wanted to tell Bryony about them too when she came, but I haven't the time at all because you've already come to ask questions. What an awful night was last night!" she exclaimed.

"May I ask who was killed, please?" Miss McNeil asked feeling her heart crunched a bit because she didn't like to hear about such things at all.

“We’ve found a young girl beaten up and stabbed in the Dobbs’ yard last night and then we found Mrs Dobbs killed in her living room this morning”, answered McNamara in a harsh voice even though he wasn’t aware of that.

“Oh, poor Mr Dobbs, what’s he doing now?” McNeil asked worried for Mr Dobbs’ health, although, of course, she was grieving for the two women having lost their life so tragically.

“Well, he’s doing absolutely nothing”, McNamara answered dryly. “He also died last night”.

That moment, Bryony felt really hurt because of his tone and his deliberate brutality and, therefore, she said as brutally as he did, even if it was not in her nature:

“You might feel hurt because I’ve not recognized two policemen in civil clothes or you might disregard me because I knew nothing of the crimes that took place. However, I think you cannot be so insolent with the people you are questioning, sir, due to your official position”.

McNamara had to admit the woman was right, but he did it only to himself and answered nothing to her. He kept looking her boldly and the same time with the same look in the fox’s eyes that still-hunts to catch a hen. He also admitted to himself that he felt a malicious joy seeing that he managed to drive her crazy a little. He had the feeling that she was too well brought up and polite and warm and he didn’t believe for one moment that she was like that for real...

On the other hand, James was quite astonished: he'd never heard his boss speaking like that to a possible witness. He did it only if he had had the certitude he was talking to the person he was going to arrest, and as far as he knew, Miss McNeil wasn't a suspect in their inquiry and he didn't even imagine how she could be. Therefore, McNamara actually didn't have the slightest reason to talk like that to the woman and that confused him very much.

Nevertheless, Mrs Stevens had her own opinion about what was going on between the two of them, and, as she'd learnt for some while, she didn't keep her thoughts to herself for a second and said loudly trying to clear things up:

"Is Bryony somehow a suspect, sir?"

"No, ma'am, she's not", answered McNamara. "She's not for the moment. We'll see later if the case is", he added, letting Bryony understand that her pretty face didn't take her out of the list at once, even if she'd thought that.

Bryony felt much more furious than she'd been before. She knew the policeman was naughty to her and openly and she didn't get it why. Then, fear overwhelmed her soul and she wondered if, by chance, he didn't consider her guilty.

"What do you want to know from me, sir?", she asked fast, wanting to get rid of their interrogatory as fast as possible and thus finish for good that absurd duel whose meaning she couldn't get.

"I'd like to know everything of Patsy Porter, for instance", he replied.

"Patsy Porter?" she asked completely amazed. "What relation could Pasty have with the crimes?"

"This is our business, ma'am", he answered impolitely. "Yours is to answer my questions as exactly as possible, if it is possible, of course. By the way, your name is...", McNamara questioned her insolently again.

"I'm Bryony McNeil. Are you also interested in my daily life?" she asked as insolently as he did. "Well, I own a small bookshop in the town. And you must know that I know nothing of Patsy or at least I know nothing of her now, I mean", she tried to explain herself. "She left some time before and I've heard nothing of her ever since", Bryony answered imposing herself to keep calm not to offer to McNamara the satisfaction to see that he'd upset her. However, she knew that indifference was the best weapon always because it hurt more than anything else.

"What kind of girl she was, in your opinion?" James asked with a conciliatory voice, to appease the asperities he'd felt in his superior's voice.

"I haven't paid her much attention, I must admit", Bryony answered to him. "If I think well, we had absolutely different interests and I didn't like what she was doing. She seemed to flirt with every man in the street and I didn't have a good opinion of her. However, I saw her quite a little, I must tell you. Most of the time I'm in town where my bookshop is and in the evening I come at home quite late and most often I see Mrs Stevens but I don't see anyone else if someone doesn't happen to be in front of my house. Only on Sunday I see people in the street and sometimes not even then if I have work to do".

"That's true", Mrs Stevens said interrupting her. "Bryony is a very busy girl. She opened a bookshop one year ago and she wants to make it successful and therefore she works a lot, even too much in my opinion. Usually, she comes very late at home in the evening and she spends most of the time here, alone or with me. You know, actually, I happen to be a very good friend of the aunt that brought her up and therefore, we're very close we two", she said, holding out to Bryony that took her hand.

"I see", said McNamara nodding. "Maybe you have someone with whom you spend time, miss?"

"I'm afraid this is not your business, as long it's not related to the case you're working on", she replied to him caustically.

"I want you to answer my question, Miss McNeil, to not waste my time investigating your situation", he told her roughly. "I'll decide if there's a connection or not to the case I'm working on. Should I understand you don't like the question?" he provoked her maliciously.

Bryony didn't like at all how the man was asking questions, but as she didn't want to have problems with police and she didn't have anything to hold back, so she said:

"No, I don't go out with anyone in town or anywhere else. I don't have time to meet people or to socialize. I work alone in the shop because I don't afford to hire anyone yet, and I keep my ledgers by myself too, so I have quite a lot of work to do. And after seeing so many people all day long and talking to so many people, I prefer staying alone at home in the evening or maybe with Mrs Stevens, the tops. But, however, work comes on first place in that concerning me, if I want to get rid of all debts I have at the bank and make myself a steady situation, as much as possible".

They watched each other and for a few moments silence filled the room.

"But you Mrs Stevens?" asked McNamara the old lady turning to her, realising that Bryony wasn't going to offer him any other pertinent information. "What do you know about Patsy Porter and about what happened last night?"

"Patsy was a very naughty girl, you must know young man", she started vehemently. "I didn't like her too much, I didn't like her at all, I may say. I can't go very well, you know", she said covering the two men with her sharp look and pointing to her stick. "Therefore, I spend most of my time reading near the windows to the yard and sometimes I can see things. I saw her many times making eyes to the men of a certain age in the street and she was wearing too short dresses and used to show too much of her skin, to like her. In my time, girls had more common sense. Patsy would flirt with everyone and would promise to become something else than a good girl. I think she'd come a light woman, I'd better say. She didn't seem to like school and work either. I heard more people speaking about her and you may believe me, I heard nothing good. Everyone would say she's naughty and an easy flirt. She'd drive her mother crazy with all the problems she'd cause".

"We've also heard Mr Porter left home because of her. Is it true?" asked James.

"Absurd! I don't believe a thing!" exclaimed Mrs Stevens. "His wife might believe it. However, Mrs Davidson came to have tea with me last week and told me she'd been in town two weeks ago and seen him with a woman on the bus. By accident, she was sitting exactly behind them and heard what they were talking. It was clear they'd been living together and they didn't seem to have met recently. She'd clearly heard the woman telling him she'd like to go again in a place they'd been six months before. So he lied when he said he'd been leaving 'cause of Patsy. The truth is he seemed quite bored with his wife and family life. Well, when he'd come home", she turned up her nose, showing clearly what she was thinking of him. "He didn't care of Patsy at all, but at all, listen to me. He wasn't made to be a father, that's it. He wouldn't do anything in the house or garden and he'd come quite rarely at home at weekends, saying he'd travelled a lot 'cause of the job. He was a sort of salesman, I think, but I don't know for sure, 'cause I wasn't interested to find out"

James wrote everything down thinking he'd imagined that was actually the cause for his leaving. Afterwards, he watched McNamara to see if he wanted to ask more questions, but he noticed, completely astonished, that his boss was more interested in the long and slim legs oh his young hostess turning up under the skirt over her knees than in the conversation.

"Sir, do we have other questions?" James asked him. He couldn't explain himself anymore the behaviour of his boss, who seemed to not be himself anymore. James hadn't ever seen him behaving such unprofessionally, and McNamara had a solid reputation among his subordinates in that concerning the way in which he would lead an investigation.

"I don't think he has other questions", Miss McNeil answered a little peevishly in his place. "He's more interested in something else, aren't you, sir?" she addressed ironically to McNamara. "And as I see you don't have other more questions and I'm quite tired, maybe you can come another time, do you agrce?", she dismissed them quite angrily, thinking that maybe next time she'd be luckier and the policeman would find her in trousers not to stare at her legs anymore.

"Ok!" said McNamara standing up, realising, finally that he'd passed over the edged long time ago, quite unusual thing for him. "Please, madams, get in touch with us if you remember something else of Patsy", he told the two women offering them his card. "But, by the way", he remembered suddenly, "didn't you hear anything last night when Mrs Dobbs was killed?" he asked Mrs Stevens.

"I don't know... I'm not sure it's related to that. By three, some time after the police left, I think, I got out of bed and went to the kitchen to drink some milk, 'cause milk helps me sleep better. While I was warming my milk, I watched through the window thinking of the girl I'd heard you found in the Dobbs' yard and of poor Mr Dobbs I'd found out he died the same night. Then I saw a tall man, maybe as tall as you", she said pointing to McNamara, "jumping over Bryony's garden fence and then heading to the gate of her yard and I lost him of sight. If I stay and think well, it was something quite familiar in his walking, you know. It was something in his posture too, not only in his walking, I think, but I couldn't figure out what it was. However, I didn't see his face 'cause he had something on the head, a black cap, I think".

"I hope you've said nothing to anyone about that", jumped James realising what that could mean and that the old woman might've been in a real danger if she'd said something about the person she had seen in the garden.

"No, I haven't. I wanted to tell Bryony now, and that's it. I don't talk too much to the people in the street".

"Then, it's all right", said James again, more restful now. "I don't think there'll be problems in this case".

"No, it's not all right", burst out Bryony whose mind was quite fast. "Did you turn on the light before getting into the kitchen?" she asked the old woman.

"Of course, I did", the answer came. "How could I've warmed the milk otherwise?" said the old woman annoyed.

"And you were standing right in front of the window, didn't you?" continued Bryony to ask her friend. "There's your gas-stove in your kitchen, isn't there?"

"In deed, I was right in front of the window", Mrs Stevens admitted.

"Then, he saw you", she said almost whispering, and then turned to McNamara, white-faced already. "Don't you think, sir, she's in danger? It's impossible she'd not been seen, and of course the man might think she'd seen him coming from the back of the houses. He can't know she didn't recognize him if there's someone we know, that's sure".

"Of course, Mrs Stevens", said McNamara sitting down on the sofa again. "I think the man saw you and might've thought he couldn't surprise you that very moment or maybe it'd been too much what he did for one night. Therefore, he might've put aside his plan to silence you the same night. I think you're in real danger and I'm really afraid you can't even move fast enough to face a possible attack", said McNamara watching meaningfully the old lady's stick and then the fingers deformed by arthritis, with no intention of being ironical this time, but strictly professional.

"Don't worry, my dear", Bryony told her at once, tapping her older friend's arm with affection. "You can come to stay with me for a while, until police finish the investigation and arrest the criminal. I know you can't use the stairs and, therefore, I'm going to prepare you a bedroom here, in the drawing room, and I'll sleep in the living room on the sofa. Thus, I could hear any noise and act if anything happens. What do you think?"

"I don't know, Bryony", she answered. "You know very well I don't like leaving my house and being an intruder, a burden, in someone else's house", also told her the old woman rashly and one could see on her face she'd love independence too much to leave it aside, no matter what.

"Don't be dolt!" burst out Bryony, excited and forgetting about common sense for the moment. "You know very well you're not an intruder in my house, and you shouldn't even think you'd be a burden to me! I'm glad to have you here, where I can watch over you! Don't you realise you're in real danger?" she said almost shouting to the stubborn old woman.

"Well, and when you go to work she's still in danger", noticed McNamara, bringing her back to earth in a second.

"Oh, yes, in deed! What can I do?" Bryony started to think of a solution feverishly to a solution. "I'd better ask Mrs Brown stay with you while I'm not here".

"She can't, dear. She's the cook of the pub, you know it. I don't think they can do without her, no way, especially now when they have no help there, since they fired the last boy".

"But Mrs Randall? What do you say of her?"

"Do you think Mrs Randall would come to stay with me?" wondered Mrs Stevens. "She's not a very kind woman, you must know it, and however, she doesn't like me too much for some time, as much as I've seen. I told her a few words once and she can't forgive me on any account for them. And, however, I don't think I could stand that stuffy individual for five minutes at least, but an entire day!"

"Then, I'll take you with me at the bookshop", Bryony said determined. "I've four armchairs and a sofa in the shop and moreover I have a room at the back where I keep ledgers and I'm sure I can find an extensible armchair to put there for you. So, you can lie whenever you'd like or you'd need, and in the evening I bring you here back with me. This is the best solution, I think", she said nodding determined, satisfied that she found the solution. "We'll take lunch together, you'll see it'll be amusing", Bryony also told her, trying to seem excited, as if she'd planned a going out to a picnic not a plan of dcfence.

"I don't know, dear, it's so much bother", argued Mrs Stevens with a doubtful voice because she didn't feel able to face a day like the one the girl described.

"Don't worry for any bother", argued Bryony too, without realising that the old woman had another reason for not taking her offer. "It's no bother, you must know. We'll feel very well and you'll be safe, you'll see. Don't you think I'm right inspector? What do you say?"

"Chief Inspector, by the way", answered McNamara having a chance more to see her scowl because she didn't like his way to draw her attention on things that had no importance to her. "Yes, it is the best solution, Mrs Stevens, even though it might be a little tiring for you. However, if you want to stay at home, I may send a policeman to stay with you during the day. It'll be less tiring, in deed, what do you say?"

"I think it's better this way", accepted the old woman at once. "Don't get upset, Bryony", she said turning to Bryony, "but you have a lot of work to do at the bookshop and I'm sure you'll feel that you have to stay with me, not to let me get bored, and you know very well you can't leave your work aside. And in the evening, you'll be twice tired than you're now. And, however, I'm an old woman, you know very well I have my habits during the day and one of them is to lie in bed as much as I can. But I move with you over the night, all right? Thus, the police don't have to send another man".

"If you want", said Bryony with a little anger in her voice. She was very angry with McNamara because he spoilt her plans.

She liked to be helpful whenever she had a chance. She felt that she could offer something in return for what she'd got years ago.

"Then, everything's settled" concluded McNamara. "However, I'll also send a policewoman for the night and even starting today", he said quickly not to let time to

Bryony to fight his decision back. “We'll leave now, and, please, be careful”, he also told the old woman. “You shouldn't mention anyone our conversation”.

“I'll see you off, gentlemen”, said Bryony and stood up again showing them to the door.

At the door, McNamara stopped and said:

“I might have to ask you more questions, Miss McNeil, so we might see each other quite soon”.

The woman nodded she understood and had nothing to object, but answered nothing. However, the man had the satisfaction to see a flash crossing her eyes, and knew she was really furious with him because he managed to ruin her evening. Without caring at all, he smiled at her sardonically, and waving to her ironically, he headed to the street.

Chapter Eight

"I hope you won't mind, sir, but what happened there?" asked James reluctantly, but effectively he couldn't refrain himself and not ask him.

"What do you mean?" asked McNamara apparently absent, although he knew well what his subordinate meant.

He was aware he jumped over the edge there, with Miss McNeil, but he couldn't have stopped himself at all. He had a real satisfaction from the mute duel of their wills.

"You know sir, I'm sure you know", James insisted, although with some reticence, fearing McNamara's reaction. "You've talked to Miss McNeil as if you suspected her of a relation with the crimes, although, as far as I know, nothing like that turned up.

"Oh, no, James, I can't consider her a suspect. I can't suspect anyone yet because I've no enough data for that. I only didn't like her behaviour at all. She seemed so superior when she opened the door that I wanted to show her what I consider it'd be her place. I didn't want to let her mock of us, that's all", replied McNamara in a voice showing absolute indifference.

"I didn't think she thought she was superior to us, sir. I thought she was only tired. She looked as if she needed some spare time or maybe a good bed to sleep, that's all. She didn't put on airs..."

"You're wrong, James", McNamara contradicted him roughly to clear himself. "The woman clearly played a game with us. I'm more than sure about that", he said although he knew he was lying because there was no sign of this kind and he felt he got angry with that woman again. He didn't like to lie and now, because of her, he put himself in the situation to lie to his subordinate.

James didn't answer anymore. However, he was sure the woman hadn't had such behaviour and he was almost sure that McNamara had actually liked her quite a lot but he didn't want to admit it. However, as he could see, his boss watched the woman's body too much and much more insistent to be right now in his words.

Nevertheless, as James had been taught he shouldn't ever upset his boss, however good or right he might've been, he preferred to keep his mouth shut. He'd learnt his lesson well.

His father had done it in the past and the result hadn't been too good. Even at all. He had to look for another job for two years afterwards and he couldn't find one because he had no good recommendations and no one would hire a man of his age with no recommendations. In the end, when he couldn't stand the shame to live on his wife's expenses he looked for an end. He killed himself.

“What will we do now, sir? James asked chasing his sad thoughts away, because however he had enough things to think of.

“I’m sure there’s a relation between Patsy Porter and the girl found. They seem too alike as face but also as behaviour. They were part of the same group and had the same occupations. In addition, I’m almost sure our killer must live in this street, James, or at least must have a connection with someone in the street. Therefore, we still have to ask questions over here. I asked Mike to check Thompson because he seems a real stud and Donna checks Graham and his girlfriend. Mark must find Porter and Jo must find Patsy Porter. When we have all these results, we’ll know for sure how things are” said McNamara. “Meanwhile, let’s talk to Ann Goddard. You’ve seen she’s one of Thompson’s lovers if we believe what people over here say”, McNamara continued. “I say one because I’m sure our man wouldn’t have been stuck with only one. There must be others too, as he doesn’t stay home too much. He’s the lecherous type, to be sure”.

***

Ann Goddard opened the door and smiled at the two men she saw in front of the door, and that thing made McNamara think that her smile was more appropriate to welcome two policemen than the ironic words of McNeil. However, he realised the two women were not of the same quality, and that McNeil really seemed superior to this one who appeared to be a mere coquettish woman, if he was to consider her clothes and the perfume she was wearing.

He showed the woman his ID and then asked her to let them in to ask her questions. Of course, he faced no opposition, and soon they found themselves in a room of the same size as McNeil's drawing room, but in opposition to that one, which was functional and comfortable, here there were coloured cushions everywhere and the curtains were pink with small roses on them.

The room was full of pink and flowers. Even the sofa was covered with such a counterpane. It was a feminine room in a way, but there was too much pink for his taste. It hurt his eyes, and, for a moment, McNamara had the feeling that his brain stopped working for good.

Ann obviously had exaggerated with the decoration of the room. McNamara, but James also, felt that their eyes hurt because of too much pink and so many roses, either painted or natural everywhere. And then it was also the smell. It was too sweet and heavy. Even the hostess had used too much perfume and her perfume had an overwhelming smell that was heavy and dizzying in the ugliest sense of the word.

They sat down trying to leave everything aside, while their hostess excused herself for a few moments and left the room to go to the kitchen.

While she was away the two men watched each other and smiled thinking of the same thing: that was the room of a woman that hadn't grown up enough and kept living a sort of fantasy of her adolescence, despite her thirty years, at least, if they remembered well her data.

Ann Goddard came back into the room bringing a tray with three coffee cups. After getting in, she gave a cup of coffee to each of them and then, holding a cup in her hand, she also sat on an armchair that was opposite to the sofa.

The men watched her a few moments and were surprised to see that she seemed younger than she should've been. Although she was thirty-two, she seemed only to be twenty-five. She had blond-red hair and her skin was so white that seemed almost transparent.

They saw some freckles on her cheeks and thought they made her look as if she was a playful little girl not a grown up woman. She wasn't tall but she had a quite elegant posture, despite the fact she didn't seem to be too sophisticated. She was wearing a coloured dress matching the colours of her drawing room.

McNamara seeing her thought the woman had gone too far with the theme of the flowers and colours. Someone should've told her, but he couldn't be that one because he'd already messed up with McNeil and made James suspicious.

"I think you've come to ask me about the girl from the Dobbs' yard, haven't you?"

"In deed, Miss Goddard", said James, catching McNamara's sight. He'd made him sign to undertake the lead of the interview. "You live practically next door and we've thought it'd have been impossible not to hear or see what happened last night".

"In deed, I live next door, but last night I typed something in the kitchen and then went to bed early. Actually, I was waiting for someone to come and when I got a phone call to put the date off, I was so furious that I decided to go to bed at once. I didn't fall asleep right that moment because I kept thinking of the ruined date, but I, once I fall asleep, I sleep heavy like a log, as my poor mom used to say. However, I woke up when I heard that awful scream. I'm not a too courageous woman, you know, so I didn't even move under the blanket of fear. I didn't have the courage to go downstairs to see what was going on. Only after I heard people talking outside, I went downstairs. I thought that if my neighbours had woken up and gone out too, then I'm not alone anymore and nothing bad could have happened to me, you know", she explained them.

"Didn't you watch out of the window at all?" McNamara asked her watching her very carefully to see if she was lying to him, but he could swear she wasn't the type of person to play hide-and-sick games and keep silent upon things when she was directly asked about them.

"No, I didn't, and even if I had watched through the window, I couldn't have seen too much. When I went out, I saw that the body was actually in the other side of the yard, and I couldn't have seen anything because of the Dobbs' house".

"Did you get closer to the body?" McNamara asked her.

"Oh, no, I couldn't have", she said apparently shocked because of the enormity of such a presumption, and the policemen could clearly hear fear in her voice. "I've just told you I'm not very courageous and I couldn't have stood to see the body of someone killed. I know I couldn't have", she replied defensively. "I haven't ever got closer to a dead person, and so far I haven't had a chance to see someone killed!"

"Have you seen someone that shouldn't have been in the street?" asked James.

"I can't say that. There was Mr Thompson, certainly. I noticed he was the only one dressed in his usual suit. He never goes out otherwise if he's not perfectly dressed and neat. He's a real gentleman, you should know", she said, and the two men watched each other, McNamara raised his eyebrows a little to convey his opinion to James. "Then there was Mr Reid", she continued without noticing the looks the two men exchanged. "Mr Reid was wearing something brown over his pyjamas, I think, and Mrs Reid who had a very light and short gown on. I even thought she must be nuts. If her husband had even glanced to her, he'd have killed her on spot with rage. He makes a big scandal for a short skirt, but for a transparent gown, I don't know what he could've done!... Ah, and of course there was also Mrs Thompson, who came a bit later, just after me, because she took her time to change her pyjamas or what she usually wears at night. There were the Davidsons too. Mrs Davidson was wearing a very ruffled training costume, I think she'd slept in it, although I can't figure out how she stood it, and Mr Davidson wearing a white bathrobe... I saw no one else until police came", she said after a few moments of thinking. "Oh, yes", she remembered, "the Browns were also there, but the Randalls came only when the police came".

'Did you hear anything from Mrs Dobbs house after the police left? Or did you see someone getting into the house afterwards?" McNamara asked her watching her attentively.

"No, I can't be sure, but I stayed at the window of my bedroom for a while and because I couldn't sleep I had the vague impression I saw someone sneaking on one side of the Dobbs' house to the back door. I'm sure it was a man, because a woman wouldn't look like that".

"What do you mean, Miss Goddard?" McNamara asked her.

"Well, the shoulders were too broad and hips too narrow. No, the body wasn't of a woman, definitely. A woman would look absolutely differently, you know it".

"Did you recognize the person?" asked James.

"No, I don't know who was, but I'd the feeling there was something familiar in his posture and gait, even if he was walking a little bent. I only can't realise who he exactly was".

"Did you hear anything then? A noise, a scream or something like that?"

“Oh, no! I heard nothing like that. I stayed at the window a few minutes only and then I went to bed ’cause it was very late and I usually wake up early in the morning”.

“When you watched through the window, was the light on or off?” asked McNamara to see whether she was in danger, remembering of the logic game Bryony had made.

“The light was off, why?”

“Then, it’s ok. He couldn’t see you”, replied McNamara. “We were afraid you could be in danger, but if the men didn’t see you, you aren’t. Could you tell us a few things about your neighbours, especially the Thompsons, the Davidsons, Mr Graham and the Reids? Ah, and of course the Porters”.

“Well, Alice Thompson is a very boring woman, in my opinion. I don’t have what to talk to her about. She knows only two things: to take care of the house and her husband so that he missed nothing, forgetting to offer him what he needs most: love and, especially, physical love. She’s a stupid cow, that’s clear. No one in the street is too interested in talking to her, excepting Mrs Reid that calls on her when she gets bored and had nothing else to do, although I don’t understand what she could talk to her, and Mrs Randall. She’s that kind of very severe and pickled, narrow-minded woman”, she said grinning. It was as if she’d tasted unripe grapes. “Mrs Randall has some very firm opinions about how a wife should be and, apparently, Alice matches her principles entirely. She's even her favourite, as anyone in this street could say it".

"But, Mr Thompson, what does he feel for his wife?" asked McNamara curious to see what the woman would answer knowing she was Thompson's lover.

Ann blushed and seemed confused a little. The two policemen waited patiently for her answer, presuming what was going to come, though. In the end, she told them:

"I know he's annoyed with her and wants to leave her but he tries to find a better way to tell her, you know, to not hurt her", she answered in a low voice in the end.

"How could you know it for sure?" asked James, curious to see if she was going to confess.

"Well...you know, I and Mr Thompson...are involved in a sort of relation...we're going to get married...as soon he's divorced her. Actually, he loves me, and wants to live with me", she said slowly.

"Mrs Thompson knows it?" McNamara asked her patiently, imagining it was quite tough for her kind of woman to admit a relation with a married man.

"Not really... Not yet... He said we should keep the secret for now... You know... He doesn't want to hurt Alice, after all she's not guilty 'cause he doesn't love her, he says, and I agree with him, after all", she said quickly even though she didn't seem to agree with Thompson's idea.

"How long have you been together?" McNamara asked again.

“We’ve been together for three years or so. They moved here five years ago and after my mom left to live with my sister in Liverpool, I started meeting him, in Edinburgh first, where we both work... Then we started to meet at me in the evening”.

“So, Mrs Thompson knows about your relation”, concluded James.

“Only if he told her, ’cause otherwise she couldn’t find out”, said Ann.

“How it comes? Do you think she hasn’t seen him coming to you so far? There’s only one way to here, and it passes right before their house. She couldn’t have missed him. She must’ve seen him, even if only once”, McNamara contradicted her.

“Daniel comes to me twice a week and he comes through the gardens, at the back. First, he gets into Mrs Stevens’s garden because at that hour she’s either inside or at Miss McNeil’s and can’t see him. It is quite very easy to get into Miss McNeil’s garden. The other garden doesn’t have an owner here now so there’s no danger, and the Dobbs spend their early night in their drawing room, and therefore they couldn’t see him. So, you see, Alice couldn’t find out he comes to me, in no circumstances, only if Daniel had told her and he didn’t. I’m sure she doesn’t know anything. Sometimes I wait for him and he can’t come ’cause either Mrs Stevens or Miss McNeil is out in the garden. Mrs Dobbs wasn’t ever in the kitchen at the time he would come. They would eat early in the evening and then watch TV. Yesterday he couldn't come at all. I think one of these might've seen him when he came back and therefore, he didn't come here last night. Usually he's very careful not to be seen by neighbours. He doesn't want Alice hear anything until he tells her".

"I see, Miss Goddard", answered McNamara, although he didn't understand how she could be so stupid and not realise that Daniel Thompson was making a fool of her, especially because he knew that, in principle, women had more intuition and didn't let them fooled so long. "Now, could you tell something of the Reids?" he asked coming back to the subject, they were interested in.

"He's a nice guy, in my opinion. He leaves at work in the morning and comes back around six in the evening every day. He doesn't go anywhere without his wife. I rarely see him in the corner pub with someone else, usually with Mr Graham or Mr Randall. With Mrs Reid is another story. She's a very lazy woman when it comes to household jobs and seems quite indifferent when Mr Reid gets angry with her and he does that almost daily. I hear she writes some stories for magazines, I think they're nonsense, but I don't talk to her at all and I can't say anything about her. Alice Thompson knows her better, 'cause they spend time together. It's quite weird their relation, in my opinion. They've nothing in common these two women, I can certainly say", said Ann.

"But about Mr Graham what could you tell us?" asked McNamara realising she liked talking about her neighbours.

"I haven't spoken to him much", she said reluctantly. "When he came here, he tried to make friends with me, but I didn't want to have a relation with him. I'd already had a relation with Daniel and I'm not that kind of girl changing men like socks. Therefore, now Graham doesn't speak to me at all. He might've felt hurt of my attitude. We greet each other when we meet and that's it. One day I saw him in town, recently. He was together with a young woman. I think she was about twenty-two, twenty-three. They seemed very close. However, I don't know anything else of him".

"Do you know anything of Patsy Porter?" James asked her seeing she was so willing to tell them more.

Her face turned red with anger. She seemed not to like the girl at all and to have quite a lot against her.

"She's a bad girl, even very bad. I don't like this kind of girl. I was glad when she left from here, you should know".

"Why don't you like her?" James asked. He was curious to see why she got so angry suddenly.

"She thinks she's the most attractive girl in the world and she makes eyes to all men of a certain age. She tried to charm even my Daniel, but, of course, he didn't pay her attention. He used to say she's a stupid girl with whom you cannot speak and she isn't even beautiful as she thought".

Policemen said nothing, even if they had already heard that Daniel Thompson went out with Patsy at least once. They wanted her to talk as much as possible and therefore, they preferred to keep silent than annoy her telling her about Daniel's indiscretion.

"I see", said McNamara. "Now could you tell us something about the other neighbours of yours?" he asked being interested in finding something out about everyone to have a general idea about the people in the Nightingale Street.

"I don't talk to them too much, you know. I've my work and I also have Daniel, and I don't need more. I prefer reading a book to speaking to my neighbours with whom I've nothing in common.

"But Miss McNeil's got a bookshop, doesn't she?" McNamara asked her curious to hear her opinion of McNeil. "If you say you like books..."

"Yes, she has. But she pretends she's very busy... She comes very late at home in the evening, you know", she told them and then kept quite for a while. Then she continued: "And however, I haven't spoken to her since she made eyes to my Daniel. She was so shameless that she came here to tell me to be careful with him because he tried to propose her to become...well, you know, his lover", she found her words with difficulty. "We two were friends then, but when I heard all those lies about Daniel, I couldn't stand to be in the same room with her and talk to her. She's a very mean woman and I'm sure that she's envious on my life with Daniel and therefore, she tried to steal him from me. She's got nothing so nice in hers, as we have... And she dared to tell me she came to warn me 'cause we were friends. I'm sure she actually wanted me to leave him 'cause she'd imagined that if I left him, she might have him. Of course, her swindle didn't last for a second, I tell you. When I told Daniel what she'd told me, he told me she was the one who tried to draw his attention", Ann stressed to make herself as clear as possible. "But he didn't even want to pay her attention, 'cause, as he told me, he had me and besides he didn't find her pretty at all. He told me that Bryony was probably too upset with him 'cause he hadn't answered to her flirt and therefore she came to me to tell me all those lies... Of course, I believed him; after all, we were together for some time and I trust him... So you see, I can't tell you anything about her 'cause I don't know anything of her anymore. We broke our friendship and for good. She wasn't too much of a friend. Maybe these days she's trying to break another relation 'cause she doesn't have one of hers", she said maliciously. "She's too caustic with men and she's not too feminine, so she can't have success".

James seemed quite stoned of Ann's accusations. He'd just seen Bryony and he could be sure she was one of the most feminine women he'd ever seen and she wouldn't have needed an artifice to make a man to like her or be hers. And certainly, she didn't seem that kind of woman that would have needed Thompson. She knew better what he could do.

"Ok, Miss Goddard", said McNamara, sick of hearing her defending the vicious Mr Thompson and seeing how stupid she could be. “Maybe we’ll come back later or tomorrow to you. However, by then, please, don’t tell anyone that you saw something last night”.

“Of course, I see”, she replied without being too sure she’d take his advice. “However, I wanted to tell only to Daniel, but I haven’t seen him yet. Of course, when I see him, I’ll tell him”, she decided. “I don’t think women should hold things back from their men, and, however, I’m sure Daniel isn’t involved in this mess. He’s too kind and loving to do such a horrible thing”.

“Please, don’t tell to him either”, McNamara asked her. “It’s better no one knows. You could be in danger, you know”.

She nodded, but didn’t show she’d been convinced at all. McNamara was sure she wouldn’t take his advice. He was sure she’d mention what she saw to Daniel Thompson, and he didn’t know what to believe of his innocence. However, as he couldn’t do anything with her, he tried to propose her something else:

“What do you say if we put a policeman here, with you, to protect you?”

“No way”, she replied vehemently. “I don’t accept that. I don’t like to have my life invaded of anyone. However, I don’t think anyone would attack me, exactly me”, she said, actually thinking that Daniel mightn’t have come to her if he’d seen a policeman in the house and she was missing him too much to risk not seeing him. However, she was more than sure no one would attack her.

McNamara saw he couldn't do anything more with her so he stood up and left with James.

After they'd got out of the house, James turned to McNamara and said:

"I'm sure the vicious Daniel Thompson made eyes to Bryony and she didn't accept him, not the opposite. She told her friend the truth, I'm sure".

"Yes, she might've said the truth, but Bryony might also have tried to have a relation with Thompson. I recall his face from last night. If I'm not wrong, he's a handsome man and women like this kind of man a lot. A pretty face makes more than anything, as far as I've noticed", he said ironically. "And you must think that he already has two loyal women here in this street, Goddard and his wife, and God knows how many others he'd have in town".

"Do you really think Miss McNeil would do that?" asked James quite shocked because he had the feeling the woman was of a certain quality.

"Maybe she could", answered McNamara thoughtfully, although he wasn't sure of that. He also noticed the woman didn't seem that kind of simpleton men like Daniel Thompson could've wrapped their head.

Hearing him, James recalled the meeting with Miss McNeil and started to suspect his boss of something else. He imagined, probably, that he liked the woman too much and he didn't want to ruin his image of tough man he tried to keep before his men. That was a good explanation for his completely inappropriate behaviour towards Miss McNeil.

McNamara figured out that James was thinking he liked Miss McNeil and he was afraid he wasn't too far from the truth. Therefore, he frowned to him and said roughly:

"Stop dreaming, James. We still have a lot of work to do, if I'm not wrong. You'd better call to the police station and ask to have two policemen sent for survey: one for McNeil's house and the other for Goddard's. I don't want any unpleasant surprises. Both of them must be here in half an hour. A policewoman will stay with McNeil in the house, because I'm sure she won't be against. She knows better than that. The other one will guard Goddard's house at the back of those trees over there", he told him pointing to the trees across from Goddard's house. "And then, we'll go to see if one of the two, Mr Thompson or Mr Reid, has already come home. We have to talk to them too".

James looked down and said nothing more. He made the calls as he was told, and then followed McNamara across the street. McNamara knocked on the Thompsons' door and waited for a few minutes for someone to come and open the door, hoping that this one would be exactly Mr Thompson.

Unfortunately, the same Mrs Thompson came to the door and opened it, not her husband. The woman smiled seeing the two policemen again.

“Is Mr Thompson at home, ma’am?” McNamara asked her.

“I’m afraid he isn’t”, she replied regretfully. “He called me a moment ago and he told me he’d come later because he’s got something urgent to solve at the office”.

“Then excuse us ma’am. I think that in the end we’ll go to see him at work tomorrow”, said McNamara with frustration, realising the same time he had no chance to find Thompson at home too early.

Chapter Nine

They headed to the Reids' house. When they reached the door, they heard someone yelling inside. The voice was very angry and belonged to a man in climax of rage. The two men watched each other and then McNamara smiled widely. He knew what was going on: one of the Reids' famous quarrels. Everyone in the street told them about.

"Let's stop this wonderful domestic quarrel, what do you say, James?" he said ironically.

"And ruin their pleasure, sir?"

"In deed, my dear friend, let's spoil their pleasure. Why should they have fun when we had a tiring day with two bodies, hmm?" McNamara stressed the situation.

James laughed because his boos was just kidding. However, he pressed the bell and, from inside, a melodious melody was heard in total discordance with what they heard from the house earlier.

Almost instantly, the voice inside stopped shouting and in a few seconds a very big, tall and solid man came to the door. He was still angry and had a red face because of rage.

"What the hell, could you want?" he asked angrily, watching McNamara fiercely, angrily, somehow guessing he was the boss of the two of them.

"Imagine, we're the police", this one answered mildly, with a smile appeared in the corner of his mouth.

"And what would you care of our personal life?" asked he, both furious and amazed. "Has anyone complained of our discussions?" he continued more astonished than before, because he knew no one in the street cared of what the other neighbours were doing in their house. He couldn't imagine Mrs Randall or Thompson, if he were at home by chance, picking up the phone to call the police.

"Not really", said McNamara. "No one called us for your domestic quarrel. We're here with other businesses".

The man watched them a few seconds seeming to not understand a thing, and then, suddenly, he realised it. The recognition could be seen in his eyes.

Actually, he recalled the sergeant's face. He'd seen him in the Dobbs's drawing room the previous night. Hitting his front with his palm sonorously, he said:

"I see, you've come for what happened last night! Poor girl in the Dobbs' yard". In his voice, one could feel a real compassion but, the same time, some relieve that his quarrel with his wife didn't make them come all the way there.

"Not only!" replied McNamara, liking to see his face changing. He could see he puzzled him. "You see, sir, Mrs

Dobbs was also killed last night, so we have questions for both matters".

Noticing the man kept changing faces, really shocked by the last news, McNamara realised Reid knew nothing of that.

"Hasn't your wife told you anything of that, sir?" he asked Mr Reid.

"She had no chance", he admitted, somehow contritely. It was clear: he'd started the quarrel as soon as he'd got home.

"Yes, I see", McNamara replied a little caustically. "You've been too hasty. You've started your favourite domestic activity as soon as you got home, sir, and left your wife no time to say a thing".

Michael Reid blushed violently, but found no reply to fight McNamara's words back, although he should have found. He didn't think the policeman had the right to speak like that. However, he couldn't say anything else. He felt even a little ashamed, though, so he led them inside with no word.

McNamara got into the living room and found Mrs Reid browsing a magazine peacefully, as if nothing had happened. She didn't seem embarrassed at all of anything that had happened before. She stood up slowly and smiled sweetly to the two men inviting them to sit down.

"Would you like tea or coffee?" she asked them kindly.

"Anything you want to drink, Mrs Reid" answered McNamara courteously.

"I think I'd drink a coffee", she said going out of the room under the killing eyes of her husband, who had the impression she was too kind to the two men. And this time he wasn't wrong at all. Actually, the woman was quite kind and anyone could say she didn't do it only because of elementary politeness, but also because she loved seeing that tough look in her husband's eyes, as long he didn't apply it violently. And he never did that, so she could afford playing a little with him. It made life more interesting.

She seemed to know what her husband was thinking because she turned her head to him and smiled roguishly to him to show him she knew very well that her attitude would have that effect upon him.

McNamara could swear he heard Reid grinding his teeth and raised his eyebrows. James caught the gesture and understood what the inspector wanted to say. He was completely astonished. He'd never seen such a thing. He didn't know and didn't believe that such a relation could be called love. The two of them were quite awful. They liked to torment each other. That was their passion.

"With your wife, we spoke during the morning today", said McNamara, trying to chase away Mr's Reid's killing thoughts reflected in his eyes. He wasn't sure Mr Reid wouldn't apply those thoughts, despite what Mr Randall had said.

"And have you found anything interesting?" Reid asked sarcastically. "I'd be amazed. As far as I know my wife does nothing else but staying before the computer, and at night, once she falls asleep, a lot of noise is necessary to wake her up".

"No, we haven't", admitted McNamara. Actually he hadn't because he couldn't ask her a thing. He got amused too much on their expenses. However, he didn't want to tell Reid about that. So he preferred to say: "But maybe we hear from you. What could you tell us about the precedent night?"

"Not much. I heard that brutal scream that woke me up and I must say that, the same time, made my blood run cold. I put my bathrobe on in a rush and then we went out at once. I realised it was a woman. In addition, that amazed me a lot. In our street women are safe, normally. I've heard nothing of any attack so far. That is why we chose this area when we moved here".

"Was there anyone else when you came out? Neighbours or unknown people?"

"The neighbour—Thompson. I think he, actually, had just got home. He hadn't even taken out his tie. Then his wife came out and the others. I couldn't say the order. I was quite shocked of what I saw in the yard across the street. I only know I saw Mr Dobbs in a certain moment. Exactly a few seconds before he fainted or had a heart attack, better said. The doctor said so".

"Mr Thompson called the doctor, didn't he? Does he know him well?"

"Well, Alice Thompson always imagines she's got all sorts of diseases. I think it's a tactic to draw her husband's attention. She doesn't really seem sick, in my opinion. Just bored".

"And does she succeed to draw his attention?", asked McNamara curious.

"Not really", admitted Reid. "The truth is that guy is a Casanova. All day long, I see him with all sorts of women, and all of them younger than he, almost half his age".

"I see", said McNamara. "And you have often the chance to see him?"

"Not very often. Once or twice a week I go to the architect's office. Sometimes I have lunch with him in town. In such occasions, I also saw Thompson. Once we found ourselves in the same restaurant. When I was to go, he came after me, and, as man to man, he asked me that his wife hears nothing. As if I ran fast at his house to tell her. The guy is stupid, if you want to take my word for that!"

Meanwhile Mary came back with the coffee and put a cup in front of each one, excepting her husband. She gave this one a cup of tea. When Michael saw tea, his eyes got round because of astonishment.

"Has something happened? asked McNamara.

"No. Not really", managed Mr Reid answer slightly evasively trying to pass over the moment.

"I think", said Mary playfully, "that my husband is very amazed now, inspector and he can't answer you. I rarely recall of his preferences, you know. And now, here I recalled that he prefers tea, and that shocked him, didn't that, dear?"

Michael felt that his entire feeling of good ran away. Mary managed so well to make him feel bad while he still hoped, the fool of him, that one day his wife would show him a real sign of affection!

He should've believed her when she told him that if he married her he only made himself problems when he didn't have. She'd been right but he feared it wasn't so easy to get rid of his feelings for her. He took a risk and he had to go through to the end. At least not to leave her the satisfaction she made him go away, as she'd always say she'd do.

Watching him and guessing some of his thoughts, Mary felt a shadow of regret for her words. She didn't know why she was so grim to annoy Michael and why she always wanted to make him feel that safety was an illusion. However, she was like that and it wouldn't have been easy for her to change. Sometimes she didn't even see the point. She knew well men weren't steadfast. At least she could make him understand that his leaving wasn't a big loss for her.

She felt an acute loneliness at the thought of Michael's leaving. The slight pain in her heart was reflected in her eyes too and, although she turned her eyes to the window, opaque because of dark of the evening passing to the night, the people in the room saw it. Michael saw it. He couldn't understand what it was but his heart hurt for her. One couldn't care of someone so much as he cared for her and not feel their anxieties as being theirs, even when they couldn't decipher them.

McNamara saw in Mary's eyes the very look of his mother. It was identical. She looked like that whenever she would recall of his father. The echo of his mother's sad and resigned smile, brought before his eyes, after such a day, made him think he didn't need that. He tried to get rid of the bitter sensation and came back to his questions.

"Did any of you see anything after the police left last night?"

Michael felt as if someone shook his shoulder when he was dozing off. McNamara's voice woke him up from contemplating his wife, but he didn't understand the question. However, Mary had heard him perfectly.

"I've told you I saw nothing. Michael was too furious and accusing to pay attention to anything else than his voice. I think he yelled louder than just now, didn't you, dear?

Hearing her words, Michael blushed again. James had the feeling he saw a kid caught with a prank. It was something that, at his age, the mad could still arouse such feelings.

"No", Michael said after few moments of silence. "I heard nothing, and, as my lovely wife has just noticed", he added sharply watching her, "I was busy with something else. I'm sorry, inspector, but I don't see how I could help you. I don't know very well the people in the street. We greet each other, it's normal, we're neighbours, but that's it. We don't visit each other or something like that. We either go out alone or with my colleagues or with Mary's friend from college. That's it".

McNamara watched Mary, and this one stressed her husband's words:

"Yes, that's true. The only one I talk to is Alice Thompson, but I don't talk too much to her either. I'd like to make friends with the girl living next to Mrs Stevens, Bryony I think her name is. Nevertheless, she's always at work. But she doesn't socialize either. I rarely catch her to talk to her. Of course, we all know the Randalls from the grocer's... That woman is awful. Her mouth is always crouched and she's awfully moralizing. At least, she despised me from the very beginning. I don't know how her husband stands her. However, I think he has no choice. Everything belongs to her, as I understood".

"The Browns are nicer", took her husband the word from her. "We go to them to the bar now and then. They're kind and nice people. However, we don't visit them or something, either".

"All right", said McNamara and he stood up. "But, however, if you recall of something unusual happened in the area or to your neighbours, call me. Here's my card", he said holding out his card to Michael.

Chapter Ten

The policeman was hidden in the dark and cursed the storm started for some while. He was cold and the hot coffee in the thermos bottle didn't help him too much. He started his guard at midnight. He'd been there for only half an hour, but he already felt as if hours had passed. It was too much till morning. Even too much.

Moisture got into his pores despite the thick raincoat. He lit a cigarette hiding it in his palm so that the light of the embers couldn't be seen and he grumbled in his beard. If someone had pricked up, he'd have realised he was very upset. He was upset that "that stupid woman" hadn't accepted to be guarded. Now he'd been warm, as McKay. He wouldn't have been out in the rain and wind.

A branch broke behind him. The policeman listened attentively. He tried to see something in the direction from where the crack came. He made a few steps. Something hit the back of his head strongly. The pain pierced him. He recorded vaguely a slight smell of aftershave and the mint smell of the chewing gum. He fell, and the last thing he realised, was the wet smell of leaves and faded grass.

***

The wind would hit the window. The deafen noise made her start and turn her head. She saw the storm burst out strongly. She couldn't see but lightning in the deep night. Raindrops kept hitting the roof rhythmically.

The cold got into her bones and she shivered. She left the magazine on the night table and went to close the window in the next room. She'd forgotten of it. At least, she hadn't heard noise of broken glass. She hoped it'd be in one piece.

She got into the room and pressed the switcher. The light blinded her for a second and she winked fast. She went to the window and closed it. She watched the night for a while.

The smouldering of the rain overwhelmed her with a feeling of sadness and loneliness. That moment, she felt the burden of her age, and from somewhere from the dark of the past, aunt Martha's words came out. "You didn't get married till twenty-eight, let's say thirty, spinster you stay. No one takes you. You get like me: old and burden on other people's head!"

It was the first time she felt doubt. Where the hell was she thinking when she bound relation with a married man? He promised her to divorce Alice and marry her, but if there were only words in the wind?

At least, Graham was free. Then. However, who knows if he's also serious. He didn't leave that impression or at least she thought so. She might have cared of Daniel too much, that's why.

She shook a little, to chase dark thoughts away. She tried to get some self-confidence and come back to the words she said that afternoon. Daniel couldn't cheat on her, lie on her like that. He must've loved her and he'd marry her. He'd said so again, a few hours earlier, when she saw him. He was more loving than ever. He was scared for her when she told him what she saw a night before. He implored her not to say anyone. He feared the killer might want to kill her too. He implored her and swore he couldn't live after her death.

Ann smiled recalling his words. They were so sincere that she felt her heart getting warm reminding of them. She felt appreciated, wanted and necessary. It was as if she'd been given something great. It was more than she could've hoped.

She left the window close and went to the bedroom again. She got out into the corridor, and closed the door behind. She looked up and started violently. The light had gone out. She was sure she hadn't done it. She'd left it lit. She was sure. Fear overwhelmed her slightly. The switcher was at the other end of the corridor but she felt as if it was miles away. She started trembling. She could feel her heart beating strongly as if it wanted to break her chest.

She felt panic seizing her and her legs became gelatine thinking of the warning of the policeman and Daniel's words. She'd spoken, damn it. She told Mrs Reid what she'd seen. Oh, yes, Mr Graham also heard. He was passing by. Her miserable mouth! Earlier, that day, she'd also told Alison Randall!

She thought to go slowly to the study she made from one of the guest rooms and took a vase. Why hadn't she accepted a policeman to guard her? Because of Daniel, that's why. He wouldn't have come to her that day if he'd known there were witnesses. She tightened her fists anxiously.

She left her slippers. First, she headed slowly to the study. She had to pass by the bedroom. She reached the door of the room. In the light of a lightning, she saw it. It was half-open. She knew she left it widely open. She was sure! Oh, Lord, if she didn't die that night! She reached out with a trembling hand and pushed the door slowly.

The silhouette in the shadow was alert. He saw the door moving and adrenaline started to run through his veins faster. He put his right hand up. The lightning revealed the sharpen blade. The blade cut off the dark after the lightning went off and struck. The thunder came. It covered the soft scream of Ann falling on her knees. She turned her head with difficulty. In the fast succession of the lightning, she saw the black mask but she recognised the eyes, the mouth and the chin. Her mouth uttered a mute "no". Her last thought taking shape in the dark covering her mind fast was: "It couldn't be you!", and then her eyes went blind. They couldn't see anything.

One moment before the definitive dark had overwhelmed her eyes, the criminal knew she'd recognised him even if she couldn't believe her eyes.

For one moment, he was tempted to close her eyes. His lucidity stopped him. It'd have been a mistake. He left her lying on her carpet paved with roses, blood-red now and sneaked out. He had one more problem to solve that night.

***

He opened his eyes with difficulty and pain pierced the top of his head. He closed them back. Then he stayed a few minutes with his eyes closed and then opened them slowly, very slowly. He touched the top of his head. It was sticky. It was blood for sure. He tried to stand up and got dizzy. He didn't know what he should do. Then he recalled. He had the mobile phone with him. It was in the coat pocket. He took it off and dialled McNamara's number, grinning at the terrifying thought of what was going to be. The sound of the bell pierced his brains. He held his front with his hand and massaged his temples.

"McNamara's here".

He felt his mouth drying instantly. He knew his boss and he knew that everything meant trouble. He couldn't utter a single word.

"McEvan, that's your?" asked McNamara, irritated because he heard nothing else but the heavy breath of a man at the other end of the line. "Answer now, damn it!"

"Yes", stuttered McEvan. "It's me, sir".

"What happened?" asked McNamara, and from the sound of his voice, McEvan realised that the little patience of his boss was worn out. He knew his temper. It was proverbial. Everyone in the department knew they shouldn't drive him mad. And what drove him mad the most was to mess up things or he had done exactly that.

"I've been hit, sir", he said softly, his voice hardly being heard.

"What the hell?" McNamara burst out. "What were you doing, sleeping? What did I send you there for?"

"He took me from the back, sir", McEvan stuttered, leaning his head in his hand. It hurt more badly than before. His boss's shouts penetrated his scull like a knife. "I didn't hear him sir, at all", he managed to utter again.

"What policeman are you?" yelled McNamara, and the sharp shouts pierced McEvan's brains like knives, making him tightening his eyes strongly. "Do you want to get to traffic?"

"No, sir. I'm sorry sir, but simply the storm and the others..." he tried to excuse himself stuttering.

"Ok, ok!" McNamara said again. "At least, have you checked Goddard? Is she alive?"

"I know you'll be very angry with me, sir", he said as if he was crying, because of the fear, pain and guilt, "But apparently I can't stand up... I feel my head turn, sir. I think I won't be conscious too long. No, I haven't check Goddard. How could I?"

"Ok, stay there and don't stand up", resigned McNamara. "I'll send Sergeant James to you together with Mike and Jo. I'll also come at once", he said, ending the discussion suddenly.

Just in time: McEvan slipped unconscious on the ground, despite the rain blowing his face strongly. Nothing could make him wake up now. However, it was better than with that terrible headache and nausea combing his stomach.

Chapter Eleven

He was watching from the back of McNeil's house. They seemed to choose not to use the sirens this time. They came in silence. He saw Sergeant James getting off the car and heading to the trees where McEvan was lying, switching on his torch and looking for him.

From the other car, two got out: a man and a woman.

The sergeant finally spotted McEvan fallen under a tree. He bent and checked his pulse. He could feel it. Weakly, but he could feel it. He shook him but McEvan didn't come to life. He lit his head top and saw the wound. It was quite serious. He needed an ambulance. He dialled 911 and announced the situation and remained with McEvan.

From there, he watched Mike Johnson and Jo Critchet heading to Goddard's house. Jo rang the bell and waited. She rang once more, long and insistently. The house kept silent obstinately. No light went on and no slight noise was heard.

"I'm going to the back, Mike", said Jo. "Stay here. Count to twenty and then break the door".

Mike nodded and got ready. At twenty, he broke the door. Jo broke the door at the back and it sounded like an echo of the first broken door.

Jo sneaked carefully on the corridor. She glanced to the kitchen. Everything was all right there. She reached the entrance hall, in front of the stairs. Here she met Mike.

"Everything's all right there", Mike whispered pointing with his head on the left where he'd already checked.

"All right, let's go upstairs", whispered Jo at her turn and they started to tiptoe up the stairs.

When they got in front of the bedroom, they saw the door open. Jo got inside first and she felt something next to her foot. She started strongly, but she made no noise. However, Mike felt her start and tension. Jo bent carefully and felt the place on the right of her foot. When she touched the delicate and still warm hand, she realised they found what they were looking for. Ann Goddard was there, but she didn't seem alive.

"Mike, the woman's here", she whispered. "I think you can turn the light on. The bird has flown from the cage for a long time", she said.

Mike turned the light on and watched over Jo's head to the woman on the floor. She had fallen on her stomach and her head was turned aside. The stoned face showed the terror felt before death.

"You make the call or should I?" he asked Jo.

"You call!" replied Jo, with some tiredness in her voice. "I don't feel like telling anyone about what's before my eyes".

This was the only thing she disliked in her work. She liked gathering information from here and there and build up a case, discover causes and motives, and, evidently, she had an enormous joy to catch the criminals. But she couldn't stand to look at victims. They had the bad habit to stay before her eyes for days and days.

Mike took his phone off and dialled McNamara's number. This one answered the phone at the first ring. He certainly had the phone in his hand.

"Say it, Mike!" his voice thundered in the phone.

"We found her, sir. She'd been stabbed twice, I think. However, she's dead".

No answer came. Mike didn't push for one. He knew his boss hadn't ever liked to lose a witness. Actually, he didn't like to have more victims during an inquiry.

"All right!" the answer came after a few moments. "Stay there. I'll come now. I'll call the prosecutor and the coroner. You call the forensics".

"Very well, sir", Mike said briefly, but however, no one listened. McNamara had already turned off his phone.

Chapter Twelve

Bryony stood up from her chair and closed her portable. She was tired, and the sound of the rain striking the tiles on the house and the windows made her want to go to bed. She went to the window and watched a few moments outside trying to distinguish something in the dark. Nothing seemed to move. She didn't notice the silhouette hidden in the shadow of the tree in the corner of the house. She didn't realise she was watched. A few minutes later, she went out of the room and tuned off the light.

She went into the kitchen where the policewoman was browsing a magazine. On the table in front of her, there was a pile of magazines to keep her over the night. When Bryony got into, she looked up.

"Haven't you gone to bed yet, young lady?"

"No, I've had work to do. I'll go to bed now. But I think we agreed not to be so formal", Bryony smiled to the policewoman.

"I know", the other one said, smiling back. "But it's difficult to get used. Not all people are as kind as you are. Usually, we have a different treatment".

"I'm sorry to hear that. I'd have thought people appreciate your effort", replied Bryony, while her eyebrows rose with amazement. "You defend their lives, don't you?"

"Yes, we do, but they don't often realise that", the other one smiled a little awkwardly and shyly. "For instance, two months ago, I had a nightmare night. I had to stay with an older lady and I had no peace at all. She was watching me continuously. She was afraid I'd steal from her. You should have heard what she told me".

Bryony remained completely puzzled for a moment. Then she burst into laughter:

"It can't be! You were representing police!"

"Oh, yes, it can!" answered the other one amused. "She told me that there are no honest people in this world and therefore, she had to be very cautious".

"I see", replied Bryony, even though she couldn't understand. She found it absurd. "Would you like some more tea?" she asked.

"Don't bother, I'll make it", she answered. "You seem quite tired. You'd better go to bed".

"If you want, it'd be great. I feel as if a car ran me down. Believe me, it's awfully hard to run a business alone, no matter how small it is".

"I believe you, I couldn't do it. Actually, I think, I wouldn't have enough courage to take the risk. Now you'd better go to bed, dear. Good night!"

"Good night! If you need something, anything, you're free to look over here, without thinking of anything. You can look into the fridge or cupboards", answered Bryony smiling at her, and then she went to the door.

She went out of the kitchen and tiptoed to Mrs Stevens's room and knocked softly to the door. No one answered. Although she disliked the idea to invade someone's intimacy, she pushed the door open to make sure everything was all right.

For a few moments, she looked at the old woman, who had fallen asleep with the light on the night table turned on. She smiled. It was all right. She knew the woman had a tough evening with a lot of pain. Then she stepped back, closing the door behind.

She went to the stairs and started to go upstairs to her room. She got to the room. She didn't bother to turn on the light. She was too tired for that. She took off her gown and remained in her nightgown. She got under the blanket and closed her eyes. It was too difficult to fight and keep them open even for a second.

Despite her tiredness she didn't manage to fall asleep at once. Maybe she was too tired and lots of thoughts bothered her. They jumped from one to the other and she couldn't focus too much on only one idea.

She thought of Mrs Stevens first. Then she thought of the policewoman watching downstairs, in the kitchen. Then, suddenly, McNamara's face turned up in her mind. Accursed man! Full of airs and stuffy! But she couldn't stop a smile thinking of him. He was an interesting guy. Quite very interesting!

The very moment she thought she'd fall asleep, she had the feeling she head a muffled thud from downstairs. She didn't pay attention. She felt too tired to get up and go to see what it was. But then she also heard the noise of a door shut against the wall. The sound was distinct. She couldn't imagine the policewoman had started to make noise.

With fear in her heart, she got up. Bare-footed she went to the door. She tried hard to think of something to use as a weapon in case of something. She had nothing like that at hand in the house; maybe just the knives in the kitchen but she imagined that there might have already been problems there. She couldn't get a knife. She was looking anxiously for a solution when she recalled. She had something at hand: the scissors. They were on the shelf in the bathroom.

On tiptoe and barely breathing, she got into the bathroom and with the top of her fingers she looked for the scissors. She was afraid she'd drop something and make noise. She managed to find the scissors and grabbed them.

Then she sneaked downstairs. When she reached the bottom of the stairs she held her breath. She heard a distinct gasp from the kitchen. She headed there. Then, more distinctly, she heard a creak in the floor in the opposite side, where Mrs Steven's room was.

She felt her hands like ice. She seized the scissors with her fingers better. Her fingers trembled. She feared she couldn't hold them well. She'd drop them. She kept going to Mrs Stevens' room. In the kitchen, she couldn't do a thing. She went as fast as she could, trying to remember the same time where was the place where the floor was creaking.

She seemed to succeed. She remembered well. She'd already got to the door and heard no creak. She leaned against the jamb. The emotion held her throat and her heart went small, small. It was lost somewhere, there, in the chest, although it beat amazingly fast.

She bent a little in front by the wall and saw the silhouette stopped almost in the middle of the room. He seemed to listen. Apparently, he was satisfied with what he heard because suddenly left the still position and jumped to the bed.

Bryony saw the shine of the blade. That moment, although she wasn't sure if her legs would help her, she rushed like crazy, to the bed, without thinking of noise, with the scissors prepared. And she struck. The other one didn't have the time to turn entirely. The scissors hit him in the shoulder. He screamed. The knife fell down and rolled down under the bed. Bryony dashed again.

Chapter Thirteen

"Go and check Mrs Stevens, James. McKay doesn't answer at all", said McNamara anxious. He was afraid that something happened there too.

Sergeant headed to McNeil's house without saying a word. Hardly had he made a few steps, than he heard McNamara behind him.

"I'd better come with you".

James nodded. Another time he'd have smiled. He could have guessed why McNamara decided to come along. But he couldn't smile. Not now. A deafen pain tightened his heart. He was afraid for McKay. She was a good girl, too good for this job.

He made big and fast steps. McNamara hardly could keep his step. If he hadn't had his own thoughts, he'd have guessed what was going on with James. Maybe he'd have made a joke.

But McNamara tried to chase away the thought that at McNeil's also happed what had happened to Miss Goddard's. The criminal had already become too bold. He wouldn't have had problems to strike another policeman.

He'd done the beginning. The way to murdering one was short from now on.

The two men got in front of McNeil house. They climbed the stairs. When they wanted to ring, the door opened suddenly making them start. Bryony got out. Her blond-red hair was dishevelled. Her eyes ran everywhere, as if they'd have looked for something along the street, or maybe for someone. Her look tried to hold on something. Only then she saw them.

Both of them got stoned. They couldn't believe their eyes. The girl had the face white as the paper excepting an ugly bruise flourishing on her right cheekbone and the blood running down.

Blood was flowing from her nose and, in the corner of her mouth, she had an ugly and bleeding wound. Her lip had already bloated. She tried to say something but she had difficulties in uttering sounds. She had something in her throat. She'd wanted to get rid of it. She feared, though, that then she'd have burst into tears and she couldn't have stopped. She'd have cried for hours.

When she recognized them, finally, she tried a weak smile, reminiscence of the good and constant education received in her childhood. But a whimper burst out at once on her lips. It hurt when she smiled. It hurt quite badly. She lifted a trembling hand. She held out to McNamara.

McNamara was still stoned. He couldn't realise why he didn't have before his eyes the slightly ironical and spiritual girl from that afternoon. Despite his surprise, he managed to catch her hand. He squeezed her fingers, as if he wanted to give her a little from his strength. He succeeded.

The girl finally pulled herself together. She composed her posture again and raised her shoulders and head. She regained something of the allure of the girl he recalled. With a voice like a rasp, and that sent some echoes in McNamara's head, she asked:

"How did you know to come? My phone's dead. I think he cut the line first. I'm afraid I hurt him badly, you must know. I think I hit him very badly. But, really, I couldn't do otherwise. Oh, and Claire's on the floor in the kitchen, I'm afraid. She hasn't recovered yet, I think. She's still unconscious. And hurt, I think".

They could see she felt bad talking, but she couldn't stop. Everything she was gathering in her mind, she had to say. She had the feeling that if she hadn't spoken then, she couldn't have ever spoken. Despair could be felt in her voice.

"Calm down, now", McNamara told her, trying to be calm to make her temper herself and bring her to normal as much as he could. "Let's get into the house. It's windy and rainy here".

Only then, the girl realised the storm hadn't calmed down. It was still raining and wind kept blowing. Both men had their hair and faces wet. She stepped slightly back and let them in.

"Come on", said McNamara, "let's get in and see everything. You say you hit him?" asked he leading her into the entrance hall.

"With the scissors. I hit him in the shoulder first", she replied with a trembling voice.

She started trembling again. Nausea got into her throat again. She suddenly came off from the hands of McNamara, who had held her shoulders, and surprisingly sure on her feet, she ran to the ground-floor bathroom. She hardly managed to reach the water closet, than she started to throw up. Oh, Lord, she didn't believe she could stop anymore!

McNamara, surprised, remained still watching her, but only for a few seconds. Then he imagined what happened and he felt sorry for her, for everything she had to do.

"Sir, I'm going to see what's McKay doing", said James with a tensed voice. "Shall I call the forensics?"

"Yes, it's for the best", answered McNamara, and then he looked at him briefly. Something on the sergeant's face, made him change his decision. He knew James wanted to do something else before. Even if his men had the impression he was focused only on his job, he saw the other things too. He couldn't do otherwise, as long as he had a department to run. And he was up to them in everything he did. Therefore, he tried to pay attention too all his men without letting them notice.

"Leave it, I'll call them", he said. "You'd better go see McKay ".

Sergeant nodded briefly but one could see relieve on his face. He couldn't think he'd have endured anymore.

He went to the left into the kitchen, leaving McNamara alone in the hall.

McNamara went to the room prepared for Mrs Stevens. He got into. He felt relieved. The old lady was sleeping like a log. He could hear her heavy breath. Maybe she'd taken something for sleep or pain.

However, around, there was a real mess. A chair was down in the middle of the room and there was full of blood near the bed. Exactly near the bed, there were the scissors full of blood. Their image brought back into his mind Bryony's devastated face.

"I'm sorry", Bryony's voice was heard from behind. "I couldn't abstain".

McNamara turned back and watched her. She seemed to come back to her senses a little. She didn't have that lost look anymore. Her eyes started to be more alive.

"Your friend slept all this time?" he asked amazed showing around.

"She had awful pains this evening", said Bryony, as if she'd excused her. "You know, when it rains, pain is more intense. Therefore, she took some stronger calming pills and she also took a sleeping pill. Quite strong, as I could see on the box. Otherwise she couldn't have slept at all".

"You realise, I think, I must do something to wake her up. I must call the forensics. There's a lot of evidence in this room and all must be checked", McNamara told her watching her as if he couldn't believe she'd recovered so much. Apparently, the woman, although she seemed fragile, had enough strength.

"Of course, I mean I think", stammered Bryony. "I'll try to wake her up", she continued, heading to the bed.

"Take care not to disturb the scene too much", McNamara told her taking his phone off his pocket. "I need it the way it is. It may tell us a lot and maybe we'll get a more consisting line."

Bryony nodded and leaned over Mrs Stevens. She shook her and called her name reassuringly. She seemed quite decided and she was. She realised it was vital that the policemen could do their job. She didn't intend to let that guy off the hook. Not after the crimes he'd done in so much cold-blood. Not after he forced her to do what she'd done. Not after he tried to kill her friend. These thoughts made her try harder.

Meanwhile, McNamara called the experts team by phone. He gave them little explanations, but he knew the people would understand it was important.

CHAPTER FOURTEEN

"Ok, boss, we'll come now", said a massive man in the microphone and then hang off. "Boys", he told the others, "I and Georgie are going to Miss McNeil's house. I understand it is a little down the street. It seems to have been a circus there too. Bloody night! he exclaimed angrily. "Tom, Lisa and Joe, you stay here and collect every pertinent evidence", he said and then gathered his kit carefully.

He took his gloves off. He crumpled them and threw them in a plastic bag prepared for that. He made a sign to Georgie to come with him and went out. Georgie followed him greeting his colleagues.

The two men got out in the yard. The massive one took his cigarettes off his pocket and lit one, protecting the flame of the lighter with his hand because the wind was still blowing. Georgie didn't smoke and watched his colleague reproachfully. He disliked this habit of his, he felt it was disgusting.

After the first smoke, Steven looked at the sky and saw it was clear. It'd been only a usual storm for the end of the summer and beginning of autumn.

"Steven", started Georgie, "do you think we have another body there?"

"I hope not", answered this one smoking eagerly. "I've heard McKay was in the house. I hope nothing happened to her. I don't know what James would do. I've seen them together in town. They've seemed quite bound. However, boss's voice was tensed but not as tensed when he had a body. He didn't say anything of coroners".

They passed by the yellow band surrounding the Dobbs' house. They went further without paying any attention. They were too used to that. After a few moments, they stopped before McNeil's house. Steven took two other smokes and then threw the cigarette.

"Bad habit", he said, knowing his friend completely approved. "I know I have to give up, Georgie", he said surprising his accusing look. "Don't bother me too. Come on inside".

The door was left open so they didn't have to ring. They got into the house and Steven called out to McNamara.

"Where boss?"

"Here, Steven", the answer came from somewhere on the right of the house.

The two men went on the corridor on the right. The very moment they reached the door, a young woman came out leading carefully an old woman with a walking stick. Passing by them, she told them very politely and smilingly, despite the way her face looked:

"Good evening, gentlemen!"

Steven and Georgie were so surprised that they couldn't answer. Usually, they didn't meet so polite people. It wasn't usual when they worked in that line of work. If they thought well, usually they met only nervous people that would forget the most elementary norms of common sense. The woman was something, to be sure.

McNamara's angry voice woke them up from amazement.

"Do you intend to come in, boys, or you want to stare after her till tomorrow?"

"Now, sir", came Steven's rushed answer. He knew his boss very well. He shouldn't provoke him with any remark when he was like that.

Steven got into the room followed by Georgie. He saw the blood all over the place and asked:

"Where's the body, sir?"

"Fortunately, no one was killed here", answered McNamara harshly. "But I want you to pick everything and especially what could lead to identify the killer. Most of the blood you see is his".

"He was hit well. Who did it?"

"The young lady that had just passed by, with that scissors there".

"Brave girl, sir", murmured Georgie in his beard.

"Brave, but with no brains", replied McNamara sharply. "She should've gone out for help, not fight a guy with a knife in his hand", he burst out watching the disaster on the floor, without seeing the change of looks Steven and

Georgie exchanged. “But, that’s it”, he said dryly. “Do your job here, gentlemen. I’m going to talk to the girl and see how everything happened. If you need more people, Steven, you have free hand to call them. Tell it to Shorty”.

McNamara didn’t see Steven nodding in approval. He already had gone out.

Steven and Georgie put their gloves and prepared to start their work.

“We need at least one or two people for the exterior”, said Steven thoughtfully. “Georgie, call them, while I’m watching around”.

***

McNamara headed to the kitchen. He arrived in front of the door and looked inside. The sergeant managed to make McKay regain consciousness. His hand was shaking while he was checking her wound at the temple. That moment, the policewoman groaned because of the pain. Her hair was full of the blood starting to coagulate. Her face had an unhealthy white colour and her eyes, as much as McNamara could see, were glassy, sign of the head concussion.

The woman’s eyes barely stayed open. She kept closing them intermittently as if the effort to keep them open had been too big. She had a serious wound at her chest, probably. He couldn’t see it, but he saw the blood still flowing. The haemorrhage didn’t stop at all and McNamara feared she’d lost too much blood. He hoped she could be stabilized.

"Have you called the ambulance?" McNamara asked the sergeant knowing that only in hospital McKay could be saved given the way she looked.

"Yes, sir! I've announced we have two people hurt. I thought that Miss McNeil should be seen too. She doesn't look as bad as Claire, but she doesn't look too good, in my opinion', the sergeant explained himself.

McNamara approved him, nodding, and then he watched Bryony who got into the kitchen. She managed to keep straight. She tried to smile to Mrs Stevens, she'd helped to sit at the table earlier. This one was still dozing. She hadn't passed over the effect of the pills.

Bryony had brought her a pullover to put around her shoulders, to protect her from the chillness of the night. If one looked carefully, he could see pain smouldering deep in the young woman's eyes. Her hand throbbed now and then. On her arm, one could see the signs already blue, showing aggression.

"Would you like some tea?" she asked. "I know I'd like some", she said, going to the gas-stove.

"Sit down", McNamara said roughly, almost prepared to take her by force and make her sit, if necessary. "I'll make that bloody tea, if you really need one", he said angrily and stood up from the chair he'd just sat on.

"What happened?" asked Bryony calmly, trying to make him calm down.

"Nothing", McNamara answered, but he didn't seem to believe his own words. "Who tamed you, tamed you well", he continued. "Nothing to say. He'd done a good job".

"What do you mean?" Bryony asked a little hurt because of his words, and the same time, she started massaging her temples. Her head was about to blow up. The pain was the same as before, but more bothering. She was about to see herself lying with migraine. She hated those states. She didn't have migraine too often, but when she had, it lasted for days, no matter what she did. It was the last thing to miss now.

"I think you'd offer us a tea even if you were to lie on the kitchen floor instead of McKay", he continued with the same rough voice, "You wouldn't think someone else could make it or that people might understand you aren't able to make it".

He started making tea under her amazed and hurt eyes, but McNamara avoided her sight artfully. He knew he could read in her eyes something else not only pain. He could read humiliation. He'd been malicious, but he couldn't be otherwise thinking of hat happened to her and when she looked like that.

The silence was getting unnaturally long and even intense. It seemed a spring ready to get loose and hit each of them. Finally, McNamara broke it.

"You'd better tell me what had happened", he told her without looking at her for one instant.

A few moments no answer was heard. McNamara turned and looked at her. He met her eyes. And then, he realised the girl didn't want to speak. It was pure stubbornness. He sustained her look for a while, but despite exhaustion, Bryony didn't turn her eyes at all. His will struggled hers. No one gave up.

Bryony could perfectly understand what was going on. But she also knew that what she had to say was important. More important than their childish game that seemed completely puerile given the circumstances.

Keeping looking at him, she started speaking. McNamara turned to the gas-stove and then a smile flourished on his lips. He got the message. However, he knew she was going to talk in the end, for a reason or another. He'd realised she was a too responsible person to keep being obstinate, especially when more important things came first. He listened to her carefully. She spoke with some difficulty, but she went on. She didn't give up at all.

"After stabbing him with the scissors in the shoulder, I pulled them out fast... I knew they were my only weapons. I couldn't afford to lose them... Then the knife fell from his hand. Because of inertia, maybe. I think I heard it hitting the floor... The man groaned weakly, and then slapped me with the back of his hand. He threw me down. Then I think I hit my right hand. It hurt terribly. Actually, it hurts right now, too", she said trying to move it easily... "Then he jumped on me", she shook the memories off with horror... "He tried to strangle me... Then I hit him with the scissors again, but in his arm. He hit me with the fist over my mouth with his other hand... Sincerely, then, I think I got dizzy for a few moments... I started to get conscious when

I felt he was trying to take the scissors from me... Then I lifted my knee and hit him in his groins with all the strength I still had. He slapped me again, after shouting loudly... Then, he rose off me with difficulty. I could see he had awful pains. I seized the scissors better but he left out of the window".

"You saw his face, I think. It was light in the room, wasn't it?" asked McNamara turning off the gas-stove. The water had boiled.

"Yes, the night light was on. But I couldn't see his face, you must know. He had a ski mask.".

McNamara felt he got angry. He'd thought they had a chance to clear things up. He tried to calm down and only then he turned back to her.

"However", he insisted, "I think you can tell me something of the attacker".

Bryony could feel his frustration. It was tangible. She was sorry she couldn't say more to help him. Then, the whole nightmare would have ended. But she didn't have anything to say. The guy hadn't even talked.

"He was a man, for sure. It wasn't only the stature and shape. You understand, I hope!" she blushed slightly, getting, finally, some colour. "When he came over me, I felt he was a man", she stumbled.

She drank a little of the tea put in front of her. She was embarrassed and she didn't know to hide it at all.

That moment, Mrs Stevens, who stopped dozing and managed to listen to everything Bryony had said, watched her carefully. Now she'd woken up for sure.

“I hope he’d done you nothing else”, she said roughly, trying to see in her eyes whether she’d tell the truth.

“Oh, no!” Bryony denied vehemently. “However, I don’t think he had such intentions, you know. I think he wanted only to kill me!”

“The eyes, you must’ve seen his eyes”, jumped the sergeant.

“I was too scared and busy to stay alive”, came the answer dryly.

The sergeant blushed and said nothing more. In deed, the girl had been alone before the criminal. No one protected her even if police had a man inside.

“They were green or brown”, she said quickly, suddenly, realising what James was thinking. She didn’t want him to think so. No one was guilty for what had happened. “I don’t know for sure”, she went on, and for the first time uncertainty was felt in her voice and quite well.

“No problem, I’m sure. You might recall later”, Mrs Stevens tapped her hand to comfort her.

“Has McKay recovered?” McNamara asked James, trying to pass over the embarrassing moment faster. He didn’t think McKay could recover. She couldn’t do it.

But the sergeant didn’t have the time to answer. The ambulance siren was heard. McNamara came out of the kitchen and went to the front door. He opened the door and let the doctors in.

“We have two women hurt”, he said. “A policewoman and a civil one. The police woman is worse”.

He went before them with big and fast steps. He showed them to the kitchen. One team dashed to McKay, who was unconscious again. The towel pressed on the chest wound was full of blood.

The other team went to Bryony. Her eyes had got a slightly glassy shine. Physical and mental exhaustion showed their effect. She couldn't resist anymore. Her fingers trembled on the cup.

Chapter Fifteen

Ann Goddard was already in the bag. The zipper had been pulled covering her face. The coroner had finished his work on spot. He had only to do her autopsy. However, he already knew the cause of death: a knife blow in the back, in the region of the heart. The blow was extremely precise. The killer got experience and trust in himself and he'd probably had the advantage of surprise.

The other people sprayed luminol on walls and floor to identify the slightest traces of blood, to determine the exact position of the aggressor. They powdered the door handle and the switcher in the room to draw prints. A wet print of the foot sole was seen on the board floor behind the door. The forensic specialist was glad. It was the first good sign. It could lead to the criminal. He drew the print carefully and photographed the floor parquet.

They found a thread from a black training suit in the door. Probably the killer had leaned against the door and then advanced. They put the thread in a small plastic bag and then they sealed it to send it for analysis.

"We've finished", said an old short and thin man. "I don't think there's anything left here to be of use. Ned, have you checked the other room entirely?"

"Yes, sir! However, there we've found only half of the print of a shoe. Probably he stepped with the other half of the shoe on the carpet, because we haven't managed to draw any print, unfortunately".

"The entries? Have you checked them all? Inclusively the windows", asked the short man who seemed to be the boss. This was a habit of his, to check everything, even though he was sure his men knew their job.

"Yes, sir! There's no trace. He was wearing gloves, certainly", said a middle-aged woman with white-spotted hair. Her voice didn't seem angry at all because she'd learnt her boss's small habits.

"Ok, then, we can leave", said the short man, who was dominating everyone with his authority.

Hardly had he got out the room, than he heard steps on the stairs. McNamara was climbing up the stairs. When he saw the expert, he asked:

"Have we got anything, Shorty?"

"Oh, yes, sir. Of course, we have. If you catch him, we've got enough evidence to kneel him, don't worry", he told him knowing that the inspector was very careful with that. He disliked having a criminal released by court because of lack of tangible evidence. "Are there other people necessary there?" he asked pointing with his head to Miss McNeil's house.

"No, we've covered everything. You may go now", also said McNamara. "However, the night is almost gone. You can catch only a few hours of sleep".

Shorty accepted his encouragement nodding slightly. He was tired. McNamara was tired too. It was written all over his face. He'd been up for too much time and he'd thought of too many things. His workday hadn't ended for him yet, though. He had something else to do. He couldn't afford to let anything uncovered.

While Shorty was gathering his people and left, McNamara massaged the base of his nose. As if he could get rid of stress and tiredness so easily.

He was effectively angry because too many people had already been hit. He couldn't deal with the thought he couldn't do anything to prevent the last two deaths. He knew he couldn't prevent the girl's death. It was as frustrating as painful for him. He never happened to have so many successive victims in a case without having the slightest idea on the identity of the killer or of his reasons, at least partially, because he knew why Ann Goddard had to die. He also knew why Mrs Stevens was attacked. But he didn't have the slightest idea why Diane had to die. Or why Mrs Dobbs was killed, although he suspected she saw the killer.

He shook off the thoughts bothering him and went out of the room, turning off the lights behind him. Then, he went out of the house, lifting the yellow strip the policemen put there and passed under it. He closed the door carefully, although he shouldn't have had to worry for anyone there. No one was there. Then, he headed to McNeil's house and arriving here, he knocked on the door and waited. Sergeant opened the door after a few moments.

"What's she doing", he asked James pointing to the woman in the house.

"She's sitting stiffly on the kitchen chair, sir. I'm sorry but she didn't want to leave with the ambulance. She said she needed only an ice compress, that's it. She said she doesn't stand hospitals and she wasn't going to hospital for so little".

"I could swear. No problem. Did she put it? The compress, I mean".

"No, she didn't. She doesn't seem to have the strength to go to the fridge. I offered. Mrs Stevens offered too, but I'm afraid that either she didn't hear or she didn't want to hear us. She doesn't seem the kind that stays and let others take care of her".

"I see," said McNamara with no intonation. "Could you take Mrs Stevens to her house? I don't think she wants to sleep for a second in that room. I hope you can stay with her till morning. Then we'll see what we do.

"Yes, sir, no problem", said James. "Of course I stay with her. I don't want we have any other unpleasant surprises. We've already had enough. What about Miss McNeil? Is she going to stay alone or should I take her with me?"

"I'll stay with her, no worry", said McNamara categorically, admitting no further discussion and then he entered the kitchen followed by James, who got McNamara's massage quite well.

Here he saw Mrs Stevens trying to comfort Bryony tapping her hand nicely, as if it was of any use, he thought. Bryony had already passed over exhaustion. Now she'd reached the stage when she didn't seem to have a bit of life in her. She even didn't notice the two men getting into the kitchen. She seemed completely detached from reality.

"Mrs Stevens", he talked to the old woman, "Sergeant James will show you to your house at once. I guess you don't want to sleep in that room anymore", he said pointing to the drawing room. "Sergeant will stay with you till morning, OK?"

Mrs Stevens approved nodding slightly. Then she stood up and went hobbling to the door. Suddenly, as if she'd just recalled of that, she stopped and turned to McNamara.

"What about Bryony? I don't want her alone", she said with determination. "She'd better come with me".

"I'll stay with her", he answered coldly. She could see on his face that he disliked admitting that he'd be the guardian of the girl over the night.

"I see", the old woman said but she didn't like the situation at all.

She watched McNamara incisively. Her look was narrow.

"I hope there'll be no problems, young man," she went severely. "I hope you realise, young man, she's very vulnerable now".

"I don't think it's the case to bring such a topic into discussion now", McNamara replied, as severely as she was. "It's not appropriate at all and you're miles away from the truth', he also added angrily. "I don't think you want to say I've got some impure thoughts with your friend! I'm a policeman, for God's sake!

His eyes revealed a strong fury as well as indignation. His fists were tightened on one side and the other of his body. He was tensed and was making a serious effort to refrain himself. He was too tired and frustrated to accept a moral lesson from Mrs Stevens.

He offered to stay with Bryony because he didn't have any available man to put there in the house. He needed them next day. He needed people able to work.

It wasn't like he'd have liked the girl, he thought. She was too stuffy and too self-confident. He preferred more flexible girls, who needed help, and when they needed help, they asked for. He watched Bryony. She didn't seem too self-confident now. She seemed small and helpless, actually. But he knew better, though. It was only temporary. She seemed small and helpless as effect of the night she'd lived and of what she'd done. McNamara felt a little sorry for her. He was also sorry because he couldn't do a thing to help her.

Mrs Stevens got out suddenly saying goodbye. She knew she was defeated that time and she couldn't do anything. And she also realised she'd vainly said anything to Bryony that moment. She didn't seem to hear anything of what happened around. If she'd heard, she'd have intervened in the discussion. She wasn't that kind of girl that shut up and let others fight for her.

McNamara and Bryony remained alone after the two others left. They heard the front door, and the safety lock locking the door automatically.

McNamara got closer to her and lifted her chin. He looked deeply her in her eyes and he was surprised to see that she was also studying him attentively. He had been wrong thinking she was completely run down. She still had strength in her. She only couldn't speak. Not yet. Then he saw he was wrong again. He heard her voice:

"You needn't have stayed", she said in a low and tired voice. "I'm sure he's not coming back this night. I don't think he's got either force or courage".

"You might be right, and I think you are, but I don't want to take any risks. You realise you're on his black list now. I think you've just made the top. I can swear he hates you to death. Any man defeated by a woman must hate her and especially this kind of man. He killed only women so far".

"Maybe, but now he's hurt and I don't think he wants to mess up with anyone this night", she argued with a weak voice unconvincingly.

"It makes no sense we talk, hypothetically, Bryony. I stay, so get used to the thought. Don't be afraid, tomorrow I'll send someone else, I won't bother you with my presence".

"Ok, then... I think you should take the bedroom opposite to mine, in this case. You shouldn't stay in the kitchen. I'm going to make your bed".

"You needn't. I'll stay here. Go upstairs and I'll bring you a compress for your face".

"You needn't. I can take it by myself", she shook her head.

"Yes, I know. You've been taking it for half an hour. Try to do what you're told, at least for once. It won't be tough, I assure you. You won't be knocked down".

"Ok, but then you also sleep upstairs, in the guest bedroom, all right?"

"We'll see, don't worry, I'll manage somehow".

Bryony frowned and then she tried to stand up. When she stood up, she got dizzy and leaned against the table weakly but McNamara caught her.

"I'd better carry you".

"No, I can climb the stairs", replied the girl hesitatively.

"I'm sure you can, but let's say you'll do it for my sake", he said ironically, taking her up in his arms.

"I'm not very light, you know".

"I know now, but don't be afraid, we'll get upstairs somehow", he said smiling but she didn't see his smile.

Bryony had closed her eyes and leaned against his shoulder. He carried her upstairs and put her on the bed. He pulled the blanket over her and said:

"I'll bring a compress at once. Stay here and be good".

He went to the door. When he realised, he got no answer, he turned back. He watched her attentively. Suddenly he realised she'd fallen asleep at once. He smiled. He was sorry, but he had to wake her up: that compress was necessary.

He went downstairs to the fridge. He took some ice cubes and wrapped them in a towel. He climbed back upstairs and approached the bed. He saw her sleep was agitated and she was murmuring something. He pulled her hair away from her face and caressed gently her temple and the cheekbone where she already had a big bruise. She groaned slightly and tried to move his hand aside. He put the towel on the bruise and because of the unpleasant feeling of the ice, the girl jumped up. McNamara laughed, unwillingly, and then he soothed her.

"Be good, I've just put the compress on your face. If I don't put it, tomorrow you'll look worse than now".

"All right", she managed to say, "but I want to tell you it's awful. This must be your revenge, mustn't this?"

"Don't be stupid, I gain nothing if you keep this on your face, but instead, you'll look better tomorrow", he said quite angrily.

"I prefer to look awful, but sleep now", she replied with as much fury as his.

"All right, then. I'll bring this downstairs and I'll leave you alone", he got much angrier and left.

Bryony tried to see his silhouette going away in the dark, but she couldn't keep her eyes open. She fell asleep.

Chapter Sixteen

He tried to stop his bleeding but he didn't manage too well. Bloody woman! Next time he'll kill her! It wasn't enough he'd had so many problems with the other two! It was good that his wife was sleeping or he'd been doomed. How could he have explained to her what happened? He couldn't. Nothing plausible came in his mind.

He followed by sight the cars going away in the night. He realised that neither McNamara, nor James had left. Probably they stayed with the two women. Stupid people! They couldn't imagine he'd come back that night! He'd expect a second chance. He must have a second chance. It couldn't be otherwise. He'd been lucky so far, hadn't he?

If the small parasites had been satisfied with what he gave them, it would've been good, but they wanted more. And he didn't have more and he couldn't find more anywhere.

He was caught in the net, damn it! He defended himself, that's all. He knew it wasn't good what he'd done, it wasn't as if he had been mad! But he couldn't do otherwise. He had no choice. He started feeling sorry for Diane. She was a great girl for what he needed. But she was so greedy! She had to pay for her greed. And the rip also stole Patsy's bag when she ran away. But he got the better of her!

And the proud Patsy wasn't so proud now. He'd taken care of her too. He effaced that ironic smile on her face. Now she couldn't make a fool of him. He had the last word, he laughed recalling everything.

They were not too smart these people from police. They didn't know to look for where they should. And it was right under their noise, if you think. It had been better if Diane too remained there where she should have remained and hadn't tried to escape. But he paid her back. And he paid her well.

Well, that's it, he thought then, he shouldn't bother for her now. The harm was done and there was no way of turning back. However, he'd really liked to know what Mrs Stevens saw that night; whether she recognised him or if she saw where he was coming from. No, she couldn't see where he was coming from and she didn't realise who he was. The policemen would have arrested him already. But she could recall, the shrew!

Because of his agitation, blood started flowing again, although it had just stopped. He pressed the compress better on the wound in his shoulder but he didn't have enough force and the blood was gurgling under his fingers. If only he didn't lose consciousness! That would really be a tragedy. His wife would find him in the morning and everything would flow away. And he'd tried so hard not to reach there, didn't he, he said himself, trying to press the wound harder, decided not to quit.

He took other two calming pills and in a quarter of an hour, he felt better. He didn't feel the pain piercing his shoulder. He promised himself not to let the bitch, who'd done that to him, to go away. When he thought he'd respected her and even liked her, he scowled. She must die.

He hoped his wife wouldn't notice the missing clothes. He wrapped them and put them in a sure place. He couldn't throw them at the garbage now with all police swarming around. He couldn't keep them in the house either. His wife, who used to rummage everywhere, would find them and everything he'd done, would be vain. Damn woman! She must know everything. He couldn't have a place of his.

He dozed a little. He woke up after half an hour. The bleeding stopped, but pain was constant, although deaf now due to calming pills. At least the scissors hadn't got too deep. McNeil hadn't had enough force. He wouldn't have imagined she'd have. She was quite small and thin.

Now, that the bleed stopped, he made a ball from the plastic bag on which he lied not to bleed on the bed, and he wrapped the remaining stained clothes in it. Now he had to find a place for them. He couldn't go to his hiding-place. He knew the policemen were still in the area.

Chapter Seventeen

When the phone rang, McNamara woke up a little puzzled and watched around. He passed his hand through his hair and over his face, and then took the phone he'd left on the night table next to the bed.

" McNamara", he said briefly.

"Chief, it's me, Jo", he heard from the other hand of the line. "Have I woken you up, by any chance?"

"No, problem, Jo. I'd wake up, anyway. Say! Is there something new? What time is it?"

"Chief, it's ten, didn't you know?"

McNamara made a grimace hearing her. He slept only a few hours, three, more precisely. He tried to stay awake. Last time he'd watched the clock it was over six. He must have fallen asleep afterwards. The truth was he'd had a nightmare day before.

"Ok, Jo, tell me what's the problem", he said slightly reproachfully, not because he'd been woken up because he had to wake up, but because she reminded him that it was late.

"I've seen you gave no sign and I've decided to call you", tried Jo explain herself. "We've got information from the country and I've also discovered something in the database".

"Go on", ordered McNamara, hoping that a breach came up in their case. He had already woken up for good and he was ready to start work.

"The guys in the country were to the two girls at home. They spoke to them and to their parents and, apparently, their parents decided to move out because they'd discovered their girls joined a sort of organization, escort girls sort. They said a guy runs it, apparently, named Daniel. One of the girls, who seems to have changed lately and become good, said that the other name of the guy is Thompson. I heard an alarm bell hearing the name. Apparently, Patsy got them into the combination".

"Good, girl, you've found out interesting things. We have to take care of this guy Thompson. He's managed to get out of our way so far. What have you found out from database?"

"One of the girls on the list, Linda Peterson, disappeared too. She's on the list for two weeks. The other two we couldn't find them at their addresses, and parents know nothing of them and they don't seem to care too much. I have them looked for sir"

"Well done, Jo".

"Mike helped me too, sir", said the girl fairly. "Now he's at one of the addresses we've got from a kid in the neighbourhood. He seems to have seen one of the girls quite often there. The kid always sells newspapers on the same street corner, so it seems credible to think the girl's living there if he's seen her so often.

"All right, Jo. James and I are coming later. I want to see what's with this Thompson; he seems to have spotted the guy. If you hear of something, call me".

McNamara put the phone down and went to the bathroom to wash himself. He looked at his red eyes and told himself it'd already got a habit. The cases he investigated required fast investigations, not to let the traces disappear, so the sleepless nights were not unusual. And, however, why would he rush home? No one was waiting for him. His mother had gone one year ago and he hadn't found anyone to share his life with.

Suddenly he thought of the girl lying in the bed next door, but he chased the thought away fast. He wasn't allowed to think of her like that. At least not as long she was part of an investigation in a way or another.

He went to her room and opened the door. He saw her sleeping, although her sleep seemed to have been agitated. The blanket was down and the sheets were crumpled.

A smile came up on his lips while he was going downstairs. The girl wasn't a bad sight. He liked to watch her. And she had some spirit and especially verticality. He couldn't intimidate her easily.

He went to the kitchen and put water to boil for coffee and tea the same time. He thought that, maybe, when the girl would wake up, she might want tea.

Up, in the bedroom, Bryony opened her eyes. She felt she was watched and couldn't sleep anymore. She'd hardly stopped a fear scream. Then she saw McNamara's back when he went out and wondered what he might have wanted from her.

She closed her eyes again. She was still very tired. She felt as if someone had beaten her. She couldn't sleep. She opened her eyes again and looked for the clock by sight. It was already over ten! She didn't sleep so much even on Sunday!

She got out of bed and went to the bathroom with some difficulty. Each bone hurt at each step. When she watched herself in the mirror, she started. Of Lord! She must have listened to McNamara. She looked awful. She couldn't open the bookshop like that. Only if she wanted to have no customer left, and her interest was different. She didn't want to scare her clients. She should have hired someone part time at least.

Then she recalled the student that came to her last week. She promised to call her up if there was a chance to hire her. She had her phone number in the bag, in the kitchen.

She washed herself fast and went to get dressed. Then she went downstairs to the kitchen. Halfway the hall she stopped. She heard the merry whistle from the kitchen. Apparently, McNamara was feeling good. She smiled.

Reaching the kitchen door, she stopped a moment. She stayed in the door and watched McNamara preparing the coffee and teacups. He'd already prepared some toast and put butter and jam on the table.

"Interesting, inspector", she said, "you seem very efficient in the kitchen. I wouldn't have thought. You don't seem the kind".

McNamara stopped a curse on his lips when he turned. He felt so good in the small bright and clean kitchen, so different from his kitchenette at home, that he left his guard fall. Or he didn't like to be caught without the invisible tough wall around him. He never let people he ran into during an investigation to know him too well. He didn't allow that to his own people, even.

"So, you've woken up", he said sharply. "Too early, but whatever. You could've slept a little more, I think".

"Yes, if you hadn't come into my room, I could have", she replied. "I didn't take any sleeping pills last night, and my sleep is very light. I hear any move", she said going to the banquette where she'd left her purse.

McNamara watched her frowning, but said nothing about.

"Coffee or tea, what would you like?"

"I think I'd drink coffee first", she said. "I haven't woken up entirely and I'm pretty grumpy until I drink the first cup of coffee", she continued without watching him and looking for something in her purse. "I don't think you'd like to see me like that. It might be really unpleasant. An unforgettable experience, as my room-mate at the college would say".

McNamara scowled but said nothing. He took the coffee pot and poured coffee in cups while Bryony held out to the phone against the wall.

"What do you want to do?" he asked a little alarmed.

"To make a phone call, can't you see? she replied without looking at him while she was dialling the number.

"Who do you want to call? I hope you don't want to wake Mrs Stevens up. I assure you she's all right; she's with James, isn't she? And James is very efficient, you must know".

"I bet, don't worry. James seems very good in his job and if you think a little he's also kind. I'm sure Mrs Stevens is fine"

McNamara felt hurt. He knew what she was talking about, but he didn't let her any satisfaction.

"Then, who do you want to call?"

She didn't answer and put her hand up to show him to shut up. He had only to hear her conversation although he didn't hear anything but her part in the dialogue.

"Hallo, Meg, Bryony McNeil's here, from the bookshop. I need a shop assistant full time for a few days, and then I promise to keep you half time, do you agree?... Good, then. But you must come and take the keys... Yes, right now, if you can... Write down my address" she gave her the address ad then she said "All right, I'll wait".

Bryony put the receiver down the hook on the wall.

"Do you hire anyone?"

"Yes, of course. You can't believe I can stay at the counter as long I look like that. No one will buy anything. Everyone will run away", she said drinking from her coffee. "You make good coffee, McNamara. By the way, don't you have another name? All people have a first name, usually. What happened to yours?"

"My first name's not your business", he snapped. "Maybe you haven't noticed, but I'm not in a social visit here. I've just been your nanny for one night, that's all".

"You're impolite again, McNamara, and I'm already furious with that idiot last night. He costs me a lot of money".

"You won't get poor if you pay a poor girl a salary", he said grumpily.

"You can't know it, you know. You don't run a business to see how difficult is to deal with", she replied also grumpily. "However, now I have to hire someone. I can't do otherwise. I'd lose too much. I'd lose my credibility too".

There was silence. Both of them focused on coffee and toast till his phone rang.

"McNamara".

"It's James, Chief. I've called to the police station to send a man to stay with the two women. They'll stay together, till night, what do you say?"

"Yes, James, they'll stay together, I'm sure. When does he come?"

"The shift? I think in an hour, chief. There wasn't anyone available now. Maybe an hour and a half".

"All right, James. When Mrs Stevens wakes up, fetch her here. Then you can go to hospital to McKay".

"Thank you, sir", answered James. Actually, that is why he called. Mrs Stevens hadn't woken up yet, but he was sure she wouldn't sleep too much.

McNamara turned the phone off and poured himself some coffee. He was stuck there for a while and he wasn't too happy.

"James has some feelings for McKay, doesn't he?"

"What does it interest you?" policeman's rough answer came.

The woman felt hurt. Initially she didn't want to say anything, but as she didn't like to be left without reply, she said:

"It wasn't just mere curiosity, McNamara. It was simply an attempt to make a conversation. I haven't happened to have breakfast with someone as taciturn as you".

"And do you often have breakfast with men?" asked he despitefully.

"Not that's of your concern McNamara, but usually I have breakfast alone.".

McNamara didn't have time to answer because the bell rang. McNeil stood up and went to the door, but McNamara stopped her. He went to the door. In front of the door, there was a flapper with glasses and her hair lubberly on her shoulders.

"Yes", he said, "Who are you looking for?"

The flapper got intimidated but she managed to say:

"Miss McNeil. I'm Meg McPherson. She called me earlier and told me to come here".

"Oh, yes, come in", said McNamara and showed her to the kitchen where Bryony was.

When she heard them coming, Bryony looked up. She smiled to the girl and said:

"You've got here fast. That's good. You must go and open the bookshop for me. You'll manage alone, I hope. As you see, I've had a small accident", said Bryony.

"I think you must change your friend", said Meg boldly, pointing to McNamara. She wasn't the kind of girl that accepted physical abuses from men.

When he heard her words, McNamara blushed with anger.

"Listen, girl", he started but he couldn't continue because Bryony jumped.

"Calm down, please", she asked him. "Meg, I'm sorry but McNamara isn't the one who beat me up. He's a policeman and he's here to defend me. I was simply attacked".

"I'm sorry", said Meg. "I'm sorry, sir. I didn't know how the things are, and as you seem to be at home..." she said but she stopped when she saw the man's eyes.

But Bryony couldn't resist and burst into laughter.

"Oh, Lord, McNamara, if you could see you face... Be calm, no one has proposed to you. However, let's finish playing. We must talk of serious things", she told the girl and invited her to sit down. "Let me explain you fast what you have to do. McNamara, are you kind to pour a cup of coffee for Meg, please?"

McNamara looked at her to see if she was mocking of him. Seeing her serious and already wrapped up in explanations, he said nothing and poured another cup of coffee. He filled their cups too and went to look out of the window. Then he saw. He turned suddenly and asked:

"McNeil, doesn't anyone live next door?"

Bryony wanted to burst out furiously because he interrupted her, but seeing he was so serious, she realised he didn't play.

"No, of course! The house has been empty for five months already. I haven't seen anyone here ever since", she said a little excited feeling his tension. "What's the matter?"

"Finish your explanations because I must go and call James. I don't want to have indiscreet ears around", he said showing Meg with his head.

Meg felt hurt, but she had no reply. So, she said:

"Leave it, Miss McNeil, I've understood and I've already seen how you work. I'm sure I manage".

"All right. All my hopes are in you. And I've asked you not to be so formal. My name's Bryony, ok?" she said seeing her off.

When she opened the door, she found James just fetching Mrs Stevens.

"You've already come, James. Good morning. You too, Mrs Stevens".

"Hallo, girl", she said not letting James answer. "That policeman", she said pointing inside the house with her head", "has just called, when we already were at the gate. You realise this boy rushed me as much as he could", she continued making poor James blushing.

Bryony smiled. She knew Mrs Stevens well, and for some time, but James had hardly run into her. She could bet on her last penny, she'd made his life a living hell that morning.

"Who's the girl?" asked the old woman suspiciously.

"I've just hired her at the bookshop", answered Bryony smiling to the young girl completely confused. "You realize I can't go to work like that".

"Yes, you're a little too colourful", said the old lady roughly, in complete discordance with the tears in her eyes. She really cared of her young friend and she also felt guilty. She'd have been in her place.

Bryony guessed what she was thinking and, touching her arm, she said:

"Don't you dare to blame yourselves, do you hear me? You're not guilty for that, but the scamp that came after you", she continued, but she suddenly stopped seeing Meg's curiosity. She disliked everyone knew about what happened to her, and, however, McNamara had already told her that it wasn't good to be known outside the house. "However, Meg, once again, I count on you. Tonight, please, just call me. You shouldn't make the way here. Ok?"

"Don't worry! I'll take care of everything. Be sure, I'm grateful to you. You've offered me a chance to have a job. You realise I've had some hard time so far".

"No problem", said Bryony with her heart crunched.

It was the first time when she'd left her business on other one's hands. And it wasn't easy at all.

Chapter Eighteen

"You've come, James, good. I've seen that the door from the other house, the door to the garden, is a half-open. So far as we know, and Bryony has just confirmed me once more, it should've been empty. Yesterday we didn't think to check this house, let's do it now", said McNamara.

"Of course, sir. Do you think we could leave the ladies alone for a while?"

"I think so", he said, looking at Bryony, who approved him nodding. "However, we won't be gone for too long. Ok?"

"All right, no problem", said Bryony. "It's daytime and I don't think the man will repeat last night's experience too soon. He must have had problems with the two wounds I made him".

McNamara agreed and made a sign to James to follow him. The two men went out through the door at the back of the house and jumped over the fence in the garden of the next house. They reached the back door there and McNamara made a sign to James to wait.

They listened but heard nothing. McNamara opened the door more and got into carefully, ready to surprise the smallest noise.

They went to the kitchen but the strong smell hit them and they turned back. There was a door on the left. McNamara recalled he saw at Bryony's a similar door when they searched the house last night. It led to the cellar. He opened the door carefully, James covering his back. When the door opened, the smell hit them strongly. The same moment they felt nausea. They knew the smell, even if it was mixed with the smell of wet and mould from the cellar.

McNamara climbed the stairs down, after making a sign to James to stay upstairs and watch the door, and then he lit his torch. Arrived downstairs, he swept with the torchlight the space from an end to another. In the left corner, he could see an indistinct shape and from there came the pestilential smell. He headed there and when he got close enough, he saw something similar to a body, wrapped in plastic bags, stuck with scotch band. Near this pack, there was another one, a little bigger. He supposed the height was different. Next to them, there were some clothes gathered like a ball. He lit them with his torch and saw they were covered in blood. When he reached with the torch light to the left, he saw the spots of blood and down near the wall there was a kind of bunk blooded too.

He studied carefully the cellar and realised it must have been very well isolated phonically. He thought of a possible scenario. He wanted to check to be sure and climbed up the stairs and told James:

"Stay here and I'll close the door. Be attentive and tell me what you've heard when I'm back. Ok?"

"Yes, chief, no problem", James replied.

McNamara went back into the cellar and shut the door behind him. He went to the left wall. Arrived there he started shouting. He shouted "help" for five times, but James didn't rush on stairs to help him so his idea made sense. He went up again and opened the metallic and heavy door of the cellar.

"Did you hear anything, James?"

"No, sir, why, what should I've heard?"

"I've shouted "help" for five times. Haven't you heard anything?"

"No, sir, I swear".

"Well, if you from here heard nothing, you realise that from the street or next houses, people couldn't stand a chance to hear anything. By the way", McNamara said, "we have to call the team. We have two other bodies downstairs, and, I presume one belongs to the girl that had disappeared and about whom Jo told me, and the other might be of Patsy's. Besides that, we have a lot of blooded clothes and a miserable bunk. I think this is our killer's nest, James".

James nodded he understood and he took his mobile off his pocket.

"Leave it, we may call from outside too. It's useless to stay here in this smell", said McNamara and went out followed by James.

Once out in fresh air, James took the phone and called to the station. He called the forensics and the coroner, explaining shortly what was about.

The two of them stayed still and expected the operative team. McNamara said:

“I think you can go to hospital to McKay, James”.

Seeing the amazed look of the sergeant, who wouldn’t have expected so much understanding from McNamara because work came first always, McNamara added:

“Someone must ask her about what she saw. I supposed you can do it”.

The sergeant smiled and wanted to say something, but he decided he’d better keep his ideas to himself. He nodded shortly to McNamara and headed to the car he’d parked the previous night near Goddard house.

Behind him, McNamara smiled, because he didn’t imagine McKay could have seen too much, being hit from the back first time, and this blow should have grown her eyes dim. However, he knew he couldn’t rely on James all day long if he hadn’t left him go and make sure McKay was all right.

Chapter Nineteen

"What do you think, doc?" he asked.

"These two were beaten and raped too, as the other one, apparently. One died more recently, the red-haired one on the right", he said pointing to one of the bodies. "I can't exactly know, but both of them were killed a few days ago. After I perform the autopsy and check the stage of larva on them, I'll know more and I may tell you exactly when they died. Of course, he did the job with the same knife. It's that knife the guys found at McNeil's last night. It matches to the shape and dimension of the wounds on Diane's body. I'm sure it will match these two girls' wounds too.

McNamara thanked him and then went to Shorty, who, together with his people, was ransacking the cellar systematically for the slightest trace.

"Have you found something we can use, guys?"

"Enough, but the case won't be solved only with this evidence and you know it", replied Shortly, slightly nervous. He was quite tired after the previous night and he had already had too much evidence to check at the headquarters. However, he couldn't do otherwise, he thought. He himself chose this job. No one pushed him from the back. His mother told him not to expect a normal life. She knew from his father. He had been a cop too, until he died on duty.

McNamara understood him. He was as tired and nervous as his people. He felt Shorty's reproach. He knew it was his duty to find the one who'd done all of these. Shorty couldn't do anything, but helping him with marginal matters. His work was essential in building a case against the killer, but it was useful only afterwards. If they didn't have the killer, his work was useless.

Therefore, McNamara left his people do their job, without bothering them anymore, and went back to Bryony, jumping over the fence to the garden and getting inside from the back to shorten the way.

He left the door at the back open not to disturb them when he'd come back. He reached the kitchen and found the two women. Both were very silent and thoughtful.

"What was it, McNamara?" asked Bryony. "What did you see there? I've heard the siren of the police car".

"We've found two other bodies", he said directly because she'd have found the news from the neighbours. "Apparently, that was the favourite playground of our killer, his nest. Have any of you seen anything suspect these last two weeks, or maybe someone who doesn't belong to this street?"

Bryony started thinking seriously, but nothing came in her mind, however she was searching in her memory. Instead, Mrs Stevens recalled something and said:

"I saw a girl, two weeks ago, at night fall. I think she was reddish and tall. She drew my attention because she was looking for a house number. She passed by my house and then I lost her from sight. I haven't seen anyone, you must know. No one has passed by here".

"Well, that night, before or after the girl passed, who did you see?"

"Mr. Graham passed first, I think", she made an effort to recall. "Oh, yes, Mr Reid, in deed. Afterwards, a few seconds after, I heard shouts from their house. I don't know what he didn't like that time", she turned her nose. "However, it was an uglier scandal than usually. You know, Bryony, you heard it too, you told me, even if you were working in the kitchen", she addressed to the young girl.

"You were in the kitchen and saw no one?" wondered McNamara. He must have passed before your windows".

"I saw only Daniel Thompson. He went to Ann Goddard that evening Mrs Stevens talks about. Actually, that time, he had a period when he was going to her almost daily. Rarely, he skipped an evening. I used to see him all the time, although they were sure no one knows about their affair. And earlier I saw one of the Randalls' children. Mr Randall came and shouted at him. He told him not to find him there anymore because he'd skin him alive.

"Why?" asked McNamara, hoping he found something.

"He's a man with fear of God and his wife", answered Mrs Stevens, smiling. "That's why. He's afraid of his shadow, if you want to believe me".

"Oh, I see", McNamara laughed stealthily and mockingly. "By, the way", he asked Bryony, "didn't you see anything interesting, for instance someone getting into the house next door?"

"No, I didn't, but I didn't watch carefully, either, did I?"

"Usually, this girl doesn't look carefully at anything that doesn't interest her", observed Mrs Stevens. "I've told you, dear, sometimes, you should watch around. You can't know what you see or who you see, dear".

"If I had the necessary time, I'd do it. But for now, I have others on my mind", replied Bryony with a propitiatory voice, although she'd have liked to tell her to mind her business, because she understood the clear massage.

McNamara figured out what the girl meant and felt even amused. He wondered how she took such discussions that, probably, took place daily. He didn't see Mrs Stevens to drop it. She wasn't the type. He didn't doubt she was stubborn. If she had something in her mind, she'd follow it to the end and, apparently, the old woman decided to see Bryony together with someone, at least, if not married.

Actually, Mrs Stevens was part of the old guard. For such women, generally, a husband ensured steadiness and, possibly, wealth. They didn't think life might suppose more. Usually, they got married and most of them left their jobs to stay at home to take care of husband and children. They considered that making a career was useless for a woman. Man was supposed to take care of her, to provide her everything she needed. They didn't think a woman should have had their own interests.

But McNeil was of a different kind. She was the kind of woman that would make her way, like Mrs Reid. The difference was that Bryony didn't seem completely against men, as Mrs Reid. She didn't seem to have started life with incommode luggage or prejudices and didn't consider that a man was absolutely unfaithful, sure that he'd leave his wife and house one day for sure. But she thought that she had to be on her feet first, to start a partnership on equal basis.

It was hardly to suppose that she might become a victim easily. Mary would rather get in that posture, although she would try hard to avoid that very thing. Mary didn't know to take things the way they'd come. She tried to push them up and as result she might reach an unwanted end sooner than she'd thought.

McNamara didn't imagine Michael could bear that daily treatment too long. Love would vanish one day, leaving bitterness and sourness instead. No one could keep his feelings intact as long as he didn't get anything else but bitterness in exchange. He couldn't do exact prognosis, he couldn't say he was an expert in the field, but he considered that in a few years, the Reids' marriage will go away.

Bryony, instead, if she'd reached marriage, she'd have fought to make it work, as she was fighting for her small business now. She was the fighter type. She wasn't that kind of woman giving up before the fight took place, as Mrs Reid.

The girl's voice, loud and clear, with no trace of resentment, brought him back to real world:

"No, I'm sorry, I didn't see anyone. And to be honest, I didn't hear anything from the house next door, either".

"You couldn't", said McNamara. "The cellar is completely isolated phonically. Nothing can be heard from the house, so you couldn't hear anything from here".

"However, it's awful what happened. I wouldn't have expected", said Bryony. "Our street seemed so peaceful! On Sunday in summer or in the evening, you hear only the neighbour children and the song of birds. It's so quiet as if you weren't near the town".

"You can't say that it's been too quiet these days", Mrs Stevens replied dryly. "We've heard nothing else but sirens, and, I'm sure, people are suspicious about the others. Although they want to think that someone from outside is guilty, they still fear that evil lives here in this street".

"Possibly", said McNamara, without getting too involved in this discussion. "Well, I'm leaving now. I must ask some things to the people in the street".

Bryony stood up to see him off.

"I'll be here", she said. "I work easier in the kitchen. If I can't go to the shop, at least I can catch up with the books".

"Don't you think you'd better sleep some more? You can't say you had a too peaceful night", replied Mrs Stevens peevishly.

"No, I couldn't. I'm too energised after so much coffee", the young woman said. "But if you want, you may go to rest in my room. I'll help you go upstairs".

"No, I don't feel like tormenting my legs now", said the old woman also peevishly. I prefer staying here with you".

"As you wish", replied Bryony calmly, although she was boiling inside. She wanted a little peace and she feared she wouldn't have any.

Mrs Stevens didn't seem in a too good mood that morning and she could bet she'd bother her with all her ideas. Usually she could bear her, but today she was quite tired and her head hurt badly. However, the old woman was more peevish than usually.

McNamara let himself seen off to the door understanding young woman's thoughts perfectly. He could imagine she wouldn't have a calm day with the old woman. When he reached the door, he turned towards her and stared at her eyes. The girl's pupils reflected her headache perfectly.

"I think, you'd better lie down. If you want, I'll send two policemen, one for you and one for her", he said, moving his head to the kitchen, where the old woman was. "So you could have peace and she may go to her house".

"No, it's not necessary", Bryony refused the offer. "I'll handle her. I'm sure you need all your people. Don't worry, I'll manage".

"I don't worry, I wanted only to be helpful", he said a little tougher than he'd wanted. But he didn't want to leave her the wrong feeling he'd have cared of her more than any other policeman.

"You shouldn't get angry again", she said tactfully, touching her temple that hurt because of his voice. "You've done it enough this morning. Be calm! I haven't made any ideas if you feared that", she continued, inferring McNamara's thoughts perfectly. "I'm just interested in seeing punished the person who's taken so many lives so far".

"Well, then", he tried to fix up the situation. "I'll probably call on here later to see if you're all right".

"I don't think you have to", she refused him dryly. "If we have an emergency, I'll call you. You've given me your number, you know".

McNamara moved his head shortly, understanding he'd been dismissed and left with a slight regret and anger in his soul. He disliked seeing that his gestures were rejected like this. However, he couldn't do anything. He stated his position clearly and he couldn't take it back. He didn't know why he'd do it, actually.

Bryony looked at his back for a while and smile flourished on her face, despite the deaf headache bothering her. Then she went back to the kitchen, but she wasn't aware that she still had the smile on her lips.

"You vainly smile, girl", said Mrs Stevens making her start. "I don't think you've chosen too well, if you want to listen to me. This man is among the ones that don't stay at home too much. You can see for yourself. He's in the street all the time. Nothing's worse than a salesman or a policeman, listen to me. You need someone that leaves at work in the morning and in the evening comes back home, not one who goes God knows where".

"I think you shouldn't think of that", Bryony replied at once. "Besides I'm not going to have a relation with anyone now, I have other things in my mind, I haven't even thought of him".

"Nonsense! You can't hoax me. I've seen sparkles between you two. But that might be only because the situation is like that. Don't pawn your heart now. Wait to see what comes next. Maybe when he finishes here, he disappears and doesn't ever come again".

"You needn't tell me that. I know very well how things are. I'm not just born. And I repeat it for the last time: my intentions don't go in this direction".

The old woman tried to say something, but Bryony picked some documents up from her bag and pretended she started to read so that the woman shut up, although she couldn't stop the feeling that it wasn't right. She shouldn't fall in for that man that seemed not the steady type, a woman needed. But, she admitted reluctantly, she might be wrong.

Bryony regretted the toughness of her words and gestures. But sometime, the woman managed to drive her crazy. She liked too much to get involved in her businesses and to give advice. The biggest problem was that she also expected to have her advice followed, whichever it was. And she wasn't always right.

Yes, maybe McNamara attracted her a little. He seemed tough and taciturn, but she didn't think things were so black. However, she felt he was a man she could rely on, ultimately. He didn't seem the shallow kind, but the deep one and he was taking his duty seriously. She could see he was responsible and actually this was an important thing to a person. Not many are like that, especially the ones between twenty and thirty. They dream of tommyrots and they didn't take any responsibilities.

Chapter Twenty

James came to McNamara, who had just got out of McNeil house. Seeing his face, McNamara could realise that McKay was doing quite fine.

"How's McKay, James?" he asked.

"She's well, sir. They managed to stabilize her and as she hadn't lost too much blood, though, so she recovers just fine. I asked her what she'd seen last night, but unfortunately, she hadn't seen anything. However, at least she's tough. After the guy had hit her in the head, she still had the strength to stand up once more and fight back. Unfortunately, the knife strike stopped her".

"So, she'd seen nothing of her aggressor's face", concluded McNamara.

"Nothing, sir. She told me about the same mask that McNeil told about too. Brave girl, McNeil! Too bad, she couldn't figure out more. By the way, you should know that I've just found out at the headquarters that they found Peter".

"Good and what's the boy saying?"

"Apparently, Patsy told him to elope together. She came with the idea. They stayed together only a few days, during which the girl was mostly out and didn't want to give him any explanations. Then, she told him she had someone else, who's not an unfledged kid, as he is, apparently, these were her exact words, and she left him. The kid says the girl used him as a cover. He realised it too late, though".

"Did she say who she was with?"

"Yes, apparently she told the boy that Mr Thompson rented a flat in town for her and she'd live there with him. Thompson was going to divorce his wife and marry her".

"Interesting! Very active this Mr Thompson! He promised Ann to marry her and then Patsy. He should have told something to Diane, too. Anything else?"

"Nothing special, sir. The coroner's report shows exactly what he said this morning. With the mention that one of the girls died two days before the other one. You realise how awful was for the second one to lie there with her friend's body around! I can't even imagine what she felt. I think she'd have gone crazy. Patsy was the second, sir".

"I see. Let's go and make a short tour to the neighbours and then go to this Thompson. So far, he's the best in the role of the killer, even if he doesn't seem to match the profile", said McNamara going up the street to Mr Graham's house.

At Mr Graham's home, no one answered. When they were about to leave, they saw Mrs Porter, who was just coming back from the morgue. A lady in a quite elegant outfit was accompanying her.

The woman with her seemed to be around forty, but time was quite gentle with her. Seeing the two men leaving Mr Graham's house, she commented:

"He's not at home at the hour, try in the evening".

"We're from the police, ma'am", said McNamara, taking his badge, as usually. "You?"

"Oh, yes! We haven't seen each other so far. I'm Brown. Mary Brown. You came yesterday and talked to my husband when I was at Mrs Porter's", she said pointing to her friend that seemed completely run down and didn't notice anything around.

"I'm afraid this is not the appropriate moment to talk", noticed McNamara.

"No, unfortunately", the woman replied to him smiling. "I'm sorry, but I must bring Mrs Porter inside and take care of her for a while. I'll call her sister to stay with her. She'll be here in half an hour, the tops. Then, I'll go to the bar, 'cause lunchtime comes. You may call on there. You have lunch with the occasion", she said kindly. "I don't boast, but everyone likes my food and I'm sure you need something warm now and then. What do you say?"

"Thank you, ma'am", answered McNamara, smiling.

He was already charmed by the woman's charm and naturalness. Mr Brown hadn't vainly boasted with his wife the other day. He seemed not to have to long for other women, in deed.

"We take your invitation. We'll come in an hour, maybe an hour and a half", he told her.

“Perfectly, sir, by then I have time to prepare one of those chicken pies”, she also said, showing Mrs Porter inside, then.

This one hadn’t reacted for one moment to the exchange of replies. She hadn’t even noticed that Mary Brown would’ve talked to someone.

James, touched by woman’s tragedy, shook his head, regretfully, and then he addressed to McNamara, who was watching Mrs Porter too:

“What a waste, don’t you think? Such a young life! Moreover, the only child!”

“What can you do, James? This is the result of a bad guidance, of a wrong education and I don’t think there’s an excuse for that, James. My poor mom managed by herself, but she’d never let me go on a wrong way. And I can’t say I felt too trammelled in rules. I’d lie”.

“I see your point, sir, but apparently not everyone has the samc talcnt”, said James, thinking of how many girls had chosen to take a wrong way with Patsy.

“That’s it. However, it’s useless to think of that now. Let’s do our job and then we’ll see”.

The street seemed to have been a peaceful one before, if he had to believe Bryony’s early words. But, now, McNamara noticed, the street was awfully silent. Not even the song of the birds was heard anymore. They seemed to have felt the misfortune having overwhelmed the street.

Chapter Twenty-One

Mary Reid came to the door only after they'd already rung four times. They knew she couldn't be anywhere else but at home and after having failed at the Thompsons', they couldn't believe the same thing happened here.

"Oh, good day, gentlemen! I knew we'd see each other today again", she said ironically. "For a few days now, a lot of things have been happening in this street. Before, you could wait for long to have something to take this street out of torpor".

"Does this fret make you happy?" showed James his surprise.

"You've misunderstood me, sir", replied the woman suddenly serious and in a cold voice. "I haven't meant this kind of fun. I don't like useless loss of human lives. Not more than you do, and I can't stand unwarranted violence. Yes, I enjoy my quarrels with my husband, but I know for sure he wouldn't touch me with one finger. He bursts out fast, but he also regrets what he says. He doesn't even curse. He only uses a louder voice. However, I keep you at the door, I'm sorry. Come in", she stepped aside.

Her sudden seriousness made the two men understand that she was something more than a mere moony woman that likes arousing her husband's jealousy. The woman seemed to have also some social values and certain principles, she would hide under the mask of a frivol woman and that's it. Reid had probably found it out for long, and therefore, he didn't give up this marriage that seemed not to bring to much joy for his heart. Or maybe it did. They couldn't judge that. He was the only one who could know what he wanted in life.

They followed her in the same room in which she had shown them the previous morning. The music was filling the room and then they figured out why she hadn't heard the bell the first time. Her work seemed to have advanced enough. There were more printed pages on the desk.

"Has your story advanced, ma'am?"

"Yes, quite well. Actually, I've just finished now. I'll ask my husband to take it to my editor tomorrow".

"Do you trust him to do it?" asked James unwillingly, and watched McNamara at once to see if he upset him.

But McNamara didn't seem upset at all. He only seemed very interested in the woman's words.

"Of course! I trust him. It's not such a big deal. He knows very well that he won't solve anything if he sabotaged me and, however, he encouraged me every time. He doesn't mind my writing. He minds only my clothes and behaviour".

"And then, why don't you change, ma'am?" asked McNamara this time, his curiosity clearly aroused.

"Because I don't give him the satisfaction to do what he wants, not because of anything else".

"But don't you think that now and then you should do things in his way?"

"Of course, when it's something important. I don't see why should I bother otherwise".

The detectives couldn't understand the woman's logic. Therefore, they abandoned the discussion and McNamara said:

"So, you heard what happened last night".

"Well, it was difficult not to hear. I was here downstairs and I was writing when the cars came. Michael also came downstairs. The noise woke him up. He even said that two nights in the row is too much. And then, exactly when he wanted to leave this morning, because he left later today, he saw a lot of cars again. He even said that either this criminal is a maniac, or all criminals in the world had come in this very street. He even already regrets we bought the house here. We thought it is a quiet area, you know. Nothing announced such a thing".

"If you were still working here, did you see anyone or anything?" asked McNamara again.

"Nothing unusual... Mr Graham passed by at eleven, eleven thirty. Usually he comes late. I think he's got someone in town. He's got a junk car and it's impossible not to hear it. Of course, that made me look up and, as my desk faces the street, it was impossible not to see him. Mr Thompson came by twelve, a little after or before. However, not very late after Mr Graham came because I hadn't turned back to work yet. I heard his car, you know. Then I saw him parking it into the yard. Who knows where he was, because he wanders a lot. Then Mr Randall passed. I think he made an inventory or something. His wife almost all the time asks him to make inventories. She keeps him henpecked and he doesn't dare to move. She's a very rough woman. Then, no one passed until you came".

"All right, ma'am. Your husband didn't see anything until we came?"

"No, he was sleeping. He was very tired. He had a hard day at work and he didn't have a quite loose evening at home", she said biting her inferior lip.

They could see she regretted a little what she'd done a day before, although it was useless now. Time couldn't come back.

McNamara stood up, but before leaving, he asked her:

"By the way, do you know where Alice Thompson is? She doesn't answer to the door".

"She came to me an hour ago, maybe an hour and so. She said she wasn't feeling well these days, and she went to the doctor. Well, it's something usual for her. At least once a week she goes to the doctor or calls him here".

"Yes, I see", said McNamara. "The house across the street was put on the market?"

"Some time before, as soon as the owner had died. However, the heirs were asking too much and they didn't manage to sell it. They left it in a waiting for, so that the price increases. The heirs are in Africa or Australia, I don't know where. They left two or three months ago, maybe. With their job, I think".

"By the way", asked McNamara, "do you remember if a stranger to this street passed by during the last two weeks?"

"I don't think so", she said thinking of that. "Oh, yes, there was a young woman. I saw her turning around the empty house across the street. I thought she'd be a buyer, although I doubted she could buy the house. She was well dressed, but not enough for how much they asked for it".

"How did she look?" asked McNamara.

"Tall, red-haired, the coquettish type, I think... I'm sorry, I can't remember anything else".

"All right, ma'am, we thank you", said McNamara. "For now, we'll go to speak to the Randalls at the shop".

"Mr Randall isn't there. I saw him leaving by car early this morning. He takes his car only when he has to go to town. Probably, he needs supplies. They don't have all their merchandise brought here".

"Thank you, ma'am! Success in writing", said McNamara in his way to the entrance door.

Mary smiled to him and thanked. When she opened the door, Michael was exactly in front of the door, with his key in his hand. He was unpleasantly surprised seeing

McNamara. He had the feeling he'd be a potential rival. He looked good, in the tough sense. Then he spotted James behind him, and he calmed down.

"Good day, sir", said McNamara. "I'd have a question for you. Did you see or hear anything before the police came?"

"I went to bed only at twelve, maybe one or a little after one, I think, even if I went upstairs earlier", he said. "I couldn't sleep, so I read for a while. When I put the book onto the night table, I thought to close the window a bit, not to let rain inside. It was pattering quite hard. It thundered quite loudly and I saw a shadow before the house across the street, the one that is empty now. The person was trying to hide behind the trees. It seemed to be quite tall. But I think it was your man, isn't it?"

"No, sir, it wasn't our man. If you could recall anything of him, anything..." said McNamara.

"Unfortunately, I don't recall much", Michael seemed in confusion. "I saw him only for a fraction of a second, I think, when it thundered", he seemed to think. "It was someone quite tall and massive... He didn't seem to resemble to Mr Graham... I'm sure of that. I can't tell you more", he apologized. "I know he was in black. He was leaning against the tree, you know, almost half hidden", Michael Reid tried hard to recall more.

"OK, sir", said McNamara. "I hope you won't think it's too much, but may I ask you what are you doing at home at the time", he asked him.

"I didn't have too much to do, and I thought to invite my wife to lunch, at the pub on the corner. I know she doesn't eat too much when she's alone and she's got work to do, and she could use a good meal, couldn't you, sweetheart?"

The woman, sincerely flattered, nodded.

"I'll come right now", she said forgetting the other two. "Wait for me to take a sweater on. It's chilly for this blouse".

In deed, her blouse was pretty light and sleeveless. In the house was also cold for such a blouse. McNamara was amazed she could stand cold dressed like that. She seemed a real weird woman. Nothing seemed normal in what she'd do.

Greeting them, he left followed by James, who seemed to think of the words of the two people.

"I think it's one of the three, sir: Graham, Thompson or Randall. But I still think it's Thompson. Graham seems quite coward and Randall doesn't seem to have a reason".

"You're right, James, but we must check them both, to see who could did it, even if everything leads to Thompson".

They went down the street thinking, and for a few seconds no one said anything. Then, McNamara spoiled the silence:

"You know what, let's have a good meal to the Browns' at the pub, and then we'll go to the station in town to see what they found. And you go once more to McKay. Maybe she recalled of something".

James approved nodding. He couldn't realize if his boss sent him to McKay because he saw he had some feelings for her or because he hoped to hear something new. However, any of these worked for him. He wanted to see McKay and any pretext was good.

Suddenly, McNamara changed his mind:

"You know what? We haven't asked anything the two Davidson. We've completely forgotten about them. Let's see what they do", he said and headed to their house followed by James, who already regretted the lunch promised.

They rang at the door and in a few minutes, a dark-haired woman, with an attractive body, came to the door.

"You're the police, aren't you?" she said. "I've kept seeing you in the street. I've been even thinking when you might come by here".

"We have a lot of things to check, ma'am", said McNamara indifferent to her reproach. "Are you alone at home or is your husband here too?"

"I'm alone. He left to Plymouth yesterday. He told that for the police and also left the phone number of the hotel where he can be found. For you, because I don't have why to talk to him", she said, leading them inside. "And by the way", she turned to McNamara, "he's not my husband anymore. We divorced some time ago".

"But you still live together", noticed James amazed.

"Yes, we haven't finished the partition. I'm afraid we have to sell the house and split the money in the end. He doesn't want to leave it to me, although I got children's custody".

"Where are your children?" McNamara showed his curiosity.

"I took them to my parents yesterday. I didn't want them stay here and listen to what people said about what happen. Mrs Randall also called her mother in the morning to take the children. It is not a sure place for them now".

"I don't think they were in trouble", said McNamara, although, who knows, a child might have come too nosy or found something and then the killer might have killed it. He didn't think the killer had so many scruples.

"Did you see anything related to murders, ma'am?"

"I'm afraid, I didn't. I don't have the habit to spy people. If poor Mrs Dobbs had lived, she could have told you everything you wanted. But now... I haven't seen anything these two days".

"But before? During the last two weeks?"

"I don't think anyone unknown was here. I saw only Patsy, of Mrs Porter".

"When?" jumped McNamara.

"A week, maybe a week and a half, I think. I went out with the children to buy them ice cream. It was about seven in the evening, maybe seven and a half. She was with a kid a little taller than she but also blond. Patsy pointed to me and told something to the other girl and they started to giggle. I think because of the house, but, really,

I don't have where to go for now. With my salary, I can't get too much".

"Didn't you see anything else, ma'am? Where they went, what they did?"

"They were going up the street. However, there wasn't anyone in the street. At the beginning, I thought they went to Patsy's house, but Mrs Porter didn't say a word of that, and I didn't think it was appropriate to ask her".

"But about the people in the street, do you know what they were doing or where they were that moment?"

"Mrs Stevens was at the window, I spotted her", she said making a big effort of concentration. I think Bryony was somewhere in the house, I didn't see her. I didn't see the Reids or the Thompsons. I know nothing of Goddard, the Dobbs or Mrs Porter. I passed by the grocer's and spoke to Mrs Randall" she reviewed in her memory. "Her husband left to talk to a supplier, I think she told me. About the Browns I can only presume they were at the pub. There's a lot of people after six. Really, I don't know what else to say".

"It's enough, ma'am" McNamara smiled to her. "You offered us a good description of the picture. We should have come to you yesterday".

His words made her feel important. She'd been missing that feeling for a long time. She led the two men at the door and remained watching after them while they were heading to the bar. McNamara felt her looks in the back, but said nothing.

After a few moments, in a low voice so that only James could hear him, he said:

“She knows a lot. If we had asked her yesterday, we’d have known Patsy was here with her friend. Damn it!” he said getting into the bar with James behind.

Chapter Twenty-Two

They sat down at a table after making their order and expected someone to wait them. A few moments, they didn't know what to say to each other. Michael was looking at her, and in his eyes, there was a sort of sadness. He couldn't understand why they were behaving one with the other in the way they were doing.

Mary was looking through the window although she didn't have anything to see. The pub was exactly on the corner. Beyond the corner, there was a square and after the square, the madness started. People wouldn't pass by there too often, only the ones living in the street. But there were trees in front of the pub and across the street, too, on one side of the grocer's, and the colours of the beginning of autumn were in their entire splendour. The previous night's rain made them seem even more alive.

She turned and looked at Michael and seeing the way he was watching her, she asked him:

"Why are you upset now?"

"I'm not," he answered smiling softly. "I was only thinking of us and our quarrels that seem endless. You know, I think I'd like a more peaceful life. When I think of the people having died, I realise life is too short to mock of it".

Mary watched him carefully, trying to guess what he was thinking by saying that. She felt some fear that the inevitable was about to take place.

"You want to say you leave, don't you?"

"Oh, no", he replied, "even the opposite. I don't even think to leave but I think I should give you more space and take things more easily. I should stop let anything bothering me. I don't think of leaving. If I'd wanted that, I'd have done it long time ago, don't you think? It's some time since we've been playing this silly game".

The woman calmed down a little, but not for good. She was too afraid to take everything for granted. She hadn't done it for a long time to start doing it now.

"You want to say you won't yell whatever I dress or do?"

"Not really", he grinned, his pride struggling in his soul. "I was thinking of a sort of compromise".

That moment Mrs Brown brought their order. She put it on the table, wished them good appetite and then left. They started eating and after a few moments, Mary asked:

"So, of what compromised you've thought?"

She didn't really like the idea of a compromise. She could see that he was about to make her do what she didn't like and that would upset her a lot.

"I was thinking I earn well now. You know I have bigger revenue, and however, you earn very good too. I think we can afford to hire someone for cleaning, washing, ironing and cooking... I know you don't like doing it and you have no inclination for that. Larry recommended me a cousin of his housekeeper. He said she's trustful and hard working... I think she'd be of a real help, what do you say?"

"And what should I do instead?" she replied pragmatically and even doubtfully.

"Not very much", his answer came in a few second. "I'd like you not to wear so bare-shouldered and short clothes, not all the time, but now and then... Do you think we could make a deal?"

Mary thought a few moments. She thought it was reasonable what he asked, but she wasn't sure she had to take the compromise. However, he didn't ask too much, she thought. It was quite little, especially because, however, cold came and she'd been freezing to death only to do it in spite of him.

"All right", she said in the end, when Michael had already given up waiting for an answer. "However, tomorrow I have to go to town if you want that. I need new clothes. You know what kind of clothes I have," she said smiling. She always took care of buying very short skirts and very bare-shouldered blouses. "And by the way" she continued, "as variation, I thought to start wearing trousers, what do you say?"

Michael smiled happily and holding out over the table, he took her hand and kissed it.

"It would be great!" he exclaimed. "Really great!"

A few tables away, in the opposite side of the room, McNamara and James, who had just come for a few minutes, watched the scene amused.

“Sir,” said James, “these two are effectively a disaster. Either they quarrel or they kiss each other happily!”

“Something like that, James, but it’s important they go along in their way. Moreover, I’m afraid their marriage is meant to resist, despite usual things, and Mrs Thompson’s to fail, even though more people think she’s the perfect wife,” replied McNamara with a fatalist tone.

“I wouldn’t wonder,” replied James. “If we only think of the “wonderful” Mr Thompson...” he left the sentence in suspense.

“Yes, our wonderful Mr Thompson. We have to go and talk to him. Do you realise we haven’t seen him or heard of him since the first night we came here?”

“Yes, it’s quite strange. He’s somewhere all the time. I don’t wonder everyone thinks they have a good marriage. They don’t hear quarrels in their house because his wife doesn’t have anyone to quarrel with, don’t you think, sir?”

“Oh, yes,” said McNamara.

He wanted to say something more, but that very moment, Mrs Brown came with their order and made him stop. She put the plates before them and smiled.

“How’s Mrs Porter?” asked McNamara.

“Not very well”, Mrs Brown became sad. “Her sister came just now, but I’m afraid she’s completely run down. She can’t imagine how Patsy could die in this street and she didn't see or hear anything. I understand her, really," Mrs Brown pitied her. "I think I'd go crazy if something like that happened to my children".

"Do you have children, ma'am?" asked McNamara curiously.

"Yes, I have two boys" she said proudly. "One is at the college, at Oxford. He didn't want to stay here and won a scholarship, you know. He learns well, this boy of mine," she said proudly. "The younger one became a pilot. He lives in London now. I have good boys, shortly. Nevertheless, we haven't got anyone to take the pub over when we're gone", she said sadly. "Only if Mark, this is my older son, comes back, but I don't think so," she shook her head suddenly sad.

"Leave it, ma'am, things will solve out in the end," James tried to comfort her.

"Yes, maybe," she admitted softly, although she didn't believe a word of it. "However, good appetite, and come to have a meal here, now and then!"

The men thanked her and started eating.

"James," said McNamara suddenly, "I don't think it's the case, but let's check where the Brown boys were during the last three weeks".

James nodded, showing he understood.

Chapter Twenty-Three

" Mike, I've found something interesting here, " said Jo.

"What did you find?"

"I checked what you said. I found out that the guys from "Vices" have had Daniel Thompson in sight for some time. Thompson seems to have a net of escort girls. All his girls are under age. Moreover, he's got a small company with that kind of girls on Internet. For that he's got five girls, apparently. The guys say he earns quite well. They've even been amazed seeing how much. A lot of people prefer this method now instead of picking up prostitutes in the street. Well, it's the age of information. They said they already have a quite thick file with everything. They gathered more proof and prepare to arrest Thompson.

"Interesting," said Mike. "But I'm sure there's something else not only a net of minor girls".

"Of course, dear, what you've thought? Of course, there's something else. Our man also blackmails. It's more efficient than renting the girls. Everything started with one who couldn't pay anymore and filled a complaint. He told everything. They've got a complaint from a businessman. He'd been blackmailed because he had relations with a girl under age. He'd been told to pay or his wife, as well as police, would receive the photos. Of course, there was only a bluff with police. I don't see Thompson to put himself in police's hands. But our man got scared and he preferred to step forward not to get into trouble. To be sure, he sent his wife on vacation in France. You see, like a present of her anniversary".

"So kind of him, don't you think?" said Mike ironically. "He's a smart guy. He can't have problems with his wife. If something comes by mail, he gets the letters or the pictures at once. I'm afraid our story is also related to blackmail or something," said Mike.

"Of course, Mike, it must be" replied. Jo. "Most of cases, the blackmailed people have the tendency to kill the blackmailer. But he should've killed Thompson, not the girls".

"Maybe the girls blackmailed him, though, without Thompson's knowledge. They might have thought to make some money on their own, don't you think?"

That moment, McNamara and James got into the office. Looking around, the chief inspector saw the entire room and saw Jo and Mike talking in a corner and the others at their desks.

McNamara greeted them and that moment his people's eyes turned to him.

"What's new?" he asked. "Have you moved on? Anything new came up about the case?"

"Yes, sir," said Jo. "I've got something new; actually we," she said including Mike too, because actually he started everything, and she began to tell him what she'd told Mike. 'We've also got documents, sir. This Mr Thompson seems to be a real tart, sir", she said fiercely.

"What a language, Jo!" Mike jumped. "I think you should watch your language a little, don't you think so, girl?"

"Mike, I don't feel like playing now", snapped McNamara. "You have fun with Jo in your spare time, not when we have so many stressing problems. I've got a lot of crimes here and we're not closer to the killer. It might be Thompson, but the same time it might not be. The girls could be killed by someone they blackmailed, don't you think?"

Jo blushed because of McNamara's remark, but she and Mike nodded. They'd thought of the same thing, even if Thompson stayed before their eyes. Everything seemed to point to him so he couldn't be the probable killer.

"Think that everyone said Thompson was the first at the crime scene in the Dobbs' yard," said McNamara, leaning against a desk. "He was in his suit, as all witnesses say. If he'd been the killer, he wouldn't have time to change clothes or neither James nor anyone else could see anything strange on his suit, could they?" he turned to James.

"In deed, sir," he said. "It was very clean, sir, although a little crumbled because he carried Mr Dobbs in the house. He couldn't be the killer. He hadn't even taken out his tie. If he'd been the killer, he should have had at least a blood stain on him, I say".

"So," concluded McNamara, taking his word, "we must find one of the girls' clients, to be sure. They probably blackmailed him without Thompson's permission. They'd thought it was easy to do, but, obviously, they were amateurs. If Thompson found that out, then he knows who killed them. Have you found out where's the flat he rented for Patsy?"

"Yes, sir, just now," said Jo. "I was thinking of going there with the operative team. I've already got the search warrant. I thought we shouldn't lose time any more. I was sure you'd want that".

"Of course! You've done well. Good, I'll come too," said McNamara. "Let me check what's piled on my desk. We'll leave in five minutes".

After saying that, McNamara stood up from the desk, turned and left the room. James went to one of the other guys and told him:

"Listen, Jay, please, check the Browns' boys. I understood one would be at Oxford, student, and the other one would live in London. He's a pilot. Please, see where they've been this month. If you find out something useful, call us, all right? At least we'd be sure they're not related to this thing".

The other one approved and started work. He looked for the boys' names in the population evidence and started to make calls where they should have been.

Meanwhile, McNamara left his office and made a sign to James, Mike and Jo to follow him.

"Have you called the operative team, Jo?"

"Yes, sir, they're waiting outside in the car".

"Good, you'll come with Mike. I'll come with James, so that we can move freely. Then, we may go somewhere else. However, James will be free tonight. He had a difficult time during the last twenty-four hours," said McNamara.

"And you, sir?"

"I'll manage, Jo. However, no one cries after me. By the way, who did you send to McNeil's and Stevens?"

"Clarence stays with them till tonight. Then, I assigned Phelps and Dulgon. I've thought it'd better each of them stay at her house, as last night. If something is to happen, at least we don't have two victims the same time, sir."

"It sounds cynical," said McNamara, "but true. We'd better limit disaster. Although I don't think the guy will attack this night. He's hurt. He didn't go to any hospital or to a doctor, I've checked. Therefore, he wasn't cared of too well. It's impossible to be in a too good state," he said turning to the door.

He was about to go out with them following him, when he turned back and asked:

"Has anyone read Diane's diary?"

"Yes, sir," said Mike. "I have. There I found out about Thomson and his small net. Jo checked with the guys from the vice section to find out if they know about it and therefore, we learnt that they already knew about the net."

“Haven’t you found there anything in relation with what happened to the girl?”

“No, sir. However, the diary stopped the day when she left home. Probably, she met her killer afterwards. In the diary, she only praises Thompson that he’s smart and good-looking, and she wrote she’d earn a lot of money and have a good life and have fun. She also writes about Patsy. Apparently, she introduced her to Thompson. Patsy seemed sure that Thompson would marry her after he’d divorced “that cow”. I’ve quoted ad litteram. Apparently, Thompson called his wife like that before his little friends.”

“All right”, said McNamara, and disgust could be seen on his face. “Come on, maybe we’ll find something in Patsy’s flat,” he said getting out with his people behind.

He disliked Thompson more and more. Apparently, he didn’t have only some petty affairs, as he thought, but he also used girls to make money. The same time, he seemed to mock on Alice. McNamara felt deep pity but also a little scorn for the poor woman, who believed blindly in her husband, thinking he was great, when actually he was a scamp.

If he had such a woman in his corner, he’d shown at least a little consideration. Nevertheless, he couldn’t imagine he’d marry such a woman with no charm like Alice. She was too stuffy for his taste and she had too many old-fashioned ideas related to another century.

He couldn’t stop comparing her to Bryony, who had more life and will in her small finger, than Alice had in her entire body. He couldn't imagine someone could dupe Bryony the way Alice was duped.

***

They got into the flat accompanied by witnesses. Witnesses were the superintendent and a cleaning lady. The other people were either to work or still on vacation.

It was a very stylish block of flats and probably it was quite expensive to live there. It had a warden and it was extremely clean. Staircases were bright and the lobby reflected perfectly the interior of the building.

Apparently, Mr Thompson's businesses went on well. Thinking that the other girls had left their homes too, he must have had flats for them too, not only for Patsy.

Jo had told McNamara the net counted over fifteen girls. So, there was a lot of money involved. He wouldn't have attracted the girls if he had brought them in a dump. Probably, the tariff was quite high, considering the girls were under age. Moreover small films on Internet were well paid and public liked them, at least a certain type of public. If they also considered the blackmail Thompson used to practice, the man gained quite well, so he could afford to rent pleasant flats for all the girls in his net.

Policed checked the flat attentively. There weren't too many things that could lead to a solution for their case. They didn't find any kind of documents, or at least a line written down, and that was quite off. There were no newspapers either, or at least an agenda or something.

Such things could be found anywhere, however low people were, unless they were analphabetic. Patsy wasn't.

Seeing the police were vainly looking for things, the superintendent stepped forward and, after some hesitation, he told McNamara, he guessed he was the boss:

"Mr Inspector, you should know that the other day, actually yesterday, the gentlemen having rented the flat left here with lots of things in a bag... He paid the rent in advance for six month only three weeks before, so I didn't panic... It wasn't my place to find interest in what he was doing, as long as nothing seemed illegal and he didn't disturb the others people in the block. In that concerning the girl, I've thought she left back home. I imagined she didn't like something. They didn't fool me a second with that thing that she was gentleman's niece from the country".

"So that was. Thompson cleaned here. That explains why it looks as if no one lived here," said McNamara with resignation, despite the fury he felt.

They found only a few clothes, and they were few for a girl of Patsy's kind, having that old profession asking for specific clothes. They didn't even find a magazine. Apparently, Thompson was afraid the girl made some notes somewhere and he preferred to make everything disappear.

McNamara turned to Jo and asked her:

“Do the guys from vices have people to survey Thompson and his clients?”

“Yes, they put him under surveillance two days ago. The next day we found the girl across his house, but this is only a coincidence. It’s a pity they didn’t do it earlier. At least we knew exactly what he did. But they couldn’t know what was going to happen”.

“Yep,” said McNamara. “It’s a pity. However, call and tell them I don’t care what they want, but I want them to arrest him at once. I can’t afford to drag things. His office should be checked and all places where he could have something hidden, possibly, the places where he kept the girls. They know. They must have already found them, if they have been following the business for a while. I want to interrogate him myself. If they don’t know this thing already and they yell I spoil their case, explain them that a murder comes first. However, we don’t have only one,” he also said bitterly.

“Yes, sir,” said Jo, and took her phone off her bad, getting out of the flat so that she could speak on the phone quietly.

Chapter Twenty-Four

Alice was surprised to see Mary and Michael coming back from the pub holding each other's hand. Envy and amazement made her to feel something in her throat. She wouldn't have expected that after the discussions heard lately.

If she had been in Mr Reid's place, she'd have chased that bad woman out of the house. She would waste time with Mary now and then; it was true, but only because of boredom. It wasn't as if she had to live together with her and bear her laziness and behaviour.

When the two of them reached close to the house, Alice, waiting for them from her yard, came out in the street as if she hadn't seen them before.

"Mary, hallo" she yelled to be heard. "Sorry, I didn't know you were with your husband", she lied wanting to leave Michael the impression that someone else could have been. "Never mind, I'll come another time," she showed her regret.

"It isn't necessary, Mrs Thompson," said Michael, without biting the bait. He knew his wife was smarter than Alice thought. She wouldn't have gone out with anyone in

Nightingale Street. If she had wanted to cheat on him, she'd have made it somewhere where there wasn't an informer. "However, I have to go to the yard," he continued. "I've only come to invite Mary to a meal," he said, having the satisfaction to see Alice turning white of envy.

He knew it would be like that. He knew that type of women. They were completely dissatisfied with their lives, even if they wanted to show the opposite. Alice tried to hide her misery and unhappiness under the mask of a responsible person full of her importance as a married woman.

Michael smiled in his mind. That was his little revenge for all bad thoughts Alice had had for his marriage, because she surely had some. In addition, there was for all the nagging she'd done for his wife.

In deed, that moment Alice felt she was chocking. Things weren't right at all. She was the perfect wife and Daniel never came to invite her to lunch. At the beginning of their marriage, he still used to phone and asked her what she was doing and if he had to buy something, maybe bread, but for some time now, he had never given a sign. She knew he was still there because she saw food or clean clothes run out.

They had even been sleeping separately for a while. Daniel would say it was better that way than disturbing her with his coming home late.

She didn't know what to think. Actually, she was afraid of thinking anything. Therefore, she had hidden her fears deeply in her subconscious and didn't allow herself to think of them but once in a while.

However she'd tried to call him at the office and lately, he'd been away. He'd started coming late at home in the evening and she would fall asleep before seeing her husband.

And here was Mary, who wasn't interested in anything supposing a slight comfort for her husband, and she was even invited to lunch. Mr Reid would leave his work and come from the other end of the town for her! It wasn't right! It wasn't right at all!

Injustice made her sick. She'd have liked to scream that moment, to bend holding her waist and yell her misfortune. Instead, she tried smiling and said warmly to Mary:

"I wanted to invited you to a coffee, if you wanted, that's all".

"You'd better come to me, Alice," she said. "I was to you last time," explained Mary, who didn't want to be on Alice's territory again. She'd prefer to have her fights on her own. And seeing the thunder in Alice's eyes, she could say that she'd have a fight with her neighbour.

Alice accepted somehow reluctantly and that moment, Mr Reid said goodbye to the two of them. Then, he leaned over his wife and whispered something, kissed her, but not shortly or coldly, as Alice would have thought, and that had a devastating effect on Alice. She felt overwhelmed with envy again. She felt like having no air and pain scratched her soul. Daniel hadn't kissed her for long—maybe on her cheek once in a while, in the morning when he left at work. Otherwise, he had no tender gesture for her. If she thought well, they were like two strangers living in the same house, nothing more.

Not to let them see her feelings, Alice tried to smile. However, the two, husband and wife, realised her smile wasn't sincere but bitter.

After Michael left, Mary invited Alice in the house without showing any of her thoughts. She was sorry for her, in a way, but not very sorry. Alice nagged her too much to feel real compassion for her. Mary considered her neighbour was too conceited and too full of the importance of her ideas, to stand her anymore.

She was that kind of person that would leave people to do whatever they wanted, obviously, as long as they let her too. She didn't like people trying to make her act differently than she thought. She didn't answer too well when someone imposed her to do something.

She prepared coffee for both of them although she knew Alice would have liked tea. However, it was useless to lie, but she had her little wickedness. She put a cup of hot coffee before each of them and lit one of the three or four cigarettes she'd smoked every day.

She was amused because of her neighbour's reproachful look. She knew she'd look at her like that. She knew Alice considered a woman shouldn't smoke: it was undignified.

Mary didn't think like that. She only thought it wasn't healthy but not undignified. Actually, she tried to give up the three four cigarettes she smoked every day but she didn't want to say it to Alice. She'd thought she had convinced her with her old-fashioned ideas and prejudices. This was the last thing Mary'd wanted.

"Have you seen, Mary, how full of life our little street has become lately?" tried Alice to make a little conversation, although she couldn't pass over what she'd seen a few moments before. Her heart was still throbbing because of the envy.

"I think it rather became too full of death," replied Mary caustically, as she didn't like Alice's words at all. "As much as I know, only bodies have been taken from here these days. How could you say that, Alice? Don't you have a little compassion for the killed women?" and then she continued in her mind: "Even though one of them was your husband's lover?" Actually, that didn't explain a murder, at least in her eyes.

"I was talking about the cars and people coming here," said Alice blushing, resenting the other one's reproach. "I didn't mean to minimize what happened, but I didn't mean the corpses either, as you say".

"Ok," said Mary peacefully, "I didn't want to burst on you like that. However, I resent everything going on. I mainly mind the wasted lives. Moreover, most of them were so young! However, obviously, I have a quite selfish reason: everything disturbs me from writing,' she tried to appease what she'd just said. She didn't like that strangers could figure out her real personality.

Alice made no comments but because she couldn't stand the curiosity, she decided to ask her about she'd just seen:

"Yesterday evening you seemed to quarrel that the entire street could here you. How it comes, your husband came to invite you to lunch? I wouldn't have expected. He usually keeps being angry for a few days".

"I don't know, but probably because he had to break me important news. That's why he came".

"What news?" asked Alice fast, thirsty of new things, even if they didn't concern her directly. But her life had become too dull lately, and she tried to catch whatever she could.

"He wants to hire me a permanent housekeeper so that I don't get tired working in the house," replied Mary, as if there wasn't too big deal.

"As if you were ever tired", thought Alice maliciously, even amazed that Mary could seem so indifferent about her husband's decision, but she said loudly:

"How kind of him! He's so full of consideration!"

"Nonsense," said Mary shortly and ironically, because she didn't like too much faking. She knew very well that the other woman wasn't glad for her, but the opposite. She envied her and she was sorry Mary had such a chance.

She'd have preferred to hear that Michael came to tell her he'd leave her for good.

"However," she continued, watching Alice carefully to surprise all her changes in mimic that she found so amusing, "I think he simply got sick of having cold food when he comes back home in the evening and of ironing his shirts, you know it Alice. I don't think it's about too much consideration here," she also said ironically.

"But you don't do anything in the house?"

Alice was completely astonished. She knew Mary wasn't the perfect housewife, but she didn't imagine she did nothing. She couldn't conceive a woman doing nothing, married or not. Actually, it was her house. She'd have had to take care of it, somehow. In addition, she couldn't imagine a man could pass over that. He was working to bring money in the house, even if Mary earned something from that crap she was writing. She didn't think her gain was too big. However, she was wrong. It was big. She couldn't even imagine how much she could earn with her little stories.

Seeming as if she didn't pay attention to what she could read on Alice's face, Mary replied nonchalantly:

"Only if I can't do otherwise, but usually I do nothing. I don't have domestic inclinations, like you," she said ironically. "I prefer working on my computer all day long than doing the vacuum or peeling potatoes," said Mary, completely indifferent to the horror that could be perfectly read on her neighbour's face.

Actually, for a long time Mary hadn't paid attention to anything people would say, especially her neighbour. She considered her a snob, proud of the way she took care of her house and husband, without realising that her husband was infidel and didn't respect her, treating her as if she were a housekeeper.

Alice couldn't imagine a woman could be so careless with her house, though. Now she understood why there was always dust on the furniture in the Reids' house and things thrown where you couldn't expect. Their kitchen also seemed to have been used only now and then. However, she could have sworn Mary was dusting or cooking once in a while. She couldn't do away without doing anything.

"How's Mr Thompson these days?" Mary tried to pay her in the same way. She knew well that Daniel Thompson would come at home only late in the night lately, probably when he was sure Alice went to bed and he wasn't in danger to meet her.

"He's at work, you know it," answered Alice very stuffy. "He works hard to get a promotion and he is an important person there, you know. They need him a lot and they give him most of the accounts, especially if they're difficult and other people can't manage them," she answered proud of his skills. "But people know my Daniel manages in any situation and he's the best of all the book-keepers of the company. That's why they do it. He can't say "no", you see, even if he's sick of that. However, he promised me to take a vacation soon and take me in a wonderful place to compensate all this time," said Alice, although she knew she was lying herself. She didn't think Daniel would take her somewhere. She didn't imagine he took some of his time to do it.

"Yes, I see," said Mary, actually believing nothing, knowing that her Daniel didn't go along at all with his accounting work and he didn't have the slightest intention to take his little wife on vacation. He wouldn't leave with her to not get bored all day long. He'd have taken one of his little sweethearts.

However, she had a hunch that her neighbour didn't work at all and, actually, earned his money otherwise. She had a friend who was a bookkeeper in the very company Thompson was working. She knew well his bosses disliked him and were on the verge of firing him. She had been told Daniel lost many accounts because of his incompetence and laziness and his bosses were angry, and they'd decided to fire him at the beginning of the next month. They had already sent him the notice. He brought real prejudices to the company's name, and they were an old and conservative company. They couldn't afford to let the company knocked down by such an individual.

Mary felt boredom overwhelming her: Alice never had anything important to say and invariably she annoyed. She kept saying the same things and she only praised her precious husband and her domestic work.

Silence filled the room for a while. Not one of them had anything to say to the other. Therefore, they drank the coffee silently. Alice felt she couldn't resist without saying anything and said:

"I think I'm going at home. I bought a lamb chop and I was thinking to cook it with mint sauce, you know. Daniel is crazy about that and I make it wonderfully. Everything is in spice."

"I'm not very fond of meat," said Mary completely indifferent and non-wanting to listen to Alice's recipe for the lamb. I prefer a salad any time if possible. It's easier to prepare and easier to digest," she said caustically.

Alice grinned but said nothing. She smiled softly, instead. She stood up and followed by Mary, who couldn't wait anymore to see her out, went to the door. Mary opened the door for her and smiling said: "Goodbye".

After closing the door, Mary scowled and said: "Boring woman, God! You can sleep with her, as well. Nothing would wake you up. What the hell did Thompson see in her, at the beginning? Maybe he saw she was one of the women that say nothing and he had a possibility to have as many lovers as he wanted. Yes, that must be!" She hit her fingers, as if she'd reached a very important conclusion, and afterwards, she went to her desk and forgot about Alice completely.

She preferred thinking of Michael instead. She wasn't sure his offer was meant to help her or bring him in advantage. Her mistrustful nature couldn't let her think otherwise.

She couldn't afford to be sure on him. She had a pathologic fear to not end like her mother. She was afraid of believing in someone's feelings. She learnt when she was young to defend her heart and never put it on the carpet.

She didn't want any disappointment and, as much as she could, she wouldn't have. She preferred to take the people as they were and not invest too much in them. Thus, if they were to leave her, her pain was close to the surface. They wouldn't scratch her heart because her feelings weren't too deep to be hurt too much.

She decided to start work and forget about all of these. However, it was a useless waste of time. She couldn't know what Michael would think, and therefore, she'd better not think of his reasons anymore. It was only waste of time. She never could guess the real reasons of people.

***

Alice started work in the kitchen, finally calmed down. Here, she knew what to do and no one could upset her. Although she was at ease and she liked cooking, she couldn't stop the thought that something was scratching the surface. It had been happening for days. She had the feeling that things weren't what they seemed and something serious was about to come in one of the next days. Nothing seemed solid and real.

She tried to chase her black thoughts away and get lost in her cooking. The very moment she thought she succeeded, she heard the bell, and that dissatisfied her a lot. She didn't feel like seeing anyone now. She wanted to ignore the bell, but the person at the door didn't get the message: they kept insisting.

She rinsed her hands and after she dried on the towel, she went to the door. She was amazed when she saw more policemen before the door. They weren't the ones that she saw before. They were others. Feeling fear, she opened the door:

"Yes, what is it?"

"We have a search warrant, ma'am," said a short and plump woman. "We must search the entire house".

That moment, Alice fainted.

CHAPTER TWENTY-FIVE

McNamara watched Thompson through the window of the interrogation room. He seemed sure on him. He was sure he was brought for the crimes in Nightingale Street. It was clear he wasn't related directly to them. However, there was a connection. If he hadn't been in the middle, the girls hadn't learnt the blackmail tactic from him and they hadn't paid for that.

"We'll leave him a little, even an hour or two. He'll lose some of his self-confidence" he said, knowing very well how the people brought for interrogation reacted.

McNamara left Mike watching Thompson and went in his office. He had to look through the papers on his desk. He had got the reports on the things found in that basement that morning. He still had to wait for some details, but he could be sure that when he'd catch the killer, he wouldn't escape. There was enough incriminating proof, but the most important was that they could make the DNA analysis and no one could deny this one.

The chief-inspector left the papers on the desk and went to the window. He had an attractive view, in its way. He could see a piece of the little park around the corner from the police station. Not many people would pass by there at the hour. It was even deserted. Afternoons were quite peaceful in that area, not like in the opposite side, where, two streets away, there was the heaven of the underground world, of the pimps and prostitutes.

A young woman with gold-blond hair crossed the alley of the park in his view and sat on a bench. She remained still with her hands in her leap. Suddenly, she reminded him of another girl, but red-blond-haired. He liked her apparent calm as well as hot fury. He could admit it now, when he was alone. He wouldn't have said it before his people or the girl; especially the girl. He'd have shown weakness. He disliked being seen as a weak man.

Along his life, he saw how feelings could make people get weak. He'd seen enough people who were only petty excuses of empty shells. He hadn't let that happen to him so far, and now, almost forty, he didn't think it was any more time to do it.

However, and it was a big however, it was something in that girl, something expressing trust, stability but also need, even if she hadn't ever admitted. It was something inside her that made you hold out to her and ask her to accompany you further. However, obviously, that might have been only an illusion, consequence of the previous night. Then, in a certain moment, she seemed too vulnerable, small and hurt. He made him want to hold her, to tell her he was there and she shouldn't have been afraid anymore.

But he couldn't do it. He couldn't do it now, and he wouldn't be able to do it ever. Maybe he'd offered her his friendship in the end, and if she took it, then it was Ok... If not, it was ok too.

It wasn't a big loss—even if something, behind his mind, told him, he was lying to himself, that it was a loss, even a big loss. It was true, he had never had but temporary relations. He took care of breaking any relation before women developed the feeling that the relation might have got serious. It was good for him, at least so far.

"It would be good now, too," he said leaving the window. He sat at his work desk again and started to browse the papers, trying to find a line. However, he was too absent-minded. He couldn't focus only on the case. He needed something, but he couldn't specify what. Maybe it was the need to sleep an entire night again and spend some time in the office, instead of running here and there...

Hardly had he finished his thought that James got into the room:

"I think it's time, boss, he lost his temper. He started making scandal downstairs".

"Then, let's go, James," said McNamara, glad he could get rid of his own thoughts. He expected that, though. He didn't like the way his thoughts were going. After a while, God knows what conclusion he'd reached. He'd better not let himself in their way. He should keep his mind busy with something else.

Getting downstairs, he looked through the unidirectional window at Thompson, who lost his temper. There was panic on his face and fear in his eyes. He already doubted his businesses were known. Otherwise, they wouldn't keep him here. He wondered if he hadn't better call for a lawyer. The problem was he didn't have any. He'd never thought he'd need one. He was so self-confident that he'd never seen himself in such a situation. Moreover, his businesses weren't related to legal world to make a lawyer necessary.

Now he was sure Patsy was one of the girls found that morning. Otherwise, he couldn't explain himself how they'd got to him. No one he had blackmailed threatened him or seemed unwilling to pay. The truth was that it was worth paying for a certain kind of pleasure.

He was afraid that someone was looking at him from the other side of the wall on his right. He tried to compose himself a face of a self-controlled person but he didn't manage. He was thinking it was useless after he lost his temper so seamlessly a little earlier. He effectively panicked. Claustrophobia was to blame.

McNamara and James's getting into interrupted his thoughts. He tried to smile to them like a decent person and he didn't realise that his lips made only a grimace.

"May I know why I've been brought here?"

"Don't you really know?" asked McNamara sitting before him, while James sat on his left.

The same time, Mike remained beyond the window, as McNamara told him, to survey the evolution of the interview.

"No, I don't know," said Thompson watching him with cunning eyes, trying to find out how much the police knew. He couldn't be sure of anything.

McNamara didn't answer or watched him. He prepared the tape recorder to tape the interview, as everything should be on the book. He turned it on and said the date and hour for the record and then turned to Thompson:

"We'll record the interview with Daniel Thompson. Sir," he added, "you must know you don't have to speak. If you want that your counsellor or a counsellor appointed by the court be present to this interview, you are entitled to that. If you refuse to benefit from this right, you must know that everything you say may be used against you before the court".

Thompson thought a few moments if he should ask a barrister appointed by the court, but he thought that one couldn't be smarter than he, so he refused.

"All right, then", said McNamara, "can you tell us what you know about Diane McWilliams, Patsy Porter and Anna McDower?"

That moment, Thompson realised they knew a lot, if they knew about the relation of the three girls with him. However, he decided to answer evasively:

“I’m not sure, but I think I met Patsy in town once, by accident, you know. I was coming from a client and she was with some friends and introduced them to me. I can’t be sure, but I think I heard these names too”.

“So, there is no other connection between you and them, is there?” asked McNamara.

“Of course,” tried Thompson to smile. “How could I be related to them?”

“For instance, to pay them the rent for the flat,” attacked McNamara in force, opening the file he’d brought with him and put before him on the table.

Instantly, the two policemen could see big drops of sweat on Thompson’s forehead. This one bent, but still tried to deny:

“I? I didn’t rent any flat for anyone! Where, for God’s sake, could I have the money? Everything I earn I bring home. With the late penalties, I can’t say I brought too much at home. Businesses don’t go well,” he tried to explain his incompetence and disinterest for his job.

‘Then, how would you explain these lease contracts?” asked McNamara taking up a few pages from the file to show to him. “It isn’t about only one and it isn’t about cheap leases, though. Flats are situated in good areas and have facilities. However, you didn’t pay for them from your wage. Even if you had kept working, and you hadn’t done everything wrong at work, you couldn’t have paid for them. So, you have another source of revenue,” concluded McNamara.

"Where should I have another revenue source?" yelled Thompson, losing his temper. "Do you really think you can make so much money even if you take two jobs?"

"Of course not," smiled McNamara understandable. "But when you have your own business and other people work for you, you can".

Suddenly, Thompson thought he lost the game. However, he decided not to lose it so easily. Therefore, he said:

"I don't want to answer any question now. Here the interview ends," he knocked decisively with his fist in the table.

McNamara turned off the tape recorder and said:

"Pity, you could have exonerated yourselves of murder. If you don't want, it's your business. However, we can solve the case easy. Everything points to you".

He turned and left leaving Thompson at the table. This one was turning white while he understood the implications of his words. However, he couldn't say a word, although he'd have wanted to yell after him. As McNamara had thought, Thompson was a jerk, a coward that couldn't stand the consequences of his deeds.

Chapter Twenty-Six

"Bryony, it's quite late and I'd like to go to my place," said Mrs Stevens coming in the door of the kitchen, interrupting her thoughts.

"You can't," jumped the girl from her chair. "Only when the policeman that will stay with you comes, what are you saying, sir?" she asked the policeman who had remained silent when he heard the decided tone of the old woman.

"I'm sorry, my dear," said the woman with determination, leaving no chance to the policeman to answer, "But I can't stay one moment more. I want to go at home, among my things. You're a nice girl, but I don't like to stay at my neighbours' too much, you know it. Moreover, if you want to know, I'm not afraid of that individual. I lock the doors and he can't do anything to me".

"However, I'm afraid he could, dear," answered Bryony calmly and decisively, gaining the complete respect of the young man who saw her facing the old lady all day long. "Therefore, if you really want to go, and believe me I understood you want to, you'll take him with you," she said pointing to the young policeman who got frozen for good. To stay with that crone for an entire evening wasn't too pleasant.

"What about you?" asked Mrs Stevens. "I don't even think to leave you with no guard. He has more against you than against me," she emphasized. "You are the one who hurt him literally and figuratively in his pride".

"I don't even discuss," said Bryony with determination. "You want to leave, you take him too."

The old woman thought for a while. She felt it was very selfish to take the guard with her and leave Bryony alone in anyone's hands. However, looking at the girl, she realised she wasn't an easy prey, for anyone, not even for McNamara who would watch her in that special way when he thought no one saw him.

"Ok," she accepted. "However, only if you promise me to be attentive and let no one inside as long you are alone, woman or man, whether you know the person or not. When the policeman's shift comes, you call this young man here to recognize the policeman and then you let him inside".

"All right, mom," smiled Bryony. "I'll do that. Now, go on, I see you can't wait anymore".

The old woman remained on spot undecided for a few moments, and then she told herself that nothing would happen to the girl and headed to the door. The policeman followed her with his heart crouched. He was afraid of what McNamara would say for not having listened to his order. He comforted himself thinking that at least he'd have stayed with one of them.

Bryony came back to her ledgers. She advanced a lot in her work, but she feared for what had happened to the bookshop that day. If she couldn't be there to check everything, she couldn't be sure that things were all right. After thinking for a while, she looked at her watch and saw it was a little time till the bookshop closed, and therefore, she decided to call. She was answered:

"Bryony's bookshop!" she heard a pleasant voice.

"Hallo, Meg, that's you?" she asked. "It's Bryony".

"What nice you've called! I've done a good job today, you must know, and everything is all right. I had enough clients and I cashed a lot. You won't be sorry you hired me," said the girl merrily.

Bryony smiled. The girl's young optimism was good for her. If she had to leave the lead to someone else, it was good she was there.

"I'm happy you have a good day, too," said Bryony, and her smile could be felt in her voice. "Was there anything that made you wonder?"

"Not really," answered Meg thoughtful. "Oh, yes, it was something, you know. A guy about fifty, solid and limping, bothered me a lot asking where you were, and when you were to come, things like that".

"Oh, Lord," cried Bryony in whose head a bell rang when she heard about limping. "What was he like?"

"I don't know too well," said Meg regretfully and reluctantly, "I couldn't watch him too well…he came when it was very crowded, you know. I told him he couldn't find you for a few days because you were sick… I did wrong?" she asked with a small voice.

"No, you didn't," Bryony reassured her. "Don't worry! However, if he comes back, pay attention to his face! Police would like to know what he looks like. But I don't think he will come back."

"Well, Bryony, I'll do that. What should I do after closing the shop?"

"You bring the money to the bank as I taught you and you deposit it. You keep the deposit note at you, and tomorrow you record it in the log from the left drawer, all right?"

"Ok, I got it. Shall I call you back?"

"No, you shouldn't. Call me tomorrow. Bye."

Meg thanked her once more time for the job and trust and hang off.

Bryony had just made herself some tea and toast, because she didn't feel like eating anything else, than the phone rang. She held out for the receiver and the same time she put some sugar in her tea.

"Yes," she said.

"Put Clarence on," thundered McNamara's voice in the receiver.

"He's not here," she said.

"What?" jumped McNamara from his chair like it was on fire. "Where the hell is he? I've assigned him to stay there with you."

"Yes, but Mrs Stevens didn't resist anymore and she had to go home, so I asked him to go with her."

"You, little stupid!" thundered McNamara's nervous voice and then he flung the receiver down.

Bryony scowled to the phone from which she could hear only the pulse, and then hung off saying: "Happy to hear you too!" She sat down calmly and started to drink her tea, browsing a magazine the same time. However, she couldn't focus too well. McNamara's way of talking kept bothering her. Actually, everything bothered her: everything that happened the previous night and that morning. It was something attractive in that man, but the same time, something made her wanting to not have anything to do with him. He proved himself being as changeable as weather and very hard to understand from the beginning. He had his way to hurt people and a certain way to make you feel safe and worriless in his presence.

Chapter Twenty-Seven

He was sitting in his car in a halt out of town. He was thinking. He looked for Bryony. She wasn't at the bookshop. It was sure she stayed at home. He knew exactly what she would do. He liked the woman and followed her. He'd liked her more than he liked the stupid bitches he took care of. He really wanted her and he thought that he'd have her in the end.

However, now, he had to get rid of her too. It was necessary if he wanted to keep his self-esteem. She hurt him badly and she had to pay for it. He couldn't stand anything from any woman. He got too much along his life. He'd been sick of being told what to do and to be shown his place all the time.

There was his mother at the beginning. She was nagging him all the time, preaching about the punishment he deserved for watching where he shouldn't or doing something, she didn't like. He had her on his head a too long time. She didn't die soon enough. She resisted drinking and shamelessness. She needed years to be knocked down for good. He didn't cry when she died. That day he was happy for the first time. He'd given rid of the tyrant of his life. Now he could take care of his own life. He'd left the village he lived in for twenty-seven years. He hoped to see the world, to feel it belonged to him that it was at his feet.

And it was like that for a little while. He didn't have too much money because he didn't have what to sell. They lived with a rent in a miser cottage, as his mother called it. Actually, it was a shed. She divided in two with plywood. So, that she had her space.

Therefore, he left only with his clothes on. He had to work on his way to London, a few days here, a few there. He chopped logs; he carried logs and dug gardens. However, he saved a little money and went to the capital.

He thought he'd do something for him, something big. He went to the evening school. He learnt and swotted in libraries. However, in the end, the same women made his money run out. He didn't know what they could do. Then, he learnt. He didn't know that if you didn't keep them in a leash in the way you should, they would mock on you and suck each penny from a man's pockets.

When he was left with nothing again, he thought of what he could do. He didn't have too many choices. Then, he decided to marry a woman with money, to get rid of the inhuman work. He was sick of work and miser houses and dragging his days. He wanted to find someone trustful to take care of him, wash and iron for him, and cook for him. In order to have someone that could care of him.

And he found! Yes, she really cares of him! He became a servant in his own house. Well, actually, hers. Nothing inside belongs to him. Sometimes he had the acute feeling he lived with his mother again. Only the smell of booze and of men, his mother used to bring in the house each night, was missing. Otherwise, everything was almost the same.

His wife didn't listen to him, as if he'd spoken to himself. She didn't care at all of what he said, as if he hadn't had a brain to think, even though he'd gone to school and learnt more than she had. She was only to high school. He also went to college in the evening. He'd got a diploma for God's sake!

Nevertheless, it was like he didn't even exist in the house. Everything was and happened only in her way. She knew better what to say and do. She knew where each thing should stay and when to work. However, he had to work all the time. He had enough on his head with his wife and the house that suffocated him. Sometimes he felt he had no air inside.

Then, those stupid girls came to ask him money. As if he had more money to give them or the amounts they'd wanted. He paid for the fun they gave him; it was right. That was understandable. However, he hadn't thought he should have paid for something else too: such things hadn't come into discussion. However, all his money was gone. Only the common money with his wife remained. And he couldn't touch it. The crone had seen.

But he paid them in the end. He paid them all! It was so easy. He picked them up one by one. They came to the cage willingly. Well, actually, he had to lie to them, and ask each of them to lie. But they lied. They hoped to get out in one piece. They didn't realise, the stupid girls, he couldn't let them go. He solved things with them out, with all three. He had fun for a few days, too, he thought feeling euphoric. He'd liked he still had them in his hand for a while. But it wasn't possible.

And now, that woman had to spoil everything. She had a nice face, but he wouldn't forget her. He couldn't. She didn't know who she was messing with. She didn't realise who he was, it was sure, because, otherwise, police would have arrested him that morning. But she'd still pay. She had to pay because she hurt him.

He'll wait a few days more, maybe two or three days. To let police think he gave up. Then he'll make the move. It was a pity he lost his safe nest. He could have kept her there for a while and have fun. He'd have enjoyed it. It was fun with those kids, but with her, it had been spectacular. Well, now he had to give it up. He'd kill her and then, he'd take care of that old crone, although, he was afraid, he'd do something good for her. He'd spare her any future pains and, in compensation, he'd make her suffer now. When she had to leave that world, she must know he can't be duped or ordered, as she thought. He heard her. He heard her saying he was a doggy in the leash.

He couldn't let such words passing by. Not now, when he discovered his power. At the beginning, he thought he was killing the girls not to ruin his marriage. But afterwards, he realised the powers he got. He realised he didn't need his marriage. He could do whatever he wanted. He had proven his manhood, and so many times, he thought, his eyes sparked thinking of that.

Unfortunately, he couldn't give up his servitude because he had to respect the appearances and come back home for some time, but only for some time.

Chapter Twenty-Eight

She heard the furious knocks on the door and her heart jumped from her chest. She was afraid to go and open it, but, as the knocking on the door didn't seem to stop, she dashed there angrily. Through the sight on the door, she saw McNamara, who started yelling that moment:

"Open the door, at once, Bryony! I saw you looked through the sight. I know you're there."

"Only if you calm down," she said with determination. "I don't feel I can stand a mass of nerves like yours just now. Consider I'm not in my best mood," she added quarrelsome.

"I've calmed down," he said quieter. "Now open the damn door".

Bryony sighed but opened the door. She thought smiling that McNamara wasn't included in Mrs Stevens's indications; she was sure about that.

When she opened the door, McNamara gushed inside nervously.

"Are you alone?" he asked.

"Of course, I am," replied the girl. "Who should I be with?"

“I don’t know, but I don’t see what other reason you had to let me knock like a fool on the door, with the entire street watching me”.

“I’m sure it’s not about the entire street,” she said fast and took her head out. “It’s only Mary Reid and Mrs Randall, that’s all. You exaggerate, McNamara and it doesn’t suit you, really,” she said closing the door.

McNamara looked at her frowning and then followed her to the kitchen, where, apparently, the girl set up her operations.

“I wonder why Alice Thompson hasn’t come out. You were doing enough noise,” she said amused and thoughtful the same time. “She doesn’t have too much fun at home, and your shouts must have woken her up.”

“You have no right to laugh at me. This is actually the thanks I get for coming to see if you’re all right,” he said reproachfully.

“Sorry,” she murmured, almost remorsefully, although, actually, she was quite amused of McNamara’s gesture. She wouldn’t have expected that from a man like him. He might have sent someone knowing she was alone, but he wouldn’t have come himself, probably leaving his work unfinished. She could be sure he had enough to do.

“By the way,” he passed over her excuses as if they hadn’t been uttered, “you must know Alice Thompson was very busy today and probably she doesn’t feel like having any supplementary fun”.

"What do you mean?" asked Bryony fearing inside. She wouldn't have thought Alice was in danger, not for a second.

"Don't worry," he said, realising she was thinking of the worst variant. "It isn't about her being attacked or something like that. I wouldn't have done such jokes if something like that happened. I hope you are aware of that. Simply she had a search on the book. And I'm afraid it was very unpleasant," he added, a little ironically. "No one likes such things".

"Do you think Thompson did it? I'd wonder, you must know. He doesn't have the guts. He's just a Casanova. I don't see him able to assume such responsibility."

"You're wrong, you must know," said McNamara. "He's able of something more. I can't tell you now what's about because you're part of the investigation, but take my word for that".

"So, I'm a suspect!" was Bryony amazed, feeling she was getting angry. "Do you really think I hurt myself last night? May I know how could I have done it? I'm really curious."

"Don't be stupid!" exclaimed McNamara, suddenly annoyed again. "Of course I don't think you're guilty. When I said you're part of investigation I meant you're one of the victims".

"Oh, you reassured me," said Bryony ironically.

"Do you really have to be so acid all the time?"

"As long you behave as a man of the caves when you come in my house, yes. You've never come here without getting annoyed uselessly, being cynical or yell."

"I've always had reasons, you know it," he defended himself. "Every single time something happened".

"Not really," replied Bryony making tea without asking him what he'd like. She thought he could use some sleep. "That first day you had no reason to be nasty with me, and you were, you know it," she continued.

"And you can't pass over that, as I see," he said dryly.

The girl turned back and looked at him. After a while she said:

"Oh, yes, I can. If I couldn't, I wouldn't have behaved nicely with you, as I behave now, by the way," she said smiling, turning back to the cooker.

Behind her, McNamara scowled. She hurt him. He knew the girl was right, though. Actually, she always behaved nicely with him, he had to admit it, despite what he said or did. He couldn't say anything to change what was before.

"By the way," she said turning her head to him, "I've made you some tea, not coffee. I think you want to sleep at night after the agitation you've had lately".

"No problem, I'll manage," he said evasively. "By the way, if you want, I can stay this night with you again, instead of the assigned policeman".

Bryony turned and looked at him attentively for a few moments. She didn't know what to think of his proposition.

"Don't watch me like that," he reacted defensively. "I haven't proposed you to be my lover, and I have no such intention, I hope you are aware. I meant I already came here and I don't think it's of any use that another policeman made the way here. Besides, no one expects me at home. I have no family or animals to miss me," he continued, then stopped suddenly realising he said too much of him. "However," he said to fix the situation somehow, and not to give her any ideas, "I can sleep anywhere. So, I can try your guest room once more. It's quite comfortable," he said slightly, smiling, as if he wanted to show her he was taking things the way they came.

Bryony still didn't say a thing but kept looking at him. After a while, McNamara, sick of waiting for an answer that didn't seem to come, changed his decision and said:

"Ok, I've got the message. After I drink my tea, I leave. By then, your guard will have come. I understand you prefer someone else at night with you her, not me".

"No," she said quickly, even too quickly. McNamara was also surprised. He didn't expect such a vehement answer. "You'd better call to the station and tell the one who was to come that he shouldn't", she continued. "I prefer you. However, I've run into you before and I know what to expect," she said playfully, as if she wanted to make her decision sound unimportant. "Who knows how it will be with another one".

The man watched her for a few moments trying to understand the stars in her eyes, but then, he gave up to bother. He'd better take things as they were. He couldn't figure out too much of her thoughts because the woman knew to hide them quite well.

As if she guessed what was going on behind his eyes, which were already grey now, she thought he'd better not know anything of her thoughts. Going to the fridge to see what was inside, she thought it wasn't good, and she was sure of that, to let him understand her preference for him. She opened the fridge, watched inside and then said:

"If you want, I can make you bacon and eggs and cheese. I'm afraid I don't have anything else here, and I can't see you eating toast like me. I'm sure you're very hungry", she said, thinking that if what she read in crime stories it was true, then the man had been hungry all day long, although she saw him getting into the Browns' pub at noon. He's stayed there enough, so she thought he had lunch, at least.

"Yes," he said, taking his phone off his pocket. "I'm really hungry. I haven't have time to eat since lunch. So, if you can make me a huge helping, it'd be fine", he said a little begging. "I'm going outside to call to the station, all right?"

"Yes, I know, I'm not allowed to hear how the investigation's going," said Bryony ironically, making McNamara frowning again. "You know, you look good when you frown. If you really don't want me to fall for you,

I advise you give it up," she said, almost bursting into laughter.

The first moment, McNamara stopped and wanted to reply her acidly, but then he thought he'd better leave her with no answer. She seemed too sure on him. She was sure she'd make him burst again. He didn't want to offer her this satisfaction. No, he didn't want it at all and, so, after a few moments of hesitation, he went out of the kitchen.

Behind him, Bryony's smile bloomed more. However, she didn't expect he'd leave with no reply. "Well, people are wrong now and then, that's it," she told herself.

Chapter Twenty-Nine

Alice Thompson remained standing in the middle of the house after the police left. She was dizzy and her head hurt badly. She couldn't believe such a thing could happen in her house. She couldn't believe Daniel was in the arrest of the police that moment, either.

She looked around bitterly. Her tidy house looked as if disorder had been reigning there since ever. She couldn't believe her eyes. Almost mechanically, she started putting things back.

She had no hope left that things could be better one day. From now on, they could be only worse.

She thought of what police found in Daniel's desk. She knew there were only documents he was working on Sundays. But there were other accounting logs. When she heard what Daniel was doing, she thought she couldn't ever breathe again. It would have been better than this shame... Anything would have been better.

She didn't know how she could be so blind. She had the feeling the police laughed at her when they realised she knew nothing about her husband's businesses. Her husband! What a good joke, she told herself with pain and bitter irony. Tears started running on her cheeks again. Oh, Lord, she thought she had a good marriage. She'd done everything for that, she was sure.

Suddenly, she thought of Mary, her neighbour. Oh, God, what satisfaction, the bitch should have now. Mary hadn't made a gesture for her husband and had everything, while she, having worked so much, was left with nothing. She'd been the exemplary wife, damn it, she was sure of that! But that bastard of husband of hers hadn't cared a bit.

She could see Mary coming ironically and mock of her. She would laugh and ask her what she'd be left with after putting that jerk of Daniel on first plan! Hardly had she finished her thought, than she heard the bell. She made a grimace of pain because her head turned at the noise.

First, she thought not to open the door to anyone, and then she imagined police breaking the door, and with heavy steps, she went to open. There was Mary in front of the door. For one moment, she had the wish to scratch her face but she wasn't able to do anything. Her thoughts were yelling in her head wanting to go out.

Mary took her around her shoulders and led her to the kitchen, closing the door behind her.

"Come on, I'll make you tea, and everything will be all right then. I'll help you," she said looking at the rummaged house, "and you won't even notice when everything is in its place. Damn police! They left a disaster behind!"

Alice watched her stupidly, but she couldn't say anything. She left herself led as if she had been a puppet. She couldn't fight. She didn't have any strength left and, moreover, she couldn't believe her eyes. Mary wanted to help her cleaning.

Mary made her sit on a stool in the kitchen, and went to make tea. She felt an immense compassion for the poor woman. The house she'd been so proud of was looking terrible. Things were taken out everywhere. Even in the kitchen, there was a disaster. Fools! They could have imagined they'd find nothing here. This was Alice's reign to be sure. If Daniel had had something to hide, and probably he had—otherwise police hadn't come—he wouldn't have hidden in the kitchen. Here Alice new each thing.

After a few minutes, she put a cup of strong tea before Alice.

"If it's too strong, I'm sorry," said Mary apologizing. "I've never been too good at that. But it's good for you. I'm sure. You'll grow stronger and help me around here. It's not nice of me, I know, but I'm not good at cleaning up, either."

Alice expected she started making ironic remarks and mocking of her. But Mary didn't do anything of that.

"All right," said Mary, seeing that Alice drank half of her cup of tea. "We'll start over here. Where should these be?"

Alice showed her with a trembling finger. Mary started working and in a few minutes arranged Alice's dishes showing efficiency and rapidity. Mary seemed to know to clean up, actually.

While Alice drank two other cups of tea, watching Mary confused all the time, the woman cleaned her kitchen, and suddenly, everything seemed to get back to normal.

Then, she had the strength to stand up and accompany her neighbour in the other rooms of the house. With more effort from Mary and less from Alice, in a few hours, everything was in the right place and nothing remained in sight from what had happened earlier.

Alice recovered quite well, but her bitterness increased. Her hate for Daniel that was born that afternoon increased too. She was feeling like a kettle under pressure.

"Alice I don't want to hear a refusal. I've talked to Michael and decided you eat with us tonight. I know it's over dinnertime but I don't care".

Alice tried to make a gesture of refusal, but she didn't finish, because Mary waved her hand before her eyes and said:

"I've told you I don't want to hear a thing. You must know that during all the time I was here Michael prepared dinner. He cooked especially for you, so you can't refuse."

Alice looked her in complete amazement. She couldn't believe that help came from where she'd expected less. She wouldn't have thought that Mary, who'd have done nothing in her home, would come to clean her house or that Michael, inconceivably for her, would cook, only to make her feel better.

She accepted and went out with Mary, closing the door behind, feeling that she was closing the door over an unpleasant chapter of her life for good. Actually, she didn't even know how her life was going to be from that moment on. Everything was too unclear, but she was sure her life with Daniel ended. It was of no use of thinking of that.

Chapter Thirty

McNamara was lying in bed, although he knew next day his trousers would look awful, but he was too tired after a night and a day when he was alert. He was staying with his hands under his head and kept thinking of his case but he couldn't manage to find a solution.

He knew the solution was somewhere there. He felt the answer was in a corner of his mind but he couldn't take it to the broad light yet. Everything was quite messy, maybe too messy.

Among all the suspects, he had, he couldn't eliminate at least one, maybe only Thompson. He certainly couldn't be in Bryony's house because he was already under the surveillance of the vice squad, and even if they lost him, and they didn't want to admit it, he wasn't hurt.

They kept him in interrogation quite long and if he had been hurt, he'd have shown it in a way or another. He didn't have enough character to resist.

Reid, on the other hand, couldn't be completely exonerated, although McNamara was almost convinced he was the kind of man sleeping with his wife in the same bed, and Mary could be considered anything but not stupid. If the man had been hurt, the woman would have seen at once that was something wrong with him and they'd have felt something when they talked to them even if Mary would have wanted to protect him. Although McNamara was positive, Mary wouldn't have been able to skip over so many crimes, even though she'd loved him enormously or not.

With Graham, though, it was another story and he knew they must arrest him the next day. Thompson gave them enough information to pick Graham. This one was deep in the combination. He was the one who supplied the girls to Thompson. Actually, he had the right place to find them: he picked them up directly from school; he didn't bother to look forward. Graham had tried to put Thompson in front, but only because he thought he was guilty for Patsy's death and he thought he was the next. This was the explanation for the fact the teacher hadn't stayed at home lately. He was afraid of Thompson, and Daniel Thompson had guessed that and got amused on his expenses. When he saw he couldn't get rid of the accusation of women traffic, he used the first occasion to betray him to the cops.

McNamara thought tomorrow they were going to interview Graham's girl-friend, to be sure she wasn't involved in this story, although he doubted the woman could be involved in this thing.

Actually, he didn't see Graham able of murder, but he didn't want to exclude him from the equation or at least not yet. There were enough people that didn't seem able to do it but they did it.

However, it was also Randall. He'd matched the profile, in deed, even if he didn't reveal anything from what he felt. Nevertheless, McNamara was sure it was impossible for the man not to have resentments towards women. McNamara knew that, generally, everyone dominated by someone, felt strongly their weakness in getting rid of the domination in a way or another. Randall seemed too calm not to have a torrent of resentments that should have burst out in the end, spiting out all the bitterness he accumulated along the time.

His situation was similar to Reid's only in Reid's case love could be easily replaced by hatred, thing that anyone knew. People knew why they said hatred and love were the two faces of the medal. When your heart is constantly stepped over, the same time with a man's pride, as in Reid's case, you can't keep your feelings for long. In the end, they melt and nothing nice remains. As much as he could see, Mary didn't do anything to keep his feelings intact, but she tried to make them vanish sooner. And Reid was the passionate kind of man and he couldn't bear too much.

McNamara gave up thinking of the people involved. He was too tired and had too many unpleasant surprises and he had to think of a lot of things and he couldn't go on. He was sick of everyone and wanted only a moment of peace.

He needed to sleep badly, so he closed his eyes and let himself fall asleep.

Exactly when he felt sleep caught him, he heard, vaguely, as from far, that a door opened and then he heard someone sneaking on the corridor. Suddenly, he became alert and sleep fell apart. He got out of the bed quickly and making no noise, tried to watch through the door, he left open. However, because of the darkness in the corridor, he perceived only a silhouette heading sneaking towards the stairs. McNamara managed only to see that the height of the person wasn't the alleged one of the attacker, if Bryony wasn't wrong. It was someone short.

As he didn't want to risk at all, he jumped on the silhouette and, profiting from the surprise of the attack, he immobilized the person, holding tight, and this one only groaned. However, he felt at once that his fingers touched the curve of the breasts of a woman and he guessed that only Bryony could be. He couldn't refrain himself to rub his fingers on the bulge he felt, but he tried to leave the impression his gesture was only an accident. Under his palm, he felt woman's heart beating scared, almost breaking her chest and jumping in his palm.

Bryony felt his smell, which was almost familiar to her, and after the first moment of fright and surprise, she said with a slightly throttled voice:

"Now, what you want to do? Finish what the killer didn't do last night? Let me go, idiot", she snapped.

"Calm, calm," he said softly, leaving her suddenly because he had the feeling that her hoarse voice made its way under his skin awaking all his nerves. "I couldn't know it was you," he replied slightly nervously, upset because he reacted so strongly to her voice, but more upset with himself because he couldn't control himself better. "What the hell are you doing here at this hour? Why don't you sleep?" he snapped turning her to him, with no kindness. "Why don't you sleep?" he repeated, looking directly in her eyes he guessed in the darkness. "It must be after two already!"

"I can't," she replied defensively watching him at her turn. "Sincerely, I'm afraid to close the eyes. I keep seeing the scene from last night, and believe me it isn't something you remind with pleasure," she answered sourly.

"Why? Don't tell me you're afraid he's coming back! You know I'm here for that, and, as you've just felt on your own skin, I react quite promptly," he said ironically.

"Yes, I saw, thank you," she replied dryly, and then paused. "But it's not only that," she added reluctantly, bending her head to hide her look. She couldn't look in his eyes, and, as both of them had already got used to dark, they could see each other quite well.

"What?" he asked, after a few moments, a little irritated, seeing her hesitation.

Bryony didn't answer anything and thanked providence that it was dark enough that he couldn't see her blushing.

McNamara lost his temper and lifted her chin, watched her attentively. He watched her for a few moments and then snapped:

"Come on, say it! What's about?"

"Oh, God, how easily you can get angry, McNamara. You're trigger-happy!" noticed Bryony, trying to smile shyly, although she felt relieved to see him, as he was earlier.

"Ok, then," he said, "if you can make jokes, and you have nothing serious to say, you'd better go back to sleep and think of nothing," he said menacingly. "Remember I'm in your guest room and nothing could happen to you this night," he added, leading her in a hurry to her room.

When they got before the door, the young woman stopped and didn't want to come in. She held out trembling slightly, and put her hand on his arm.

"What's now?" he snapped, wanting to hide the compassion, he felt in the moment of her touch, but he didn't manage to do anything else but make her start. He felt her start, and catch her hand, and caressed her arm softly to calm her down.

She seized his wrist with her fingers tightly, as if she didn't want to release him anymore. Frustrated because he couldn't see each expression of her face, he pushed the door with his shoulder and pulled her inside, and then pushed the breaker on the left of the door. The strong light made both of them wink, hurting their eyes, too much used to darkness. McNamara searched her face and was surprised and even hurt to see fear in her eyes.

"Don't tell me you're afraid of me," he said quickly leaving her hand quickly as well.

He seemed ready to quarrel with her for such a foolish thing, but that moment she vehemently denied such a presumption, shaking her had, and then said reluctantly:

"What would you say if... I asked you to stay with me this night?"

"But I'm with you, aren't I?" he said and Bryony could feel exasperation in his voice.

"I mean, here, in this room," she specified and blushed again.

Bryony was aware that her proposition was too bold and interpretable and she feared he'd reject it at once.

"Only to stay, that's all," she said quickly, to chase any thought that could come off in his mind.

"With you? Do you mean, with you in bed?" he said amazed and intrigued the same time, because she did such an invitation.

He wouldn't have thought of that. He wouldn't have thought for a moment he could get in her bed, when he came to stay with her.

"Yes," she repeated, "but only to stay," she emphasized the last words. "Nothing more... Maybe you could hold me," she added, and then continued in her mind: "So that I won't feel so lonely and unsure of what happens to me.

So that I feel a little tenderness and feel these strong arms around me."

"Why?" asked McNamara interrupting her thoughts, and looking impatiently for an answer in her eyes.

"Because," she replied determined, letting him understand clearly that this was a conversation, they couldn't have, and he should take things as they were, nothing more.

They watched each other in silence for a while, each of them trying to guess the other one's thoughts. Then, McNamara, as if he understood her wish, told her, unexpectedly kindly:

"Ok, then! Get into bed and I'll come at once. I'm going only to take my things from the other room, and I'll come to you".

She smiled shyly, and after thanking him squeezing his arms slightly, she ran to bed, like a child having got the toy it wanted.

The man expected to see she was under the blanket. When she saw her breasts moving under the pyjamas blouse, he passed his hand through his thick and rough hair, wondering fiercely what he got into this time. Somehow rigidly because of the trousers getting suddenly too tight, he turned and went to take his things from the other room.

After only a few minutes, he came back with his coat and mobile phone in his hand. She could see on his face he made a real effort to relax his tense muscles in his face and back, although his eyes still kept a metallic spark.

Silently, he put his coat on the chair in front of the toilet table and his phone on the night table. He surprised her in the mirror, watching his movements. He could perceive a slight fear in her eyes and he wondered if she thought he'd jump on her now, as his instinct, quite awake now, was demanding.

She watched him carefully wondering what the man actually thought of her proposition. She didn't have any experience with men and always watched out not to have a relation till the point when they should share the bed.

McNamara lay on the blanket next to her and looked her intensely, as if he wanted to guess her thoughts. She glanced back, although with some restraint, and then she asked him, somehow whispering, in a thick voice, having a strong effect on him, making chills run on his skin:

"Why don't you get into the bed in the right way, under the blanket? Nothing will happen to you, I promise," she tried saying ironically.

"It's not that," he replied annoyed. "I only can't. However, my trousers will look awful tomorrow," he also said pointing to the trousers of the suit, which had already been rumpled.

"Oh, God! I haven't thought of that at all," she said regretfully. "Don't move," she said jumping from the bed and going out of the room so fast under his amazed eyes that McNamara couldn't react at all because of the surprise.

Bryony came back after a few minutes only, fetching training trousers and a t-shirt. She found McNamara at the door, ready to come after her and bring her back in the bed. The woman burst into laughter seeing his usual wrinkle between his eyebrows, betraying his nervousness, but it fitted him so well, giving him a specific charm.

"Here you are," she said, calming down, seeing he was ready to burst out and snubbing on her. "These belonged to my aunt", she said putting the clothes in his hands. "She was almost as big as you," she added smiling, hoping to make the wrinkle between his eyebrows disappear. "I'm sorry I haven't thought earlier you couldn't sleep in your outfit. I'm getting into the bed and cover my head with the blanket so that you could get dressed here".

She left him with the clothes in his arms and ran to bed, and he followed her by sight saying nothing. However, he couldn't stop noticing the simple blue cotton pyjamas suited her, and was waving on her shapes, caressing them and making him imagine how it would have felt if his hands were the ones touching her skin.

He chased the thought away and waited for her to get under the blanket and then he undressed quickly and put the sports trousers on, glad they fitted. He tried to put the t-shirt on, but he felt it broke and gave up. Apparently, Bryony's aunt didn't have her shoulders as broad as his.

Then, he turned the light off and got into bed next to her and held her, as she asked him earlier. Bryony crouched next to him, however not very close, but after a short hesitation, she put her arms around him and got a little closer.

He found her hesitation amusing and the man smiled ironically, although she couldn't see his smile in the dark. The obvious contradiction between her earlier boldness, when she asked him to stay with her, and her present shyness, when they shared the same bed, amused him mostly.

He brought her tight against him and put her head on his shoulder to be as comfortable as possible. Feeling his arms holding her tightly, Bryony sighed softly and closed her eyes, satisfied that she felt really safe now. His smell teased her nose and overwhelmed her gradually, making her feel good and protected. After a few moments, she fell asleep, close to him.

In her sleep, unconsciously, she got closer, and her half open mouth was caressing his chest, and her hot breath made his skin shiver. His sleep went away for good. He felt his arms too full, and sensations teased him.

He'd never slept with a woman, and especially he'd never slept holding one. He always watched out the intimacy of such a gesture, because he was sure that thing would bring false assurance and a certain kind of commitment he couldn't make now. He always felt that keeping distance was sure, but now he couldn't find the point anymore. He knew he'd feel like a jerk next day, if he let the woman go and he got back to his place, far from her. However, he felt something pleasant teasing his heart and his man's pride, thinking that Bryony was so quiet in his arms, showing trust letting herself in his arms with no way out.

Although he felt too alive holding her, in the end, he yield before tension and tiredness his body felt. He also fell asleep, smiling, without realising it was the first time he'd been sleeping with a smile on his lips for a long time, actually since he broke up with childhood.

Chapter Thirty-One

Sunrays got through the window and teased his eyelids playfully. Then, he opened his eyes slightly and breathed deeply. That moment, the smell of the woman next to him overwhelmed his senses and made him look down to her, trying to lean on his elbow the same time, to see her better.

His move, even it was slight, woke her up. Her eyelids discovered her eyes looking at him directly full of amazement seeing the pure green of his iris bright in the light of the morning sun. Her lips moved, as if she wanted to talk, but no sound came out.

That moment, desire caught McNamara tight like a fist. Her face and mouth were too tempting. Her lips, half opened, seemed to utter a mute invitation, and he, not completely awake, deaf to the sound of the warning bell in his mind, bent and touched her lips that trembled almost imperceptibly and opened more. A soft sigh came from her throat and made him get tensed as a spring. Control slipped from him and he, almost brutally, took her mouth entirely, making his kiss deeper and deeper.

With a sudden movement, her hand raised and caught his neck pulling him to her. Then, he dragged her closer and became more possessive and inciting the same time, teasing her with his passion. His kiss was strong and gave as much as it asked, and he asked even insistently.

Something in her mind told her his kiss became quite dangerous, but she couldn't let go, and, she admitted to herself, she didn't want that.

McNamara abandoned her lips and his mouth caressed her neck, which arched in complete abandon before his mouth. His teeth scratched her skin sending lots of signals that made her tremble and hold him stronger.

The moment McNamara opened her blouse, the bell at the door rang, and made them both start. They watched each other for a few moments. They both wanted to ignore the bell, but it came more insistent.

"Damn it!" snapped McNamara, cursing then so badly that she made a grimace. "I'll kill whoever is at the door," he jumped out of bed nervously to go downstairs to the front door and see who was ringing so instantly.

Bryony smiled for a moment and stretched, still feeling the warm he spread in her body. Then, recalling the last moments, and finally perceiving the acute fury in McNamara's voice, she jumped out of the bed and ran after him, fearing what he could do. She caught up with him when he was opening the door and was saying angrily:

"And what the hell you might want?"

In front of the door, there was Mrs Stevens, whose lips got as tight as her look that became very severe and accusing.

Watching Bryony's face, who had violently blushed, ashamed of having been caught like this, Mrs Stevens had a pretty image of what had happened before her arrival. Bryony's lips were swollen and wet and looked as if they were kissed well, and on her neck, there was a red irritation because of McNamara's beard. Mrs Stevens watched meaningfully the opened blouse Bryony forgot to close, and the girl, with a sudden start, buttoned it at once.

Behind Mrs Stevens, there was the policeman assigned to guard her the night before. This one remained still and didn't dare to say anything because he knew his boss quite well and he knew he shouldn't talk when he was angry, and now he was angrier than ever before.

Until Mrs Stevens could find her words to express her thoughts, McNamara said to the policeman:

"Well! You can leave now. We'll talk later, and you'll draw the report only tonight. Now go and sleep".

The policeman thanked him and disappeared at once

After he saw the policeman had left, McNamara looked at the old woman and realised she was on the verge of saying some tough words he wouldn't have liked. He didn't let her speak, and, stepping aside, he said quickly:

"Come in, Mrs Stevens. I don't think you want the entire street hear you".

His voice was too calm, in opposition to his harsh look, and the opposition didn't predict anything good. The woman felt the toughness hidden behind his apparent calm and came in but she thundered both of them with her look, the man and the woman that was two steps behind him, to make them understand her firm opinion.

McNamara closed the door behind her and looked at her completely indifferently. He didn't care whether she thought he had slept with Bryony.

Bryony, instead, had blushed to the top of her ears under the old woman's accusing look, and she wasn't aware that her cheeks made her neighbour go too far with her imagination.

Bryony realised that her request that McNamara would sleep with her and especially hold her was completely inappropriate. She didn't even want to recall his kiss, because every time she thought of that, she felt her stomach crouch and she knew she would blush even more, leaving Mrs Stevens with the worse impression possible.

"Do you want to go in the kitchen and wait for us to get dressed?" McNamara asked the old woman apparently formally, but the firmness in his voice turned the invitation into order.

The woman wanted to reply to his rudeness, but watching into the tough eyes of the man she realised she had no choice but do what he had told her. She knew she shouldn't push things further or at least not then.

McNamara caught Bryony's hand firmly and pulled her after him up the stairs, but Bryony, who didn't like the situation at all, pulled her hand back angrily. She didn't manage to take it off his hand because McNamara had squeezed her hand stubbornly and unaware that she was hurt.

"Please, let me go," she whispered afraid that she might have been heard from downstairs, imagining Mrs Stevens coming after them as fast as she could and thinking a real scandal might arouse. However, her words were angry enough to make the man understand her opinion about his Neanderthal manners.

"No," replied McNamara briefly not giving her a chance to answer. "You come with me now. After you get dressed, you may go down to your neighbour. If you want my opinion, you shouldn't let her dominate you. She's got the impression she can run your life, woman! She looks at you reproachfully, and you already consider you've done something wrong and blush like a kid caught doing a naughty thing", he snapped, his fury smouldering in his voice.

Bryony felt his fury strongly, and she leaned against the wall, as if she wanted to protect herself. His green eyes were sparkling and seemed to burn her skin with the intensity of his rage. She watched him a few seconds with her big eyes without saying a word, and then she said:

"But I made a mistake, McNamara! I'm sure you think that too! I shouldn't have asked you sleep with me and hold me. I behaved like a slut" she said with despise.

"Not really!" he replied angrily. "Don't be stupid! Really! I didn't have this feeling for a second. You wanted to be with someone and that's it. I understood that, otherwise I wouldn't have come into your bed; you must know it. Damn it!" he hit the wall with his palm making her start. "Why do women have to complicate things always?" he snapped angrily.

"Well, that might be right for tonight," she found the courage to say. "But this morning?" she remind him reluctantly.

"I'm to blame for what happened this morning, if you want to blame someone. Tell the old crone I was guilty because I couldn't control myself. You did nothing," he said pulling her after him in the room.

She pulled back with her cheeks in flames and said:

"Oh yes, I did. I pulled you in my arms and answered to your kiss".

"Don't flatter yourself!" he interrupted her. "If you want to believe that, it's your business. However, I advise you not to tell it to her", he said pointing to the floor towards the kitchen. "She'll eat your soul up, and, as far I can see, you're stupid enough to let her do it".

"You know, if I let you kiss me, it doesn't mean I'm stupid!" she snapped angrily.

"I haven't said that and you know it! However, you must know I like doing it not talking about it," he said sardonically, and pulled her in his arms kissing her deeply not to let her continue the discussion.

After a few moments, he suddenly let her go, and he had to support her because she tottered. Laughing, he took his clothes and his mobile phone from the night table and went to the door. When he wanted to go out, he remained still and then turned to her and said ironically:

"By the way, if you don't know it, we're in the twenty-first century. Now, a man and a woman can kiss if they both want that. Actually, they can do more," he added and went out leaving her thinking of the implications of his words.

Bryony still stoned by his unpredictable kiss and because of his acid words, felt anger boiling in her blood. She felt like going mad because she allowed him had the last word, and frustrated, she tapped her foot nervously.

Chapter Thirty-Two

Bryony got into the kitchen and felt the hostility wave between Mrs Stevens and McNamara at once. Hostility hit her so strongly that she even moved back. For a moment, she wanted to turn back and ran into her room.

She grabbed all her courage and got into the kitchen avoiding artfully the reproachful looks of her neighbour. Instinctively, she went towards McNamara, who had already made coffee and poured it into cups. She had the vague feeling he was her only ally.

With no words, McNamara gave her a cup of hot and strong coffee, and then put one before Mrs Stevens, who was visibly smouldering of anger.

The old woman put sugar and milk in her coffee with sudden movements, and then wanted to drink some but she didn't resist and put the cup on the table so nervously that she spilled it. She said with authority, as if she had talked to two teenagers she found fooling around on the sofa:

"Could you tell me what you two had been doing this morning before I came?"

"No," answered McNamara briefly, thundering her with his look, and showing he wasn't afraid of her for one moment. "And I think I've already told you that. It's not your business, it's ours".

The old woman felt hurt and watched Bryony reproachfully. Bryony opened her mouth to say something, but McNamara turned to her, sure that the girl would try to explain herself somehow. The moment she felt his dark and rough looks on her, she said nothing, although she made a real effort to swallow her words. To have an excuse, she drank a little coffee and then went and sat down opposite to Mrs Stevens.

None of them said anything and drank their coffee silently. Then, McNamara looked at his watch and saw the policeman to guard them was about to come, so he asked Bryony to accompany him to the door because he had to go.

When he got to the front door, McNamara stopped and watched her a few moments and said:

"I hope you're not sorry. I, sincerely, don't regret anything... Maybe only that I was stopped too soon. Please, don't let that damn woman make you feel guilty. You shouldn't; believe me".

Bryony answered nothing, but kept looking at him with her big eyes, not letting him see what she was feeling or thinking, and that embarrassed him and decided he'd better go.

"A policeman will come to stay with you. His name's Mackie. We'll talk," he said and opened the door to go out.

Suddenly, he turned and pulled her to him. He kissed her insistently, and then opened her lips. He kissed her deeply and before letting her go, he bit her inferior lip softly. After letting her go, he looked closely at her and whispered somehow authoritatively:

"We'll speak later, I promise".

Then, he went out and closed the door behind, leaving her alone in the hall. Bryony remained there, completely still, and only after a few moments she turned back to the kitchen breathing deeply.

When she entered the kitchen, she saw that Mrs Stevens wanted to jump on her, and, for the first time in her life, she forgot of the elementary norms of politeness. She stopped her, raising her hand and saying harshly:

"I'm sorry for you, but, as McNamara said, it's only my business. That's it".

The old woman felt hurt, but her surprise at Bryony's reply was so strong, that she couldn't say a thing for a few seconds, even she was boiling with anger and couldn't accept to be left aside. Suddenly, she burst out, although her voice trembled because of the increased nervousness:

"I was your aunt's friend and adviser for twenty years, Bryony. She always respected my opinion. You know. I thought, you respected me too, but I think I was wrong," she said with tears in her eyes.

Bryony felt badly before the woman, but she held her position and, knowing McNamara was right and she shouldn't yield at all, she said:

"It is not like that, Mrs Stevens! You must understand that's normal that my private life remains private".

"Though, why don't you want to understand that this man could be here today and somewhere else tomorrow? Do you really believe he'll stay with you for good?" asked the woman, amazed of such a presumption from the young woman. "Girl," she shouted, "this happens only in movies, not in the real life!" she argued strongly, trying to make her see things clearer.

"I don't know where McNamara will be tomorrow, and sincerely, I don't care! He didn't promise me anything, if you are afraid of that. I know he was here last night, when I needed him, and this is enough for the moment," replied Bryony, pouring herself another cup of coffee with nervous gestures, these betraying her inner struggle.

Actually, she didn't want any more coffee, but she had to do something with her hands, to hide her nervousness.

The old woman didn't want to drop the discussion, though, and wanted to make her reason. Therefore, she told her exasperatedly:

"Really, girl, I don't understand why don't you find yourself a good boy to be with you all the time, help you with everything, with the bookshop...

"Because I'm not interested," Bryony interrupted her harshly, because she'd lost patience already. "Really, I don't want to talk about that, let's eat something. I'm hungry", she said wanting to end the conversation and went to the fridge, although she wasn't hungry at all.

***

One could see Mrs Stevens was really boiling. The policeman didn't know what to do to get rid of the tension in the air and he fidgeted pretending he was reading. The tension was tangible although the young woman seemed calm while she checked the bills and invoices a girl had brought her a quarter of an hour before.

After ten minutes of tormenting silence, the old woman said in a determined voice:

"We can't go on like that, Bryony," she tapped with her palm in the table and made Bryony and the policeman start. "We must talk. Necessarily. I must bring you with your feet on the ground".

"I'm sorry," said Bryony, leaving the documents for a few seconds. "I've already told you we don't have to talk on this subject, not now or ever. However, if you want to talk about something else, you're welcome".

That moment, the policeman wanted to stand up and leave the room, thinking that maybe they couldn't speak because of him, but Bryony stopped him with a gesture:

"You needn't leave, Mr Mackie. It's not about you. Simply, the matter Mrs Stevens wants to talk about, concerns only me," she said apologetically, watching Mrs Stevens. "Therefore, I don't want to talk about that, and really, I don't see why we should quarrel on this topic," she added, looking at the old woman, who had frowned hearing her words.

Mrs Stevens stood up from the bench decisively and said:

"Then, I'd better leave, if I'm not wanted here".

"You know it's not like that," Bryony stood up too. "You know you're always welcome here, but you only exaggerate now. There's nothing to talk about now, that's all. However, even if there is, I'm the one who should decide in that concerning me. I don't have to take all the advice given to me", answered Bryony trying to make up things.

Her words didn't have the effect she wanted over Mrs Stevens.

"Then I must really go," said the old woman upset and with no discussion further, she left limping to the door.

"If you really want to go, then you take the policeman with you. I manage by myself," replied Bryony convincingly, even if she wasn't so sure on her.

The old woman left the kitchen nodding shortly. The policeman went behind her, feeling desperate. He was thinking with horror of McNamara's reaction. He decided to call him as soon as he'd got to Mrs Stevens'.

Chapter Thirty-Three

The woman went to the basement to look for something to clean out the stains on boys' sheets. She was very upset because the boys had eaten in bed again, although she'd forbidden that. Obviously, they'd spilled the food.

Normally, the basement was her husband's domain and she'd have sent him to bring her what she needed, but he was still sleeping. She thought her man started to skip work lately. He'd got too lazy. She'd have had to wake him up and ask him to go in her place in the basement, as she used to do, she thought, shaking her head angrily. She wasn't one of the people who'd have accepted laziness in any circumstance.

She turned the light on and got down in the basement. She watched the shelves on the left, but she saw nothing there that she could have used. She looked at the other shelves and on the right corner a dark plastic bag attracted her attention. Something white with stains came out of it. Amazed to see such a thing in the basement she opened the bag.

She took out a sheet full of blood. There were clothes wrapped in the sheet and they had big and ugly blood stains. When she threw the clothes on the floor with disgust, a big hunting knife came out, and hit the floor with noise. Hearing the sound, she started seriously and then screamed but she covered her mouth with her hands, afraid of being heard.

Only then, she saw the shadow of the arm that came and grabbed her throat. Her scream died for good. Her husband was grabbing her and she was hardly breathing. She tried to get free, but she couldn't and he burst in laughter and then threw her to the floor strongly.

"Bitch!" shouted he. "You couldn't leave me this place untouched. I'm not allowed to have anything of mine, without your touch!" he yelled bitterly.

The woman watched him with frightened eyes. She couldn't utter a sound at least, and this was something new to her. Before, she could have talked for hours, without a break. She would always deliver moral lessons to anyone, who'd have listened to her. But not now. Her throat was hurting and fear suffocated her.

"You don't say anything now, do you? No problem, don't be afraid. However, you won't say anything from now on. I'm sick of you as everyone in this street. I want to have my life with no obligation of seeing you before my eyes," he said bending to take the knife from the floor.

He went to her decisively. The woman tried to stand up and run, but he stabbed her in her hand. She screamed and made a few steps with her heart struggling in her chest. Fear invaded her mind and she couldn't think of anything else but to break free no matter the price.

The knife stabbed again and knocked her down, killing her scream to come. Although she fell down, he stabbed her once more to be sure she wouldn't stand up again. He left the knife next to her and left the basement quietly, as if nothing had happened, and closed the door carefully behind him.

He went back in the kitchen and prepared himself some tea. He felt his heart light. Finally, he controlled his fate with no thorn in his soul. He was sure he'd escape from police easily because they weren't smart enough to catch him especially that lecherous inspector who was trying to pick the bitch of McNeil.

They deserved each other, he thought, grinning sardonically. She hadn't even watched him twice, the stupid bitch. She, probably, didn't know what she was losing, he laughed loudly.

But he could show her, couldn't he? He'd just seen that crone leaving McNeil's house, and the policeman left with her. Probably, the two women had a row.

Thinking of the free way, he made a decision. He'd drink his tea quietly and then go to her. He was sure the woman would be glad to see him even though she left the impression she wasn't interested in him. Actually, he had to defend his honour he'd lost the night McNeil hurt him with the scissors. He couldn't let a stupid woman defeat him.

Chapter Thirty-Four

McNamara got into detectives' office and everyone looked up to him. His face was far from pleasant that morning. He seemed even grumpier than usually, and his unshaved beard made him look tougher.

"Good morning, boss," dared Mike tell him, thinking things couldn't be so black. "It's good you've come. Your phone has been ringing for two hours. It's the big boss," he said pointing to the ceiling. "It seems important, but he wants to talk only to you."

"All right," said McNamara emphatically. "Anything new?"

"Jo went to the vices. They said they'd already picked all data, and therefore, they'd arrested Graham forty-five minutes ago, and brought his lover to interview too."

"Damn it!" exploded McNamara. "We should've arrested them, not they. Tell them to bring them here at once!"

'They can't, boss! It's order from up".

"How up?"

"McCullen, the big boss," said Mike regretfully, understanding frustration on McNamara's face.

"Why?"

"He didn't want to tell me. He said he'd speak to you. But you must know Jo went to the vices because of that. She charmed that guy there and made him let her to interview Graham. So, no worry, boss," he said playfully. "You know Jo. If there's something to find out, she's the best person to do it".

"At least that," said McNamara angrily. "Have you checked the others?"

"Of course, sir! We've almost finished. Just a little and we finish with all. You must know the Brown boys weren't in the area, that's sure. They couldn't be. The eldest one was in the campus during the entire period we're interested in, and the youngest had flights in the days of the murders and he did them".

"So, we've got rid of them. That's good! The others?"

"Reid has a usual past. His parents died after he'd got married. They had a car accident somewhere in Surrey. He inherited something but little. His wife got bigger heritage from an aunt of hers and that is why they afforded the house and the car. They gain well both of them so they don't have financial problems."

"Have you found anything to show he's our man?"

"No," said Mike reluctantly. "We haven't found anything like that. He might be but I think his wife should've known something if he were the killer".

"That makes two of us. Randall?"

"I've found out he had a bad situation in the past and he had to work a lot to get here. But, you know, his wife is with the money, not him. We haven't found out what he did yesterday. It seems more complicated," said Mike slightly frustrated.

"I see! Well, persevere! When James comes, send him to me," said McNamara going into his office.

***

The door was wide open. James wanted to knock but he changed his mind. His boss was too absorbed in his thoughts and he thought he'd better go. When he turned to leave, McNamara said:

"Come in, James, it's no problem."

"Anything happened, sir?"

"Unfortunately, yes," said McNamara leaving the window and sitting down at the desk, showing James to sit down. "McCullen called me. He seems very agitated because we arrested Thompson."

"Is he related to him?"

"No, not him personally. He didn't get in details, but evasively, he said his brother was one of Thompson's clients. Of course, he said it was only a minor mistake, he wasn't a constant client, but he didn't want his name appear in reports. You know the law for sexual relations with a girl under age".

"What did you say, sir?" asked James, without controlling his curiosity.

"I told him to speak with the Vices, because I don't think, and here I'm sincere, he's related to our crimes. He couldn't know of the empty house on Nightingale Street.

However, I'll ask Jo to check on him discretely. She knows to deal with delicate situations. If I sent Mike, he'd be able to go to McCullen with the entire cavalry after him".

"I'm afraid so, sir," said James smiling, knowing very well what his colleague could do. "The boy is as delicate as a herd of buffalos".

"Have you found anything else from Thompson?"

"No, and I don't think he knows anything about the crimes. He admitted his blackmails, and that he knew who was the girl on the Dobbs' lawn when he saw her. He's been stressed ever since, especially because three girls of his were missing, and among them his favourite. The other two friends of Patsy that didn't appear in the investigation are in Bath for a month with some clients. We've sent for them."

"And didn't he suspect anything when he saw his girls were missing?"

"Oh yes, but he didn't make a move. He was afraid."

"Ok, James. How's McKay?"

"She's recovered well, sir. I think they let her go next week".

"That's good, very good," said McNamara happy for both of them. "All right, James, see what you can find out and I'll read these reports and then we'll talk".

James went out to his colleague leaving McNamara with the reports.

***

"Boys, meeting! Everyone in my office, now," said McNamara in an authoritative voice, and then turned to his office.

In a few moments, all of them gathered in his office. Jo and Donna sat on the two chairs before McNamara's desk, and Mike, James and Mark stood.

"Well," said McNamara, "I saw that the two Brown boys can't be suspected, and Jo eliminated McCullen on the list. Now I want to hear your opinion on the others. Jo, you start!"

"In my opinion, sir, Thompson can't be the criminal and I'm sure of that. He didn't have a chance or motive," said Jo.

"In deed," interrupted Mike. "And if we think, the girls brought him a lot of money, even a lot. It's meaningless for him to kill them."

"And Reid?" asked McNamara.

"Reid seems to have only one objective, sir, to watch his wife, sir," said Jo maliciously.

"Yes," approved James. "He wouldn't have paid attention to Patsy or any other woman".

"Moreover, he didn't have a motive for the murder, I say," said Mark. "I've checked him well".

"Brown?" also asked McNamara.

"No, sir, it's not him," answered Mike. Brown's got only two interests: his wife and the pub. He wasn't related to the girls, excepting Patsy he knew because she lived on the same street. He can't be on the short list".

"Well," said McNamara. "Who checked Davidson?"

"I did, sir," answered Mike. "I've checked Davidson. In the period the two girls died, he wasn't in the area. I checked and know for sure he was in Leeds. And by the way, I also checked the women, as you told me, although we both know it's a waste of time," he added and McNamara thundered him with his eyes.

McNamara also realised he couldn't relate a woman to the murders, but he didn't like to leave anything uncovered. Therefore, he asked Mike to check them out.

"McNeil didn't have a motive, sir, or the necessary force to knock two girls down and tied them. She's a delicate woman," he added and stopped seeing McNamara's sharp look.

Mike suspected, as the others, that McNamara had fallen in for the girl, although no one of them thought it could be possible. McNamara was leaving the impression he was too cold and cynical about women.

McNamara could guess what his subordinate was thinking and he didn't like at all. His mouth curved in a severe line and said shortly and firmly:

"Go on! Anything else?"

"She was at the bookshop, sir, from morning till evening, if we believe the woman from the tea shop next door. She isn't related to a man, and she should have had an accomplice because the girls were repeatedly raped," reminded Mike to him, although it wasn't necessary. Everyone in the room knew the facts.

"Mrs Stevens, sir, can't be taken into account. She's a crone, according to the investigation, but she's got low mobility. No man visits her. Apparently, she despises everyone. She despises us, the policemen, more than anyone else, excepting the salesman, as far as I could see".

"Yes, I've noticed," said McNamara dryly, recalling what happened that morning. "Alice Thompson?"

"She didn't have a motive, sir, maybe only for Goddard and Patsy Porter, although we didn't manage to prove she'd have known of her husbands affairs. She was very shocked hearing about her husband's occupations".

"Yes, sir," said James. "She effectively made a nerve crisis, when she found out. We hardly managed to make her come back to her senses. You must also know that the other women can't be included on our lists of suspects, either. Mark and I checked all of them, and found no motive, opportunity or complicity with a man."

"Sir," said Donna shyly, as she used to be, being that kind of person that hated standing out, "from what I found out from reports and what I found out myself, the only one that could be the author is Randall. The motive might be blackmail. He had opportunities because no one checked him when he was supposed to go to his suppliers. I found out he usually solved things by phone, even though his wife knew differently."

"Yes, you're right," approved McNamara, "I also think he is, but we must find out where he was yesterday or if someone saw him. I hear he was limping, and McNeil said she hit not only her attacker's shoulder but also the leg with the scissors, even though the wound at the leg was superficial".

"No, sir," said Jo, "no one saw him. Mark checked his all suppliers and he wasn't to any of them yesterday".

"Mark?" McNamara turned interrogatively to him.

"I checked his past, sir, and I found out from one of his former school colleagues, he liked women a lot till he got married. I'm afraid he didn't give up afterwards, but you know well, his wife is ugly, and as Thompson say, also frigid."

"When did Thompson say that?" jumped McNamara off the chair.

"This morning, sir," said Mark afraid, seeing him so angry. "We interrogated him once more before the guys from vices took him. He said Randall was his client too, but he didn't blackmail him because they were neighbours".

"Do you think he is?" asked Jo, aware of what the inspector was thinking.

"Of course!" sneered McNamara. "He is! What the hell haven't I seen it so far? There were enough signs. Moreover, we knew he was limping yesterday. That's it!" he said. "We arrest him. The motive of the crime is clear. The girls tried to blackmail him on their own and they didn't know how. We search his house and ask also a blood test, because we have enough tests from McNeil's house. Come on, let's go!' McNamara rushed them.

Meanwhile I get a search warrant," he added, holding out for the receiver.

That very moment, the phone rang. McNamara picked the receiver and listened to what he was told from the other end of the line. While listening, a deep wrinkle got shape between his eyebrows, and the colour of his eyes changes and got the metallic shine of the steel.

"Good, I got it!" he said angrily and slammed the receiver. "McNeil is alone again," he told the others who was watching him with open curiosity. "That crone left with the policeman and left her alone in the house. Prepare the teams faster, James, and you Jo go to take the search warrant. I call now to ask for it. You go with it to Randall's and the others expect you there. I leave after I make the call. I go to McNeil," he said.

He didn't see the other watching each other suggestively before leaving. James went with Jo to take the search warrant, which McNamara was asking that moment, letting Mike form the teams and ask the forensics to go with them to the Randalls.

Chapter Thirty-Five

They got into cars and left to Randall's. Hardly had five minutes passed than Jo's phone rang. She answered the phone and heard McNamara's voice. The tone of his voice showed her he was very angry.

"Jo, you must make a turn to North-East. It was a serious accident here. Three cars are involved and the road is completely blocked. I'm afraid I need at least ten minutes to go out of here, so I'll catch with you," he also said, and expecting no answer closed the phone.

Jo put the phone into her pocket and then said to James who was driving:

"It was the boss. He's badly angry. He seems to have been stopped in traffic because of an accident and told us to turn to North-East. I let the others know," she said and opened the radio of the police car.

James approved nodding, and Jo announced everyone to follow another route, due to the blocking of the road.

They drove twenty minutes more, but managed to get to Nightingale Street in the end. They passed by the Randalls' grocery but it was closed, so they drove over up the street and stopped in front of the Randalls' house.

James and Jo, who had the search warrant, rang at the door and waited. Seeing no answer was coming from inside, they insisted again.

That moment, from the Thompsons' house, Mary Reid came out and she recognized James at once.

"You vainly ring at the Randalls, sir. Just now, I've come to Mrs Thompson, and I've met Mr Randall, who was just leaving the house. He told me his wife left early this morning to see her children she brought to her parents' yesterday. I wouldn't have expected that from her. She doesn't seem this kind of person. However, she's not at home and Mr Randall is down the street. I think he went to the grocer's, but I'm not sure, because this is the day when they open later."

"Thank you, ma'am," said James, obligingly. "How's Mrs Thompson?"

"Not very good, I'm afraid, but she'll recover eventually. Although she seems a weak woman, she isn't. She's got enough strength, inside," answered Mary, noticing Jo was already tapping her foot impatiently. "I'd better leave you now," she added and turned to Alice Thompson's house.

"What are we doing now?" asked Mike. „Should we break the door?"

"I think so," supposed Jo and then turned around as suddenly as her colleagues, because they'd heard the gnashing of tyres behind them.

They saw McNamara stopping his car and getting out.

"What the hell are you doing?" he snapped angrily enough to make them start. "Have I sent you to gossip or what?"

"There's no one at home, sir," said James to explain him why they were in front of the door.

"And what do you expect? Break the hell down, that door! Or maybe you expect me to do it? Can't you do it, or what?"

Mike nodded in sign that he caught the idea and hit the door with his foot strongly, right in the locker and the door opened at once.

***

Bryony poured herself another cup of coffee, although she knew she had already drunk too much, and then sat before the ledgers sighing. She didn't stand that work at all, but she didn't have anyone available to do it for her, so she had to do it alone.

She could still feel that morning's tension and she was bothering because she hadn't behaved nicely to her older neighbours. Moreover, somewhere, in a corner of her mind, there was also the thought that she had been about to make something irreparable that morning. She'd almost given to McNamara what she'd never given to anyone before.

Although her thoughts were bothering her and she didn't pay attention to the ledgers, something made her look up. She listened carefully and then she realised she heard well: someone was trying to open the back door.

A cold shiver crossed her spine and her hands started trembling. She spilled coffee on the tablecloth and on her hand. She put the cup down because she couldn't hold it anymore.

Bryony thought she had to pull herself together. She couldn't do otherwise, if she wanted to get out from the trouble in one piece. Determined, despite her legs, which were trembling so strongly that she hardly could stand but walk, she went to the rack of knives and took the biggest one with a very sharp blade.

She listened to catch the slightest noise. Now she could hear someone was trying to sneak along the wall with not too much noise. She heard only a slight noise when the intruder touched the wall.

Bryony hid behind the door and tried to keep still. She kept her breath and shut the eyes, so that she could picture in her mind each move of the other one. She felt when he got into the kitchen and then she dashed her hand with the knife before, but the knife only bit a little of the other one's hand.

In one second, Randall threw the knife from her hand screaming, and then a wide grin covered his face. Now he was content.

Bryony tried to get free passing by him, but the man slapped her so hard that he threw her with the head against the door and the door got shut noisily at impact. Bryony shouted weakly. The hit made her dizzy and she hurt her left arm. Her eyes grew dim and tears started running on her cheeks because of the pain overwhelming her entire body. She felt fainting and darkness covered her eyes.

She recovered only when she felt his hands on her blouse. Randall pulled the blouse and the buttons flew away everywhere, and the sound of the torn cloth scratched her ears. Bryony tried to hit him with her knees between his legs, but the man had already learnt his lesson so he watched out and burst into laughter.

Then, Bryony raised the unharmed hand and scratched his face with her nails, deeply and angrily. Randall screamed and loosened her blouse for a moment and Bryony took advantage and crawled away of him. She had almost managed to stand up leaning on the table because of the dizziness, when he jumped on her. He caught her and lifting her, he threw her on the table and started to tear her pants.

The woman started moving her legs, yelling and hitting him with her fist. The man didn't pay her attention, at the beginning. He was too busy in taking her pants out, but when she managed to hit him hard in the nose, hard enough to make him bleed, Randall stopped and slapped her strongly over her face and made her see black before her eyes.

Randall got closer to her face and told her with a low and threatening voice:

"Be careful, bitch! No one can take you out of my hands now! Maybe, if I like you enough, I'll let you live some more. Maybe," he said, bursting into that unnatural laughter that made her shivering.

His laughter stopped in his throat suddenly, when he felt someone caught him from the hair and pulled him back. He turned back fast, yelling, determined to kill the intruder. He tried to get the knife he had on the belt of his trousers. It was the knife he took from the floor near his wife's body before coming after Bryony. He didn't manage to finish his gesture because a fist hit him in the temple and he fell like a log.

McNamara kneeled near him and caught his hands with handcuffs. Then, he stood up and took his mobile phone off to call James to come after Randall. He didn't say anything to Bryony and avoided her look carefully, although he felt she was watching him insistently. He couldn't watch her, at least not now. He knew he'd shouted at her because she sent the policeman with Mrs Stevens, and he didn't want to scare her more than she was.

Bryony grabbed the edges of the thorn blouse and realised her fingers trembled. She saw McNamara's look avoiding her and she felt like freezing. She remained still on the table, in shock. She couldn't believe that something like that happened to her. However, she felt more hurt seeing McNamara couldn't look at her and she imagined that what he'd seen earlier, probably, disgusted him deeply.

Randall came back to his senses and started writhing. He tried to stand up and hit McNamara. He was sure he could kill the policeman with his hands tied at the back. However, he'd already shown he was smarter than the policeman, and he was sure he couldn't lose.

McNamara, without a single shiver of fear, but trying hard to control the rage overwhelming his mind, caught him from his shoulders and pulled him up, although he could bet on what Randall was thinking.

This one tried to hit him in the chin with the head, yelling like a trapped animal. McNamara only watched out and then, although he'd have wanted to kill him, told him with a voice promising nothing good:

"I advise you to calm down if you don't want I beat you up".

Randall didn't take his advice because he was sure he couldn't be defeated. He jumped ahead, but McNamara hit him with his fist in the temple and Randall fell at his feet with a deafening sound.

The same moment, James turned up. He entered the door McNamara left open when he heard Bryony screaming. James looked at Bryony in amazement. She was still trembling. Then, he saw Randall on the floor.

"Take him," said McNamara shortly. "Bring him to the station and lock him up. Too bad you can't throw the key afterwards. If he messes up, you're free to do whatever you think is right...on my account".

"Yes, sir, at, once," said James, nodding, and then he bent to pull Randall up. This one was like a sack with potatoes.

"Have you found anything there?" asked McNamara.

"Yes, unfortunately," started James, but McNamara, guessing from his voice what they'd found, stopped him with a gesture, showing to Bryony, who didn't need to hear that too.

"James, you and Mike take this guy," he said showing to Randall despitefully. "Jo will prepare the report with what you've found. I stay with her," he said pointing to McNeil. "Ah, and by the way, send someone tomorrow to fix the door. I don't think it closes anymore. I've broken it for good".

James nodded he understood and pushed Randall to the door. Suddenly, this one recovered and tried to escape from his hands. McNamara took him from one side angrily, and James held him on the other. They pulled him to the door, not paying any attention to his curses and threats.

Outside, McNamara spotted Mike, who had just got out of the Randalls' house and called him to them.

Mike, seeing Randall in cuffs, ran quickly towards them. Randall kept threatening and trying to escape from the hands of the two men.

"Calm down, you animal!" said McNamara roughly. I'm looking forward to having a good reason to beat you up until you faint so, please, oblige me."

Randall realised from McNamara's voice that he was angry enough to do what he said, and suddenly, he became completely apathetic. He abandoned fight, understanding for the first time, he couldn't win. There was total confusion in his mind, because he didn't believe he'd be caught, not for a second.

He had the conviction that McNeil was guilty for what had happened to him. She took his minds away and he couldn't take care of her when he had her in his hands. The bitch deserved to die, and even in awful torments. Thinking of that, his look became cruel.

McNamara saw his look and suspected what Randall was thinking, and his wrinkle between his eyebrows, which hadn't gone away for the entire day, got much more visible.

"My advice is you forget this woman exists, because if not, I'll make your life a living hell from now on. I'll take care you have no moment of peace, for all your remaining days. I swear!" he said thundering him with his eyes.

Randall looked at him hatefully but didn't dare to say a thing. He decided to hide his thoughts and keep them for himself, realising that it was wiser. However, he hated and despised McNamara even more than before, and he thought it would be a waste of time to speak to him anymore.

Mike and James took him and brought him to one of the police cars parked before Randall's house and put him in the back of the car.

Mary Reid and Alice Thompson, who had been watching the moves in the street behind a curtain, came out and started to whisper one to the other watching Randall, who didn't pay any attention to anything.

McNamara remained in front of Bryony's house and watched them until he saw Randall in the car. Obviously, he saw the two women who'd come out curious to watch Randall.

That very moment, he saw Jo coming out the Randalls' house and made her a sign to come to him.

"Tell me shortly what's there," he said when the policewoman got to him.

"We've got another body, sir. I think it's his wife. We found her in the basement. She's stabbed twice. The guys are still searching the house. We found the clothes he wore that night when he attacked McNeil or at least we think so".

"Good, Jo. After you finish here, you leave. I have to stay here with McNeil. I'm sure she needs someone now and I think I'm good as any other. Besides that, I broke her locker and the door can't be closed now."

Jo, who knew what she knew, nodded seriously and went to her colleagues, trying to not smile before she'd got out of his sight.

McNamara wanted to get into the house when he heard Mrs Stevens calling him. He scowled and turned back to face her. Mrs Stevens, who had assisted to the all fret in front of Bryony's door, couldn't resist staying inside and headed to him limping with determination on her face.

The policeman near her, Mackie, watched McNamara with a guilty look, but McNamara knew well that the poor man wasn't to blame. It wasn't easy to deal with the old woman when she wanted something.

"Yes, ma'am, what's now?" he asked her without caring of the rough look of the woman, watching him reproachfully.

"What happened?" she asked. "Where's Bryony? How's she? I want to see her at once, young man!" she said decisively.

"We've just arrested the criminal, so you don't need a policeman to guard you, ma'am," he said, skipping over what she'd said, as if the woman hadn't asked him a question. "You may leave now, Mackie," he told the policeman and he could read relief on the man's face. He was happy to have got rid of the crone, who had nagged him by then.

"And Bryony?" didn't give up Mrs Stevens. "I'm going to see her," she said to McNamara, in a voice that, normally, wouldn't have left place to discussion or refusal.

However, McNamara didn't yield at all and he stood before her, decided not to let her into the house. He was angry enough with her and not only for what happened that morning when she found him with Bryony.

He couldn't stop thinking that what happened to Bryony was because she left with the policeman. If she'd stayed with Bryony in the house, Randall wouldn't have dared to attack her during the day, he was sure of that. Therefore, he told her firmly, with a voice that didn't admit reply:

"Not now, ma'am, no way. You can come tomorrow and see her, but not too early," he underlined, maliciously, having the pleasure to see her frowning. "I'll take care of her and she'll be fine, so you could relax".

"But I want to see her now," burst the old woman angrily, trying to pass by him.

"No way! You can't see her now," he stopped her. "She must rest now. She had quite a tough day, don't you think?" he said and turned back into the house to show that the conversation ended.

However, Mrs Stevens couldn't give up so easily and she caught his hand. When McNamara shook his hand and turned to her, the old woman wanted to say something but then she saw the determined look of the man before her and hesitated a few moments.

McNamara took advantage of her hesitation, and, suddenly, he decided to tell her exactly what he was thinking, although he had avoided that up to then. He was too nervous to think that he could hurt her too much.

"Because of you, she was attacked, ma'am, so you'd better leave her alone today! If you hadn't left with the policeman, Randall wouldn't have dared to attack her. Therefore, at least you could leave her alone," he said resentfully.

The old woman stepped back when she felt the vehemence of his resentments. She'd also thought that her leaving led to Randall's attack she saw taken out of Bryony's house by policemen, but she pushed the thought somewhere far in the corner of her mind, being too afraid to analyse it.

However, hearing someone else expressing her fears, she felt guilt digging out to the surface and, looking into the rough eyes of the man, she admitted she was defeated and said nothing.

The woman frowned and turned back. She left and her heavy movements showed acute nervousness, but McNamara didn't care at all.

McNamara looked at Mackie, who left on the stairs and showed clearly he couldn't believe his ears. He knew his boss was a tough and direct person, but he didn't think he could hurt an old woman so much, even though he was right. McNamara watched him and told himself he didn't care what his subordinate was thinking, and then he made him sign to leave and entered the house.

***

He found Bryony still on the table where she was when he got out with Randall. The woman didn't have colour in her cheeks and her eyes had become enormous and lifeless. She had held herself around the waist and she was swinging absently.

McNamara felt a sharp pain in his soul seeing her like that. He got closer to her and took her cheek in his right palm, and he held her with the other arm and took her to his chest. He held her strongly, as if he wanted to give her some of his confidence and strength, and then he kissed her ruffled blond-reddish hair. Then, his lips got down on her cheek like an illusion and then stopped over her trembling lips.

When he touched her lips, a slight sigh came out, and her body moved closer to him, coming back to life again. McNamara lifted her in his arms and went to the bedroom with her. On stairs, he had the feeling that Bryony had said something, but he didn't understand. He'd only felt her lips moving slightly on the skin of his neck, making him tremble with desire, even if he knew it was the most inappropriate moment to think of that. He stopped and asked her:

"What have you said?"

"I've said," she answered with a stronger voice now, "That I thought you didn't want to speak to me at all, after what had just happened".

"Don't be stupid!" he replied ironically, and then he held her stronger, making her scream softly, due to the ribs that still hurt.

He laughed briefly and let her loose and then continued his way to the bedroom. Arrived in the room, he let her on the bed and then held out to the blanket to cover her, but she stopped him:

"No, please. I want to wash first, to get rid of his smell. I've got the feeling it's in my skin already, and I can't stand it for one moment".

McNamara nodded, guessing what she should have felt that moment, and then asked here reluctantly, fearing her answer:

"Do you manage alone?"

"Yes, don't worry. I'll be back at once," she said going to the bathroom.

He thanked providence for small favours. He didn't think he could have kept his blood cool and his hands at home, if he had had to help her get undressed. It'd have been too much for him now.

McNamara expected her to come back looking through the window at the little street that seemed to get peaceful again, as if nothing had troubled it before.

Bryony came back from the bathroom after a quarter of an hour, dressed in the same comfortable cotton pyjamas she'd worn the previous night.

McNamara felt her when she got inside and turned to her. He looked at her in expectation.

"Do you want to stay with me tonight?" she asked him almost begging and her words seemed to be the echo of the words she'd said the night before.

"This night, yes," he answered taking care not to make any commitment or promise something he couldn't do for sure.

She understood what he wanted to say and got into bed waiting for him to undress and come next to her under the blanket. McNamara held her and put her head on his shoulder, holding to his chest and then kissed her head and whispered:

"Sleep now! We'll talk tomorrow."